PRAISE FOR M. L. BUCHMAN

3x "Top 10 Romance of the Year"

— BOOKLIST

13 times "Top Pick of the Month"

— NIGHT OWL REVIEWS

I became completely immersed in this story and it had me at page one. Entertaining and full of emotion.

— FRESH FICTION, *WHERE DREAMS ARE BORN*

A favorite author of mine. I'll read anything that carries his name, no questions asked. Meet your new favorite author!

— THE SASSY BOOKSTER, FLASH OF FIRE

M.L. Buchman is guaranteed to get me lost in a good story.

— THE READING CAFE, WAY OF THE WARRIOR: NSDQ

I love Buchman's writing. His vivid descriptions bring everything to life in an unforgettable way.

— PURE JONEL, HOT POINT

Buchman has catapulted his way to the top tier of my favorite authors.

The only thing you'll ask yourself is, "When does the next one come out?"

Superb! Miranda is utterly compelling!

Miranda Chase continues to astound and charm.

Escape Rating: A. Five Stars! OMG just start with *Drone* and be prepared for a fantastic binge-read!

WHERE DREAMS RESIDE

A PIKE PLACE MARKET SEATTLE ROMANCE

M. L. BUCHMAN

Buchman Bookworks

SIGN UP FOR M. L. BUCHMAN'S NEWSLETTER TODAY

Other works by M. L. Buchman: *(* - also in audio)*

Action-Adventure Thrillers

Dead Chef
One Chef!
Two Chef!

Miranda Chase
*Drone**
*Thunderbolt**
*Condor**
*Ghostrider**
*Raider**
*Chinook**
*Havoc**
*White Top**

Romantic Suspense

Delta Force
*Target Engaged**
*Heart Strike**
*Wild Justice**
*Midnight Trust**

Firehawks
MAIN FLIGHT
Pure Heat
Full Blaze
*Hot Point**
*Flash of Fire**
Wild Fire

SMOKEJUMPERS
*Wildfire at Dawn**
*Wildfire at Larch Creek**
*Wildfire on the Skagit**

The Night Stalkers
MAIN FLIGHT
The Night Is Mine
I Own the Dawn
Wait Until Dark
Take Over at Midnight

Light Up the Night
Bring On the Dusk
By Break of Day
AND THE NAVY
Christmas at Steel Beach
Christmas at Peleliu Cove
WHITE HOUSE HOLIDAY
*Daniel's Christmas**
*Frank's Independence Day**
*Peter's Christmas**
*Zachary's Christmas**
*Roy's Independence Day**
*Damien's Christmas**
5E
Target of the Heart
Target Lock on Love
Target of Mine
Target of One's Own

Shadow Force: Psi
*At the Slightest Sound**
*At the Quietest Word**
*At the Merest Glance**
*At the Clearest Sensation**

White House Protection Force
*Off the Leash**
*On Your Mark**
*In the Weeds**

Contemporary Romance

Eagle Cove
Return to Eagle Cove
Recipe for Eagle Cove
Longing for Eagle Cove
Keepsake for Eagle Cove

Henderson's Ranch
*Nathan's Big Sky**
*Big Sky, Loyal Heart**
*Big Sky Dog Whisperer**

Other works by M. L. Buchman:

Contemporary Romance (cont)

Love Abroad
Heart of the Cotswolds: England
Path of Love: Cinque Terre, Italy

Where Dreams
Where Dreams are Born
Where Dreams Reside
Where Dreams Are of Christmas*
Where Dreams Unfold
Where Dreams Are Written
Where Dreams Continue

Science Fiction / Fantasy

Deities Anonymous
Cookbook from Hell: Reheated
Saviors 101

Single Titles
The Nara Reaction
Monk's Maze
the Me and Elsie Chronicles

Non-Fiction

Strategies for Success
Managing Your Inner Artist/Writer
Estate Planning for Authors*
Character Voice
Narrate and Record Your Own
Audiobook*

Short Story Series by M. L. Buchman:

Romantic Suspense

Antarctic Ice Fliers

Delta Force
Th Delta Force Shooters
The Delta Force Warriors

Firehawks
The Firehawks Lookouts
The Firehawks Hotshots
The Firebirds

The Night Stalkers
The Night Stalkers 5D Stories
The Night Stalkers 5E Stories
The Night Stalkers CSAR
The Night Stalkers Wedding Stories

US Coast Guard

White House Protection Force

Contemporary Romance

Eagle Cove

Henderson's Ranch*

Where Dreams

Action-Adventure Thrillers

Dead Chef

Miranda Chase Origin Stories

Science Fiction / Fantasy

Deities Anonymous

Other
The Future Night Stalkers
Single Titles

ABOUT THIS TITLE

When a life's passion and a Life Plan collide, things can quickly come to a boil.

Angelo Parrano's *great passion? Cooking his family's Italian cuisine in the heart of Seattle's Pike Place Market. His success definitely leaves no time for a personal life.*

Jo Thompson *escaped small-town Alaska by applying her brains and sheer force of will. Now a top-notch corporate lawyer in Seattle, her life plan runs right on track. The myth of cozy family? Not on her schedule.*

From the very first moment, they both must confront the unknown place in their hearts Where Dreams Reside.

CHAPTER 1

*J*o Thompson prided herself on her practicality and calm demeanor. It had humbled opposing counsel and convinced even the most reluctant judges and juries. It was a weapon she could wield with the elegance a chef plied her knife.

So why was she standing here feeling...mushy?

Definitely not her norm. Even a sip of the exceptional champagne, that sparkled across her tongue with the same joy as the June evening, only helped her focus a little.

The setting was glorious, a broad white canopy fluttering in the light evening breeze that drifted over the lawn. Through its open sides she could see the Mukilteo lighthouse and, sliding out from behind the brickwork tower, a large green-and-white Whidbey Island ferry nosing out onto the waters of Washington State's Puget Sound. Sunset—a path of gold on the saves—straight to her. As if it was trying to lead her away from her so-clear route through life.

The whole thing was so romantic that even contemplating it choked Jo up all over again. She turned back to the goings-on under the canopy.

Cassidy was positively radiant. Her best friend wore a cream-and-ivory lace sheath wedding dress that clung to her shape like a caress. Every time she even breathed, hidden threads of metallic silver glinted and sparkled. On a more provocative woman, or even a lesser one, it would have been indecent. On Cassidy all it did was smolder, which was clearly giving her new husband something to think about.

The first dance hadn't been a tango, but she and Russell had certainly danced it like one, as if they were the only man and woman alive in the whole world. The reception might now be winding down, but they still moved together, constantly teetering on the edge of a tangle of fiery passion.

Jo searched out the third member of their self-proclaimed "Terrific Trio." Perrin was flirting with the father of the groom, who was almost as handsome as his son. And, with her typical effervescence that exceeded even the champagne's, was doing so despite Russell's mother happily draped on his arm. Julia Morgan took Jo's arrival as an opportunity to return to the dance floor with her husband.

"They're such a beautiful couple," Perrin sighed happily as she and Jo leaned their shoulders together.

"They are." It was clear that they'd been dancing together for years. Jo had never learned, but they made it look so intimate and fun that maybe she'd have to find the time.

Someday.

In her copious spare minutes between lawsuits.

Perhaps not.

She only really managed to carve out time with Cassidy this week because she was in between cases. A situation that would be ending first thing tomorrow morning.

Lanterns warmed the scene as the summer evening slowly faded in the background. A live duo were knocking out songs that you couldn't help at least tapping your foot to. Above them, the Mukilteo lighthouse spun and cast its beam upon the June waters.

"We done good!" Perrin jarred Jo's shoulder with a sharp nudge.

"No, you did. The dress you designed for her is a marvel."

"It does make her look pretty marvelous, not that she doesn't normally. Still wish Russell had let me do something with his outfit." He stood with his best man taking a momentary breather from the dance floor.

Jo arched an eyebrow at her, "Do you think you could make him look even better than that?"

Perrin offered her a bit of a grimace. "Probably not. He's sooo hunky in that tux, but it would have been fun to try."

"He doesn't just look that hunky," Cassidy slammed into them from behind and draped her arms over Perrin and Jo's shoulders, the sweet peas laced into her hair scenting the first-night-of-summer air. "He *is* that hunky! I can't wait to rip his tux off." Then she blushed bright red and grinned at the same time.

Jo pulled her in, "You done good, Cassie. Exactly what you're supposed to be doing and who with."

Cassidy laughed. A laugh she'd rarely displayed even when they were college roommates over a decade before, but she had discovered it with Russell Morgan.

"When do you fly out?"

Cassidy grabbed a piece of prosciutto-wrapped shrimp from a passing waiter. She tried to eat it, speak, and chortle all at the same time and nearly choked herself.

Jo handed over her glass of champagne from which Cassidy took several swallows and then released a loud hiccup.

"Tomorrow morning."

"Wellll," Perrin drawled out the word. "I'm sure he'll let you finally sleep on the flight, unless you're going for an entry in the mile-high club."

Cassidy's smile and blush definitely grew. "Russell might have mentioned something about that."

"Damn," Perrin stamped her foot. "I am so jealous. I want reports. Perrin wants reports." She began counting on her fingers. "Is married sex better than single sex? Does high altitude make it, well, better somehow? Pluses and minuses of doing it in four-star hotels, Italian villas, and sailboats on the Mediterranean. Take notes. You'll be graded afterward."

"Yes, Perrin. I promise a report. When I get back from three weeks of sailing the Amalfi coast with the man of my dreams, we'll all go out, get drunk, and I'll tell you every little sordid detail about my most private sex life."

"Good." Perrin nodded emphatically. Her hair, presently dyed as black as Jo's, swirled about her pale face. As usual, she'd missed the sarcasm in Cassidy's voice.

Jo also knew from experience that Perrin would indeed be wheedling at least some of the juicier details out of their friend in due time. This allowed Jo to, without parsimony, both share Cassidy's present amusement at Perrin's expense and later enjoy the results of Perrin's somewhat voyeuristic but highly effective curiosity.

Cassidy hugged them both close, "Best friends ever."

"Best friends ever," she and Perrin repeated.

While Perrin was both more tipsy and much more emphatic, Jo could feel the truth of it once more softening her heart.

"WHERE'S MY GODDAMN CAMERA?"

"Let it go, *mio amico.* You're the best man, Russell. No, wait. You're the groom, I'm the best man, though with how Cassidy is looking in that dress, the groom really oughta be someone handsome and Italian like me." Angelo Parrano slapped Russell on the back hard enough that the groom almost snorted his beer.

"But just look at them." Russell insisted.

There was no question who "them" was.

It was almost impossible to look away from the three women friends, but he managed because he knew he'd been staring.

Russell's friends from the dock where his sailboat was moored in Seattle were mostly dressed for the Northwest, clean jeans and button-down shirts. They clustered together by the buffet table Angelo had spent most of last night putting together, eating the gourmet food with as much attention as they'd eat a bucket of chicken. He'd bet money they were talking about sailing. It was a topic they never tired of.

Near the bar stood a group of Russell's New York friends. They were dressed far more fashionably, looking dark, edgy, and wholly out of place at a Pacific Northwest wedding reception—outdoors at that, held beside a picturesque lighthouse. Clearly, in their opinions, the wedding of one of America's wealthiest bachelors and an internationally known food-and-wine critic shouldn't be in a setting more rustic than the ballroom at the Carlyle in Manhattan.

A dozen or so of the Northwest's top vintners from Cassidy's new Northwest Wines venture were in attendance.

She'd also invited a daunting slice of the restaurant world—Michelin-starred chefs and food critics with a global voice.

It shouldn't be surprising who Cassidy's friends were. Still, it was his restaurant, Angelo's Tuscan Hearth, where they'd held the rehearsal dinner. And now it was his buffet they were presently tasting and judging.

He looked away because he couldn't bear to watch, even from a distance.

Yet out of the whole crowd, there was no question which "them" Russell was referring to or why, as a professional photographer, he was desperate for his camera. The three women laughing together made an amazing picture.

Cassidy was right out of a magazine shoot. As a matter of fact, she soon would be. Angelo knew Russell was planning to use her in that dress for the next ad campaign for Perrin's Glorious Garb. Not just a boutique for edgy clothes, but now astonishing wedding dresses as well.

Actually he'd be an idiot if he didn't use all three of them in exactly these dresses. Perrin had done one of her fashion-design numbers on herself and Jo Thompson as well. Courtesy of a dye job, Perrin's hair matched Jo's, a straight fall almost as black as night to the middle of their backs. Their dresses were cut from the same cloth, but that's where the similarity ended.

Perrin's pale skin and blue eyes were offset against the light celery-green fabric by severe lines in the dress' tailoring that accented the slender lines of her body and revealed unexpected flashes of that creamy skin. She looked long and dangerous, like a racing sailboat or a Miyabi chef's knife.

Jo's darker skin, revealing her part-Alaskan heritage, was kissed by the gentle green curves of her dress. Each swoop and swirl accented her full figure and the fitness he knew she earned through hard sweat at the gym. A man could become lost while navigating among those curves until there was no hope for his return.

The three women had their foreheads together and their arms around each other's waists.

"Truth, beauty, and joy. Jo, Cassidy, and Perrin." Josh Harper observed over Angelo's shoulder even as Perrin burst forth with one of her bubbling laughs. The reviewer from *Gourmet Week* had come up between Angelo and Russell. He knew Josh from a couple of stellar reviews of Angelo's Tuscan Hearth and his habit of coming there to eat when he was in town, even when he wasn't researching for a review.

"Guess it wasn't hard to tell what was grabbing our attention." Russell noted. "You're good with words, Josh. Maybe you should write for a living or something. No, wait. Those are my words."

"I only steal from the best," Josh sighed as he watched the three women. "There are moments when being happily married really sucks."

"And moments when it's damn good." Russell took a swallow from his bottle of beer. "So what's your excuse, Angelo?"

He tried to speak, he really did. But Jo Thompson had just raised her head and was looking at him from beside the other two women. Her dark eyes inspected him as only a top corporate lawyer could, slowly taking him apart like a fine chiffonade, one sliver-thin slice at a time.

Russell's punch on his arm sent him staggering to the side. His wine, thankfully a white Oregon Viognier, spilled down the leg of his gray suit pants, and perfumed him with its warm floral components.

"Shit, Russell!"

"Sorry buddy. I'd feel bad, but I have to go dance with the most beautiful woman here." He finished his beer, handed Angelo the empty before going to fetch his wife. Having his hands full was the only thing that kept him from smacking the groom a good one.

Angelo stood there, empty wine glass in one hand, a drained beer bottle in the other, and a stain down his tuxedo pant that made it look as if he'd just peed himself. Like a lush on display. He shook his leg to try and shake loose the wet pant leg clinging to his skin. It didn't work.

Then he looked up and saw that Jo was still watching him. A soft smile, the kind that came the instant before a laugh, lit her face.

Josh clapped Angelo on the shoulder as Russell and Cassidy hit the dance floor, appearing to float several feet above it in their happiness.

"Yep! A good woman has definite perks." Josh said moments before his own wife swept him up to join the dance. All of the happily married couples dancing beneath the emerging stars was an amazing spectacle.

But Angelo couldn't stop watching Jo Thompson.

CHAPTER 2

"*Y*ou've got a special at table seven," Graziella called out as she breezed through the swinging doors into the restaurant's kitchen. She dumped a stack of empty bowls with a clatter in front of Marko the dishwasher.

"What kind of special?" Angelo didn't even bother to look up from the Veal Florentine he was plating. An almost invisible shaving of truffle, followed by a fistful of fresh mozzarella and shove it under the broiler to finish.

"Wants the chef on the floor," she had to shout a little to be heard over the typical kitchen mayhem of orders rattling back and forth and pans clattering against the stove as Manuel, the sous chef caramelized some onions in Marsala wine adding a brightness to the richer tomato overtones that generally permeated the air.

"I'm busy." 'Chef on the floor' was a stupid New York thing anyway, not Seattle. Angelo grabbed the plate as his grillardin slid a medium-rare pan-seared duck breast into a nest of slivered porcini. The dark, fatty duck and the earthy umami of the butter-sautéed mushrooms filled his senses. It was one of his favorite new dishes, because of its richness in all the senses. A sprinkle of bright green chives and purest-yellow lemon zest, as much for the color as the tang. He slid it across to Graziella.

"Told her you were, but she seemed confident you wouldn't mind," She dressed the duck with a side of steamed baby asparagus as he pulled out the veal and then she took both out with her. "She's a looker, if that helps."

Angelo tossed the latest batch of pasta with tongs, and drizzled on cold-pressed olive oil. Now he had to let number seven wait. Because if he didn't, Graziella would assume being pretty was all that was needed to get him out of his kitchen. Definitely, let her wait.

But he couldn't. He'd been side-tracked, knocked out of the groove. The second time his garde manger had a salad ready before Angelo had prepared the plate, he gave it up and called Manuel to take his spot. Manuel might be Mexican rather than Italian, but he could turn out a hundred complex dishes each exactly to Angelo's recipes and repeat it night after night. The perfect sous chef.

Wiping his hands on the towel dangling from his apron's waistband and checking that there were no flour stains on his charcoal chef's jacket, Angelo pushed through the door into the restaurant. It took a moment for his eyes to adjust from the stark white and steel of his bright kitchen to the soft ambiance of Angelo's Tuscan Hearth.

He and Russell had redesigned the dining area like a traditional Italian kitchen. A large central fireplace. Tables in small clusters scattered about the room. No booths, but comfortable chairs, tasteful paintings, and photos of Italy on the walls.

On their last trip, Russell and Cassidy had taken a number of photographs of the old Italian villages that Angelo's mother had left before Angelo's birth. But it lent an authentic feel to the room, photos of home. It was cozy and Angelo forced himself to slow down enough to share a friendly moment or two with some of the diners he recognized as repeats, and a few that he didn't.

"Yes, that's fresh basil," as if he'd use anything else.

"I used the Pacific salmon in this Cioppino, it's a gentler flavor than the Atlantic salmon," and it was more popular here in Seattle even if it was a bit less authentic. It gave patrons a chance to feel slightly superior for living out here on the "wilder" west coast.

"And what can I do..." his words trailed off as he reached table seven.

Jo Thompson sat there wearing a deep yellow blouse the same tone as the wall paint, but richer, more intense. Her black hair was back in a ponytail, leaving her face and neck exposed. Her skin and eyes were lustrous in the restaurant's soft candle-light. Her cleavage, not deeply exposed, was accented by a small dangle of gold in the shape of an orca whale on a hair-thin chain. The subtle adornment made her absolutely stunning.

"Yuri and I were hoping that you could choose dinner for us tonight."

Angelo glanced at Yuri. He was a big man, tall and broad-shouldered. Angelo wasn't that short, but he might not even reach this guy's shoulder. His face was square and rugged in a way that he supposed women would find handsome, but he could never be sure with guys.

His hands were big and rough, a working man's hands. Angelo's animal brain flashed an image of those callused hands groping Jo's beautiful skin and he felt the blood drain out of his soul.

"Of course," his voice nearly broke, it had suddenly gone so dry. "It would be my pleasure Miss Thompson. Do the lady or the gentleman have any preferences?"

The man waved one of those hands dismissively. "Whatever you make will be fine." His voice was deep and smooth, accented lightly with Russian heritage making it even richer.

Angelo went from hating him to utterly despising his merest existence.

"Jo says that your taste is impeccable and that's good enough for me." He rested an elbow on the table as he leaned across toward Jo. "Must say that my taste is pretty impeccable, too."

Clearly dismissed, Angelo turned for the kitchen. Once back in the world of white and noise, back where the sizzling of the deep fryer battled the dish boy for sonic ambiance, and oregano and garlic scented the air along with the undertones of port reductions, he let his hands fall to his sides.

Cook for them? *Non possibile!* Twice he went to step forward, but he had no idea what to make. So, he'd just make…something.

After his third attempt at a Roasted Artichoke and Venison Carpaccio Bruschetta, he had Marco send out a simple Antipasto-su-baguette. From there it went downhill. Working beside a flustered Angelo, his grillardin slid out of the groove. He ruined the last duck breast, then burned a sirloin so badly that they'd had to open the back doors and turn the fans up to full roar to avoid the charred scent reaching the dining room.

The disaster rippled through the kitchen. The friturier dropped plastic tongs into the deep fryer, which melted and permanently merged with the fry basket before he was able to recover them. They'd be throwing that basket away. The potager grabbed the salt instead of the sugar and then knocked the last of the asparagus soup across the patissier's station taking out a whole tray of Torte della Nonna.

Angelo considered going to apologize to the patrons at large, but couldn't face Jo's disappointment. Clearly she'd been intending a romantic dinner to show off her savvy in choosing his restaurant. Instead, Angelo took the coward's way out and stayed hidden in the kitchen. Tonight, he knew, he was going to be drinking far too much wine. And with Russell in goddamn

Italy, he was going to have to face tomorrow's hangover on his own.

Jo KNEW she'd made a miscalculation the moment she saw Angelo's face. Not only that, but his hands, normally so expressive, had dropped to his sides and hung there. But she didn't know how to take it back. She should have taken Yuri anywhere in Seattle but Angelo's restaurant.

Yuri had called, saying that he'd be in town and he'd love to take her out to dinner. She'd suggested Angelo's Tuscan Hearth without even thinking. The food was exquisite and the atmosphere quiet but cozy. It didn't force absolute isolation like in an American steakhouse with booths so deep and tall that you could be the only couple there. Nor the merry mayhem of the Moroccan place they'd gone to for Cassidy's bachelorette party. Jo still wasn't sure quite how Perrin had inveigled Cassidy and herself to join the belly dancer, much to the entertainment of other customers.

Angelo's offered quiet tables, the gentle strains of fine Italian singers sounding from a discrete sound system rather than an uncomfortable trio traveling from table to table. Tasteful. She liked that about his choices, his restaurant was immensely tasteful. It had seemed the perfect place to bring Yuri, especially as fine Italian dining wasn't something easily found in Alaska.

Jo had spent a lot of time with Yuri Andreevich over the last two years working on the Alaskan fisheries lawsuit. He was one of the Russians who had immigrated to the Alaskan coast seeking the rich American life. Unlike most, he had found it. Many of his countrymen had simply traded one fishing boat for another.

Yuri had used the lawsuit to leverage himself into position as a "voice of the fishermen" and proven himself to be capable and successful as such. He sounded as if he were the hero of the two-brother boats eking out a family tradition, rather than in the pay of the conglomerates launching hundreds of craft and being sued for price control by the state on behalf of the fishermen.

She hadn't much enjoyed the ethics of the whole thing, but she'd ultimately justified it to herself that the individual fishermen's claims were even more unfair than the conglomerates' practices. And the fees had been astonishing which had paid off her condo and left her little excuse to complain. She'd spent two years ignoring the sharp pinch and it was now past time where she could change anything.

Yuri's big voice was romantic, and his heavily accented English caused several heads to turn at other tables when he first spoke. It wasn't a booming voice, but it carried and attracted attention. It had also worked well in interviews and, she had to admit, on the phone with her. Jo liked Yuri, and there had been a connection there. Or at least she'd thought so.

She'd been feeling lonely after the wedding. With Cassidy out of town and Perrin immersed in another of her design frenzies from which she might not emerge for days or weeks, Jo was discovering quite how pitiful her social life had become. She couldn't even throw herself into the next lawsuit, it's opening stages were only starting to trickle in. Dinner had sounded like a fun and easy answer to an otherwise quiet Thursday evening alone.

But when Angelo saw them, he had looked as if he'd been shot. She'd known he was attracted to her. It was plain to see, but his feelings had left him awkward in her presence. And, she had to admit, it had left her awkward as well. They'd danced together a few times at the wedding last weekend but he'd said little and she'd said less.

If it had been purely physical, that might have been fun as he was genuinely nice to look at. But it wasn't her body that he was always watching, but rather her eyes. Not a good sign. She didn't need any attachments right now. Especially not one that would be complicated by being her best friend's husband's best friend.

Russell was good for Cassidy. If it had been Jo, she would have killed the man inside the first week, but he was good for Cassidy. His carefree attitude forced his wife to loosen up and relax, something she did only a tiny bit better than Jo. Jo had never "gotten the hang" of letting go. She didn't have time for it, truth be told.

Russell's ease, mixed with his ramrod forthrightness, made Cassidy face decisions head-on rather than sliding by them. It did make him the perfect man for her.

Angelo unbalanced Jo and so she determined it was best to simply not consider him at all. But she hadn't meant to wound him by flaunting Yuri in his face. She was always fumbling in Angelo's presence, a feeling she wasn't used to. And one that the confident counselor in her didn't like at all.

"This is the Earth calling to the Jo Thompson," Yuri sounded like a Russian flight controller with his gentle destruction of proper English syntax. "Where did you go off flying to just now?"

Jo shook her head.

He was about to press when the appetizer arrived. She took one of the tiny antipasto sandwiches to stall, not one of her usual tactics.

It was good, but nothing exceptional. She'd been here a couple of times with Cassidy and knew this was merely one of Angelo's standard, albeit wonderful, dishes. Clearly not the exceptional food he made for friends.

She had hurt him and he was being petty and spiteful. Yet another reason not to be attracted to him. Spiteful men always became worse with time. She'd focus on Yuri, he was her date after all.

"I was just thinking about the next case I'm taking. It will be bringing me back to Alaska." Now why had she said that? During the fisheries lawsuit, Yuri had been one of their main spokesmen. They had worked long hours together honing both the public talking points and the court messages. Jo had been particularly careful to make sure the relationship had remained professional. This was the first time they'd seen each other since she'd won that case.

She'd also only recently emerged from a rather intense, even by her standards, lawsuit regarding the crabbing practices along the U.S.-Canadian border, again on behalf of the larger fishing corporations. That particular suit had bankrolled her a splendidly comfortable savings account.

Though she wasn't sure how she'd ended up doing that. She'd started out to be an environmental lawyer, but reality had twisted without her noticing.

As she'd dressed for dinner, Jo had been uncertain of her own feelings. So, she'd chosen attractive but conservative attire, her yellow St. John blouse buttoned fairly high, with black Donna Karan slacks and sensible heels, that sent a clear message. "I will make myself pretty, but the verdict is still out on whether or not we will be spending the night together."

"Good. Alaska is very good," Yuri sounded very pleased and leaned in a little closer.

No, Alaska really sucked, but she wasn't going to say that aloud.

"You are a woman who it would be a pleasure to see more of, Jo." The momentary dip of his eyes without lingering and his smile might have been charming under different conditions. Had they been sharing sushi at the Old Power House in Kodiak, it probably would have worked.

Sitting in Angelo's, he struck her as not quite coarse. That was the wrong word. Perhaps as a touch crass.

"The case will take me more to the North Slope than

southern coastal," she did her best to backpedal. As if anywhere in Alaska was better than any other. She'd escaped it straight out of high school—her career constantly forcing her to return was not one of life's little ironies—it was one of life's steam-roller-sized ironies.

"It's about the Arctic's continental shelf rights. Who gets to drill how deep and just where do international waters begin when we're talking about the mineral rights beneath the seabed when everything converges toward the pole. The state, after losing to me so badly last year, wants me to protect their interests. They've learned that if the corporations don't get what they want, the state won't get their tax revenue."

"That is still good. You will fly through Juneau and I will meet you there. It will be good to see you more often and away from the laws, Jo." And he sounded sincere.

Jo knew what she was looking for in a man. The criteria would change in another three to five years. But for now, she was focused on her career and could afford to dally a bit here and there. When she was ready to settle down more permanently, then she'd pick a quiet, intelligent man. He'd be well-educated and have already passed through whatever crises men passed through. Then she'd think about family.

Each thing in its order. It was a safe maxim, one she'd always liked. There was still plenty of time. She wouldn't "settle" when she was making that final choice, not one little bit.

That's when she knew that Yuri would be sleeping alone tonight—or at least not with her. Despite the romance that Cassidy's wedding had briefly awakened in Jo's heart, she wouldn't settle even during the dating phase of her plan, and that's what sleeping with Yuri would be. Not only wasn't he Mister Right for the future, he wasn't even Mister Right for the present.

Thankfully, before she had to respond, the soup arrived. The aroma was rich, the fish broth revealing a depth that even her childhood-in-Alaska trained senses couldn't fault. It was a cheerful mixture of clams, mussels, and salmon.

Yuri took a spoonful first and nodded his head as if saying, "Good enough."

Jo felt a heat rise. Angelo's cooking deserved more than a "good enough." His ingredients were always the finest. The proteins were always finished impeccably and his seasoning balance was exquisite. He had been written up by so many critics that he was causing some embarrassment to the city's other restaurateurs. For six months his write-ups had commanded as much print and blog presence as all of the others competing for the high-end market combined.

She allowed herself a moment more to appreciate the scents and presentation of the soup. Even the dark blue stoneware bowl, that just happened to match the room's paint accent, against the soft yellow tablecloths promised a depth that a white bowl would not have.

The broth delivered its richness to her tongue as her nose had promised. Living through college with Cassidy, even before she became such a renowned food-and-wine critic, had trained Jo's palate well. She could appreciate the interplay of the basil and oregano and the way they complemented the clam-based broth.

Then it hit her. Square in the center of the tongue, the impossible-to-miss bright sweetness of sugar. It broke the broth. The dusky clam and the subtle salmon were washed beneath it like an ocean wave. Another spoonful from elsewhere in the bowl had the same issue.

It was good. Would have been fine in some spaghetti-house type of restaurant, but it didn't belong in Angelo's.

How could Angelo stoop so low as to destroy one of his own dishes to get back at her? He wasn't merely petty; he had no pride of ownership.

She barely paid attention once Yuri began creating a fantasy weekend of small fishing cabins along the Sitka shore during a Pacific winter storm. She'd always taken meticulous care to not reveal her past. As far as anyone other than Cassidy and Perrin knew, Jo Thompson had been born the day she arrived at college.

Yuri would have no way of knowing that she'd dedicated her younger existence to escape exactly such a place that he thought so charming. Since she escaped to college after busting her ass to graduate at the top of her class and complete a full year of simultaneous night classes at the community college, she had never been back. She occasionally met her father in a restaurant in Ketchikan when she was flying through, but she never went back to the hovel filled with too much fish and too much alcohol. At least he'd been a quiet drunk, albeit a morose one.

If Yuri thought he was painting a romantic scenario with his coastal cabin love nest, he couldn't be more completely wrong. He might have risen to a fishing consultant sought out by corporations and the media as an expert in the field. But at his core, he was still a fisherman who would be happiest out on his boat with the wheel in one hand and a bottle of vodka in the other.

After the soup, a tiny entremets arrived. Angelo had taken to adding little dishes between courses as accent marks, a common enough action in modern French cuisine, but he was perhaps the first to apply it to traditional Italian dining. Definitely the first to do it so successfully. The between-course dishes typically completed the last flavor of the prior course or hinted at the next. Occasionally, they stepped wholly out of the bounds of the meal and were brightly amusing which somehow heightened her awareness of the dishes to either side.

This appeared to fall into the last category. Two delicate shrimp tempura on a single plate, set curve-to-curve so that they nestled together like a yin and yang symbol. They rested upon the sheerest smear of what might be a blackberry sauce set off by the perfectly white plate. The dish might be Japanese in form, but Jo would wager it had some Italian twist to the flavoring.

She took hers, refusing to be embarrassed that Angelo had sent a lover's dish to her table. The first taste pleased her, she'd been right about the blackberry sauce. The second almost made her gag. A sharp bite of plastic rolled along the edge of her tongue and even a swallow of the red wine did nothing to cut the acrid bitterness. It was as if he'd fried it in plastic.

Jo was going to kill him. This wasn't only rude; it was down-right nasty.

An exclamation from the next table over drew her attention. A fork clattered down in disgust and a plate was shoved aside, though the others at the table continued to eat. The protesting patron had a different dish from her own. Something wasn't right.

She looked about the room. Most people were continuing to eat, but here and there, plates were returning to the kitchen, their purported delicacies abandoned.

That just didn't happen here. At Angelo's Tuscan Hearth, people mopped their plates clean with their bread so as not to lose the least drop of sauce. Working here as a dishwasher had to be one of the easiest jobs in the kitchen.

Not tonight.

But if it wasn't personal…

Jo began to worry.

Something had definitely gone wrong in the kitchen.

CHAPTER 3

*M*uriel, Jo's legal assistant for over five years, carried the towering woven-wicker basket into Jo's office and set it on the corner of her broad oak-wood desk with a thud.

"Shit!"

Muriel stopped and stared at her, "I don't think I've ever heard you curse."

"Sorry. You can just take that right back out." The thing was huge, brimming with flowers and sausages, bags of coffee and wedges of cheese. It was monstrous enough that there could be an entire ham hiding beneath the cheery multicolored cloth. It was late morning, only a little before lunch, and the waft of fresh-baked bread made her stomach growl. That woke up her entire system which then insisted on its desire for a deeply fatty and high-caloric lunch that it certainly was not going to receive, even if it filed a motion for summary judgment in state court.

Jo tried to look back down at the benthic map of the Arctic continental shelf that showed all of the undersea topographic ridges and valleys she'd been studying. The wicker basket's base covered from Ivvavik Park in the Yukon clear over to Prudhoe Bay and well out to sea.

"Don't you even want to know who it's from?"

"An arrogant Russian who does not know the meaning of 'just get on the plane and go home'." Suddenly Jo had far more of her assistant's attention than she wanted. Suddenly her personal life was spinning out of her control and she was in over her head as if she were being pulled down a whirlpool. This was a not-familiar and highly uncomfortable feeling. Normally it remained in the same perfect control as her career and her workout schedule.

"Sorry," Jo rubbed at her eyes. "Bad date last night. What part of 'No!' don't men understand?"

"Oh, they understand it just fine, except for its meaning and how to spell it."

Muriel Mendenbaum, despite her name, was sassy and youthful. Only a year younger than Jo, she somehow embodied a vitality that Jo kept committed to her career. The woman was also a gift in Jo's life, they'd been through hell and back over their years together.

Jo wished she was more like Muriel, so confident in all aspects of her life. Muriel talked easily about men and boundaries and good dates and bad. Jo merely felt awkward and so made a point of moving slowly. That had labeled her as overly choosy or, at times, arrogant. Neither was right at all, except perhaps for the discerning part.

She'd hit Ketchikan college at sixteen and been lost in all of the flirting and sexual confidence of the eighteen-year-old's world. On her arrival at Vassar College at eighteen, she'd found a decent guy and latched onto him for safety. Latched on so hard that she hadn't figured out how to let go of him except by graduating four years later and moving across the country. Richard had been decent, but not exciting, definitely not a keeper. A decade gone and he still e-mailed her occasionally, especially after a bad breakup, which she studiously ignored.

Muriel stood now with her short, dark hair tucked behind her ears, a pink cotton sleeveless blouse with lace shoulders, and a smart black skirt with a flirty hem. She also had her hands fisted on her hips. Jo knew her assistant well enough to know that Muriel would plant herself by Jo's desk until she had the whole story, or at least enough to satisfy.

"Whereas I see you have a date tonight." Jo tried to turn the subject with the compliment to her nice clothes.

Muriel just shook her head no. Not no to the date, but no to Jo's lame evasion.

One of the newbie associates rushed in. She'd hoped for a reprieve, but all he needed was a signature on one of the smaller research matters she'd subbed out to him. He was gone almost before he arrived.

Jo would like to claim she had to get back to work, but Muriel knew Jo's workload better than anyone, frequently even Jo. They both understood that the large map spread across her desk only meant that the first files hadn't started arriving yet. She needed to get the lay of the land, but there was no rush.

Even looking out the corner office windows over Elliot Bay and the Seattle waterfront didn't offer any nice distracting topics. Where was a blizzard when you needed one, who cared if this was June?

"Let me simply say that the meal was not good. Then I almost had to deliver a slap to force him to back off at the front door of my condo."

"Maybe you should have taken him to that place you like so much. The Italian one."

"Yeah, maybe." She wasn't going to mention that she had. The entrée at least had been marvelous, almost as good as the meals she'd had with Cassidy attending. And dessert had finally swept Yuri's attention from her to his food, he couldn't stop saying how deep and rich the chocolate torte was and how the brandy was the perfect match.

Her espresso had been scorched to sludge and the Sweet Ricotta and Meyer Lemon over Amaretti had been so sour she could still feel the dry pucker at the back of her throat. She'd have liked to taste Yuri's dish just to be sure it was okay, but by that time she hadn't wanted the implied intimacy and begged off as being full.

When she didn't eat even a second spoonful of her own dessert, he teased her about it. She'd considered digging out a bit of the amaretti cookie, but they were too soggy to make it worth eating one to shut him up. He'd put the final nail in his own coffin with some remark about her girlish figure. She knew she was a full-figured woman; he didn't need to hammer on the point.

"It was Yuri, from Ketchikan."

"Ooo, good-looking Russian." Muriel almost chortled then caught herself. "But you didn't drag him into your lair."

Jo actually laughed at the image. She'd never "dragged a man into her lair." But the way Muriel said it, perhaps she should try it someday. She made it sound fun.

"No, I didn't. I sent him to his hotel and wished him good travels. He was deeply shocked. Why do men assume that a pleasant meal is always a coquettish invitation to crawl into a woman's bed?"

"Sure, guys are like that. They go from having a sure-thing-with-an-incredibly-hot-and-voluptuous-high-powered-attorney fantasy one moment, to boring-sexless-night-all-alone-and-not-understanding-or-willing-to-admit-why reality the next. For some reason, it's always a shock to their system."

"Anyway," Jo glared at the basket towering above her. "The last thing I want from him is a gift basket."

"Well, how convenient that it isn't from him."

Jo held out her hand and Muriel dropped the card into her palm.

"PPM." Calligraphed on heavy ivory stock. The paper looked like one of those artisanal, handmade cards. "Nothing else?"

Muriel shook her head, though clearly she knew something more, she wasn't going to give it over that easily.

Jo puzzled at the card for a long moment. "I'm assuming that the Presidential Pet Museum is not soliciting my services."

"Nor the Progressive Party of the Maldives," was Muriel's comeback.

Jo wondered if she'd Googled that just to have it ready, or if the woman had already known about it, or made it up. Jo decided it was better not to know. Muriel's smile said she was clearly enjoying her boss' confusion.

But even as Muriel opened her mouth, Jo made the connection. She stood up and looked down into the basket. Whoever had assembled the basket had raided every shop in Pike Place Market. Okay, there were something on the order of two hundred of them, so they'd raided a quarter of the shops, still the bounty was amazing. The cloth covering the gifts wasn't just a remnant of fabric, it was a splendid piece of local weaving. A pound of Market Tea. A salami from the meat merchant, traditional cookies from the Italian grocery. The treats kept going as they probed the contents.

She hoped there wasn't a dead fish somewhere in the depths. She pulled back the corner of the cloth. Actually, there *was* a dead fish, but it was a teriyaki-and-ginger smoked salmon which sounded delicious. Fresh bread from the French baker's stall had been the cause of her stomach's growling.

It was a bounty on a glorious scale. Even splitting it fifty-fifty with Muriel, this was going to last a while. Maybe they should bonus some of it to the junior lawyers she'd be chewing up on the Alaska case to ease their upcoming pain.

"No other note?"

Muriel shook her head. She reached down and pulled out a local artisanal chocolate bar, seventy-percent dark with Bing cherry and marzipan filling.

"It's never too early for chocolate," Jo nodded for her to open it. They broke off squares and tapped them together like champagne flutes. They shared a moment of respectful silence as the flavors bloomed in their mouths.

"Damn!"

Muriel's soft exclamation echoed Jo's feelings exactly.

"Now, what the hell do they want?" Jo noted her own curse and ignored Muriel's pretend shock.

"Maybe the Market's administrators are just being freakishly nice?" Muriel dug around some more and held up a coupon from the Parrot Store for a free parakeet. "After all, you redid their lease agreements for them."

"That was months ago."

They uncovered several more stunning delicacies and a really nice pair of earrings that they joked about arm wrestling for, which Jo resolved by putting them on. But no further information.

When Jo's phone rang, Muriel answered it. After listening for a moment, she handed it across the desk.

JO MET Renée Linden at the Maximilien French Restaurant for lunch. The Executive Director of the Pike Place Market had deftly avoided Jo's queries on the phone as to the lunch's purpose with a skill that was easy for a trial attorney to appreciate.

They were seated at an immaculate table set on the restaurant's second story. Their table nestled up against the glass that fronted much of this side of the Market. Beyond lay the spread of the Seattle waterfront. From the giant Ferris wheel to the south, past the ferry docks in the foreground, and West Seattle rising like an island in the midst of Puget Sound. Beyond the docks lay the sweeping expanse of Elliot Bay and the majestic Olympic mountains still sporting their glittering white glacial caps despite the June heat. It was one of the finest views in Seattle and Jo let herself be swept up by it.

"I'm so glad you could join me on such short notice."

Maybe Jo shouldn't get swept up too easily. This was Renée Linden across the table.

Jo's Friday lunch plans had transformed and her stomach was going to get what it asked for after all. She'd planned on a cup of soup and a workout at the gym, a rare midday luxury that only happened briefly between cases when her schedule had a little flexibility. Now, she would be power-lunching over a three-course French meal. It was almost as well that her dessert had been awful last night, at least she'd saved those calories. Tonight she'd have that cup of soup and gym workout to balance this splurge.

Renée Linden.

Jo had researched her further in the half hour she'd had between shooing Muriel and much of the contents of the basket out of her office, and this lunch. She'd worked with Renée before and knew what a powerhouse the woman was on the Seattle scene.

What Jo hadn't known was that Renée had been behind the revitalization of Pioneer Square in the '90s. A formerly dangerous district, that lay in the original heart of old-town Seattle, had been turned into a tourist Mecca of edgy theaters with the Fringe Theater movement, fine galleries, exceptional dining, and bars that featured hot bands instead of Saturday night brawls. She'd also been on the board for the creation of Westlake Center, which drew tourists and shoppers into the heart of the business district.

A key player, and donor, to both the new Symphony Hall

and the complete renovation to the Marion Oliver McCaw Opera Hall only a few years later. The list kept going until Jo had closed the bio abruptly and turned to stare blankly at the Arctic map until it was time for the meeting. Jo still couldn't puzzle out the meeting's purpose.

They split an order of Escargots à la Bourguignonne over a glass of Vouvray from Château Moncontour and Renée remained elusive. The woman spoke only on light topics.

Jo followed right along with the informal prelude. This was a business lunch and that was at the center of Jo's skill set, barely a step down from the courtroom.

Renée told of coming to Seattle after re-meeting her husband, now the President of Boeing's business jet division, at a tenth-year college reunion at Oberlin.

"I never would have dated the man in college. He was fantastically brilliant, which I found to be quite daunting."

Jo declined to mention quite how humbled she felt in Renée's presence. Her circum vitae was enough to set even the most aggressive overachiever on her heels. Jo regretted looking up the details. It was leaving her a little tongue-tied, which hadn't happened to her in years. Often no knowledge at all was a better strategic position than too little.

"But by that time we were in our thirties. I found he had, if not mellowed, grown deeper and richer with time. He really is like a good wine, though a red rather than this white. This is far too light on the tastebuds. I'm the Vouvray to his Burgundy."

"You are at least a Beaujolais or a Bordeaux." Jo spoke before she could stop herself. That this amazing woman would think herself as of so little consequence. Why, that would leave Jo as what, grape juice?

"I had hoped that would get a rise out of you."

Jo blinked. She took another of the decadently buttery escargots to buy herself a moment.

Renée declined to explain, but the tone of the lunch shifted as if she'd passed some test.

"You did a wonderful job on those leases for us. You understood the fine balance we must strike between making money from our more successful lessees yet nurturing our start-ups and struggling entrepreneurs. And be equally fair to all two hundred plus of our tenants. That really captured our attention."

"Our?" Jo hadn't missed the word choice and rather suspected that Renée was not using the majestic plural.

Renée merely smiled and selected the second-to-last escargot.

Jo returned the smile and finished the dish.

Well, that meant that this was indeed a business luncheon. One most likely sanctioned by the board of the PDA, the Preservation and Development Authority responsible for running the Pike Place Market.

When they'd wanted help with the leases, there had been an interview in her own office followed by several meetings in Renée's office. Then Jo had done the job and presented the significant changes before the full board. She'd quite enjoyed the project in retrospect. There had been many interesting facets to consider.

Now, two months later, the basket and the luncheon.

After a brief debate, she decided to forego the Smoked Salmon and Dungeness Crab Salad in favor of the Bouillabaisse.

They were clearly courting her for something. Her hand froze halfway to her glass of wine as the waiter cleared the escargot plate. They wanted her on the board. It was a terrible, double-edged sword.

All PDA board positions were volunteer. It was for the wealthy semi-retirees who cared heart and soul about Seattle, not for a working woman gearing up for a multi-year litigation on the Alaskan North Slope. Yet serving on the PDA board also carried immense prestige. The position opened every door among the true movers-and-shakers of Seattle. Those connections would make her career.

Was she willing to trade what little free time she had, plus probably a fair bit more, for the opportunity? Not as if that particular question mattered. She clearly didn't know what to do with free time on the rare occasions she did have it. She'd been naïve enough to think that being on a date with Yuri Andreevich was going to be a constructive, or at least pleasant, use of her non-working hours.

Jo Thompson knew she wasn't exactly "owning the jury" when it came to her personal life.

"MAMA!" Angelo had to blink to be sure. But there stood Maria Amelia Avico Parrano at his open kitchen door as if it were the most natural thing in the world. She'd only been to his restaurant twice, once at last year's opening and again last week for Russell's wedding reception.

He rushed over and gave her a hug.

"You don't need to be so gentle!" She hugged him back as fiercely.

He laughed and squeezed her harder until she'd have laughed if he'd left her enough air.

He finally let her go and just looked at her. "You look wonderful." And she did. She'd always been a beautiful woman. He and Russell used to wonder that some man hadn't hounded her into marriage after Angelo's father died while Angelo was still in the womb.

The dark that curled down to her shoulders in thick waves had started to gray, and she'd let it. Her figure was generous, but looked amazing on a woman barely five-foot-four.

"It's retired life. It agrees with me."

"*Una pensionata?!*" His thoughts blanked.

If Graziella hadn't put a hand on his back at that moment, he'd have fallen to the floor.

"Hi, Mrs. Parrano, so glad to have you back in town." Graziella made sure Angelo would remain on his feet, before taking his mother's hands and kissing both cheeks.

"*Bella bambina,*" she patted Graziella's cheek as if she were a twelve-year old girl and not a twenty-eight-year-old master of the front of house at one of Seattle's finest restaurants. Graziella hurried back to her job without appearing to hurry, one of the traits that had made her Angelo's first hire even before he opened the restaurant. The customers were always given the impression she was spending ample time with them, even when it was only a moment.

"Retired?" The word choked on its way out.

"Is an old woman allowed to come in?"

That finally got a laugh out of Angelo's constricted throat. He gathered up the suitcase she'd set in the doorway and led her to the side prep table not presently in use.

"Are you hungry, Mama?"

"Good boy," she patted his cheek. "Just a little pasta and red sauce to get that airplane food out of my tongue." Her accent slid about him like home. Thirty years since she'd come to America to cook for Russell's parents, the Morgans, and she still frequently mangled idioms, which just added to her charm.

He hurried to the line, glad for a moment to collect himself. A quick glance at the order tickets and then down the line showed that they were running smoothly once again, as if last night's debacle had never occurred.

He made two bowls of pasta, sliced a little Biroldo sausage into the sauce, grated some Asiago on top, and carried them back to the table to join her.

"Retired, Mama?"

"Yes." Then, just to make him crazy he was sure, she forked

31

and twirled up some of the linguini and took her time to chew and swallow. She nodded.

"It is good. A little paprika would bring it to life, but it is good."

"But…" Angelo bit his tongue. Paprika wasn't Italian. It was Hungarian or sometimes smoked for Spanish cuisine, but not Italian. However, he had never won a seasoning argument with Maria Amelia, and he wouldn't now, so he left it be.

"Retired. Yes. My Julia and John, they have retired and are going to travel for a while. They will probably sell the big house unless Russell wants it. They say they will travel until they find where they want to live."

Angelo couldn't imagine the Morgans selling the sprawling mansion from which four generations of the family had run a global shipping empire.

"Wait, they fired you?" Angelo felt it bind in his gut. They may have helped raise him, and Russell might be Angelo's best friend, but they couldn't fire his mother. She'd been their cook for over thirty years. She'd—

"I quit."

Angelo dropped back on his stool and did his best not to look shocked.

"You…" He couldn't even finish the sentence.

"Angelo, sweetheart." She patted his cheek with almost a slap. "You know like I know, there is the point where three becomes the crowd. They were horrified when I give my notice but they were also relieved. It was *perfetto* solution. To make up for relief, they give me part of Morganson Shipping company, enough that I can do what I want for many, many years. I also make good savings."

Angelo had to look away for a moment and inspect the line. He could see the smooth flow, the pattern of two dozen lunches moving simultaneously through various stages in the kitchen. Manuel had it well under control.

And he could see Julia and John Morgan making sure his mother was taken care of no matter how long she lived. He'd bet they personally drove their cook to the airport for this visit with her son. He brushed at his eyes. They had taken in a single, pregnant Italian country girl with little English, sent her son to college, and treated her like family. He would find some way to repay them. He couldn't imagine how, but he would. He turned back.

"That's good, Mama. That's good." He took a deep breath to regain his composure. "So, now that you can afford to do anything, what are your plans?"

She merely smiled as they each twirled up a forkful of pasta. He bit down on his, agreeing that perhaps his mother was right about the paprika, the sweet, not the hot. Just enough to accent the Biroldo—

"I'm going to live with you," her eyes twinkled as she paused. Then her smile turned ever so slightly wicked. "And help you cook in your ristorante."

CHAPTER 4

*J*o had blown off the rest of the afternoon, what was left of it after a three-hour lunch, and gone to the Eastlake Gym.

When Renée Linden did a full-on opening argument, Jo had found herself at some loss to offer a clean and cogent rebuttal. And she still didn't know what her plan or intent was, making it all the more confusing.

If there were a pending lawsuit on which the Market needed her assistance, why hadn't she simply laid out the bones of the case. Not that Jo would have time to tackle it, but she'd be glad to give them a little advice and hook them up with someone sharp enough to take down whoever was messing with them.

Jo shoved the pin in ten pounds heavier than normal and began working her triceps on the machine. This wasn't her normal workout time. She and Cassidy usually came in with the other early corporates. Hard workouts to get fired up for a guilt-free day because your workout was already under your belt. Perrin never joined them. A true night owl, if she ever went to the gym it would be at midnight.

The afternoon crowd was an odd mix. A lot of mothers

getting in a quick half-hour while the kid was at ballet or wherever. There were also a fair number of guys who looked bruiser strong. Like construction workers off work at three who hadn't gotten enough exercise hefting steel girders and giant laminate beams all day.

Jo decided to just keep her head down and do her workout. And hope that she could somehow make sense of what happened at lunch.

"We're retiring," Renée had explained over the entremets of strawberry sorbet with a dark chocolate flake. "Nathaniel and I are going cruising for a while, then we thought we'd winter over in New Zealand. This is our home, but we decided it was time to travel for some reason other than business."

Renée Linden retiring. That would send shockwaves rippling through the Seattle social firmament. Jo still couldn't make sense of that, even by the time she'd worked through biceps and moved on to abs and obliques.

And Nathaniel Linden leaving Boeing management? He was the President of the custom business-jet division, had practically created it. Did a Saudi prince want his own personal 737 outfitted for entertaining? He was the man. A six-bedroom 747, with an in-flight movie theater that could seat Russian billionaire's family and friends each in their own lounge chair before a ten-foot screen with full-surround sound and a garage in the cargo bay to transport your Maserati? He'd make it happen. It was a small, but exceptionally lucrative division.

That had been enough of a shock for Jo, and she'd wager that neither Pike Place Market nor Boeing were the least bit happy about their pending departures.

Jo counted out ten more reps trying not to think, but that wasn't helping.

Her litigator instincts would bet safe money there was still more up the woman's sleeve. She was notorious for never stopping once she'd set her sights on something.

But Jo couldn't quite identify what she'd been after.

That's when Jo's brain had shut down, plain and simple. It was as fatal a mistake in court as it was at a power lunch, but she couldn't get around it. Researching the woman for a year would not have brought her to that lunch prepared for what was fielded at her with Renée's pleasant conversation and a one-two punch of kindness and gentility.

Without actually saying it out loud, Renée had made it clear that they didn't want Jo on the PDA board, which simplified that decision for her. It had been such a relief that she'd ordered the most decadent Soufflé au Grand Marnier she'd ever eaten.

No. The board had its twelve members. But, Renée let slip ever so casually, that she hadn't yet told the board that she'd be resigning as the Executive Director of the Pike Place Market. Because Jo was the first to know other than her husband, she must keep it to herself until she announced it next week.

Jo let the kick bar for working her quads drop back into position with an ear-ringing clang. Half the people in the weight room turned to see if there'd been an accident. She tried to lift it again so that everything appeared to be normal, but couldn't gather enough neurons for sending the message to her legs to do so.

Renée had simply wanted "to let Jo be the first to know. As a professional courtesy."

Jo had been so dazzled by the lunch and the conversation that she didn't even see it coming until this moment sitting at the exercise machine, her foot hooked behind a bar that was impossible for her to lift.

Renée wasn't merely retiring, she had already chosen her replacement. And, without once stating it in as many words, she'd informed Jo that she was Renée's first and only pick to replace her. She'd simply used the basket and the luncheon to plant the idea in Jo's mind, and then allowed it to have time to build and age like the Royal Oporto Tawny Port they had with the final cheese-and-pear course.

Jo blew out a breath as if at the end of a brutal workout and not just her third set of reps.

The anointed chosen successor to the great Renée Linden?

She'd never seen *that* coming. Never had a chance to react and refuse or, Jo now identified the heart of Renée's finesse, say anything she might regret later such as laughing hysterically in the woman's face. At least not until she'd had time to think about it.

The woman would have made a daunting attorney and Jo would hate to argue a case against her in court. She wouldn't stand a chance.

ANGELO HAD TRIED EXHAUSTING himself on the step machine, but though his legs burned, his mind was still churning. He went for the elliptical next and set the program to maximum cardio with heavy resistance. The gym was high above Eastlake Avenue, high enough to look over the buildings across the street and allow its patrons to enjoy views of Lake Union and steep Queen Anne Hill if they tired of the television screens while they worked out. High enough that maybe he could get some perspective on what had just happened to his life.

His mama had come to live with him. That was wonderful. Mostly. He had the room. With the success of the restaurant, he'd moved out of the tiny one-bedroom apartment and bought a two-bedroom condo with a good kitchen right in the heart of Pioneer Square. He'd fully equipped it to test new dishes, but he never did; he always ended up just going to the restaurant at odd hours for that. No matter. He'd bought it free and clear.

And the last time he'd had a girl up to his apartment...

He looked out the window at Lake Union. A cluster of sailboats were skittering across the surface of the lake that made the north boundary of downtown Seattle. He had to think back a long way to remember. Well, okay, so his mother wouldn't be cramping his style there either.

But in his kitchen? No one was as good as his mama in the kitchen. It didn't matter if they actually were, they still weren't. Paprika in the Biroldo sausage? *Sacrilegio!* Then he'd tried it after she left to go to the apartment and take a nap after the flight. It was exactly right, damn it. She'd be fussing with each of his dishes until he didn't recognize them anymore. And worse, they'd probably be better.

At least she'd never know what happened last night. Just last night? He cast his eyes skyward in prayer that she'd never hear how he'd had a total meltdown less than twenty-four hours before.

Sweat poured off him as the elliptical sent him on another hill climb.

Of course, he knew why he'd made such a mess. Too bad there wasn't a thing he could do about it. It was too late. Jo Thompson would take that meal as a personal affront and never speak to him again. He certainly would in her position. He truly hadn't intended to ruin her date with awful food.

God, he hated working out in the afternoon. He should be worrying about dinner prep, instead he was worrying about his mama. When he worked out in the mornings after he'd done the shopping for the restaurant and before lunch prep began, he used to run into Cassidy and Jo on occasion. Casual waves, polite greetings. But the heat that had coursed through his body each time he saw Jo had become too uncomfortable and he'd shifted his workouts to between lunch and dinner service.

Another hill? The machine had it in for him today. He grabbed his towel and wiped off his face and eyes. They stung with the salt from his sweat.

Another mile the machine warned him. And one last high

resistance climb. He was dying here. The only way this could possibly be worse…

He focused on a machine two over from him. The woman climbing onto her elliptical was one he'd recognize in a white-out blizzard even if she were wearing a parka and hood. Though that sure wasn't what she was wearing now. A dark maroon sports bra left her shoulders and midriff gloriously bare. It left so little to the imagination that his blood pressure was threatening to pop. Matching running shorts that exposed one of the nicest lengths of leg he'd ever seen. And lemon-yellow sneakers like the laugh line on a great joke.

Jo Thompson looked incredible. And she wasn't looking at him. Either hadn't noticed him or, far more likely, was studiously ignoring his existence.

A hundred percent snub.

There were rules in workout gyms. Everyone was in their own space, doing their own thing. You never messed with that. And it was truly bad form to stare at a woman. His own head-phones were spilling out The Boss because who else could help you with your Italian mother better than Springsteen. *Born to Run?* You betcha!

Jo was probably listening to opera. She sure wasn't looking his way. She must have seen him, had purposely left an empty machine between them, and then ignored him to rub in how angry she was about last night's meal ruining her date.

He slowed his pace. The machine began blinking the "Pedal Faster" sign at him. He slowed to a stop. She was staring up at the TV screens set above the wide glass window with the view of the lake. CNN or the James Stewart film. He couldn't tell which she was watching.

He wiped down the machine and headed for the showers.

One glance back showed him a view he'd never forget, the beautiful and brilliant Jo Thompson running away from him at high speed.

CHAPTER 5

"*H*ello, Angelo."

Jo noticed that he'd parked his Tuscan-yellow restaurant van with dark blue lettering next to her car's passenger door. They'd arrived at their vehicles almost simultaneously.

Glancing over at her he dropped his keys. He leaned down to fetch them, then stood up under the van's mirror. He whacked his head good and hard, then slid nervelessly out of sight.

She sprinted around her car to see if he was still alive.

He sat on the ground beside his dropped gym bag and keys, with his back against the van's door. His head was between his knees and his hands were wrapped around the back of it. A string of Italian that sounded beautiful, but she'd wager was actually some serious invective, streamed out into the air. She'd studied French, which gave her some of the roots, but the sound of the traffic rolling along on Eastlake Avenue muted his words just enough that she couldn't make them out, which was probably just as well.

"Are you okay?" she squatted beside him.

He raised his head enough to inspect his hands.

"No blood." He patted his head gingerly and looked at his hands again. "Feels like there should be though."

"Here, let me look."

Angelo shrugged, winced at the motion, and acquiesced.

Growing up a fisherman's daughter she'd seen enough bumps, bruises, and cuts to last a lifetime. Also enough to make a quick and probably accurate diagnosis.

"No blood. I can't feel a crack. One hell of a bump rising already though." His hair was still damp from the shower and smelled lightly of shampoo.

"Thanks, I knew that."

He sat up and lay his head back against the van door right on his restaurant's logo. "Ow! *Merda!*" He leaned his head back between his knees and reclasped his hands over his head.

Jo wanted to laugh. She knew it wasn't seemly, but it bubbled up inside her anyway. He looked so sad and helpless. She took a deep, pre-jury summation breath, then another and steadied down quickly enough.

She set her gym bag on the ground beside her own car door and sat on it to wait with him until she was sure he was okay. The brutal hour-long workout had done nothing to clear her head of Renée's offer. She'd focused her mind and driven her body until every muscle screamed, but she still didn't know what she was feeling. Even as she waited for Angelo to recover, she could feel her muscles stiffening. She was going to be seriously sore tonight.

Cassidy really needed to get back from her honeymoon. Jo needed a sounding board at the moment and found herself a bit distressed to realize that she really didn't have anyone else. There was Perrin, but her advice which would probably be, "You should totally go for that! You'd be awesome at it!" would also stand a high probability of appearing as tomorrow's newspaper headline. Perrin Williams and secrets had an...interesting relationship that was exceedingly difficult to predict.

Angelo sat up more slowly this time, keeping his head well clear of the door.

"How are you feeling?"

He squeezed his eyes closed for a moment in a hard wince, then opened them wide as if trying to make them focus once again.

"Okay, I think." He shrugged. "Mostly like a total klutz." He made a gesture slapping the back of one hand against the other, as if running into a wall. He started to stand.

Jo rested a restraining hand on his arm as he let himself slide the two inches back to the ground.

"Oh! Maybe I'll just sit here for a few more minutes. You should go though. I'm okay. Don't let me keep you here."

"No, that's fine. I want to make sure you're okay."

He nodded his acceptance but didn't say anything more. He closed his eyes and rested his head back very tentatively.

Jo checked to make sure he was still conscious in case he'd actually concussed himself, but his body hadn't gone limp, simply quiet. She'd somehow forgotten how incredibly handsome he was. His short hair, as dark as her own, curled foolishly about his ears compared to her own dead straight fall. His skin glowed with the warmth of a tan from the Italian beaches, though she knew he'd grown up in New York City. Broad shoulders but trim build. And she'd seen how fit he was when they used to run into each other during workouts, though it had been a while.

It was his hands though, presently hanging limply from where his wrists rested on each raised knee, that were his best features. They were slender for a man, but strong from cooking. She'd never actually seen him cook but could easily imagine the exacting confidence and incredible speed they could apply to each task.

"You're speaking to me." Angelo had opened his eyes slit-wide against the sun shining on his face and was studying her.

"No," she worried again about his head perhaps being injured. She hadn't said anything.

"You aren't?" He pointed at her as if there was some question who he meant even though only the two of them sat there.

"I wasn't. Now I am."

"Why not?"

Jo huffed out a breath. "Where did this conversation go astray? I didn't say anything before. Is your hearing okay?"

"My hearing is fine. I'm not hallucinating." He held up two fingers squinted at them as if trying desperately to tell how many really were there. "I thought you weren't speaking to me, as in never again."

"Oh. Why would I do that?"

"Last night's dinner."

Jo blushed. She was fairly sure that it had all been her fault. "Look, I'm really sorry about that."

"What? No, I am. I'm the one who served that food. If you can call it that." Angelo scrubbed his hands over his face. "Thank the great *Patrono* in Heaven that Mama wasn't there. She'd have murdered me."

Jo remembered the charming woman from the wedding. She barely came up to Angelo's shoulder and kept bursting out with how proud she was of him. She couldn't stop talking about how handsome he was, how beautiful his restaurant was, how amazing the food her son had served tasted. And it truly had been amazing. His mother had also clearly read every review and followed every award. Her joy of her son radiated straight from her heart.

Several times Jo had to bite back the envy burning deep in her gut at having a mother like that. A loving parent who cared about how you did, and supported it.

But she was also clearly very Italian. If she knew Angelo had served a meal like last night's...

"Yes, I expect she would have murdered you but good. Thankfully for you, she's three thousand miles away."

All Angelo did was groan and put his head back into his hands.

"Are you okay?"

"No. But that's not your fault."

"Well, last night, I suspect, was." She knew it was. Angelo had been giving her such total puppy-dog eyes at the wedding, it was impossible to miss. Then she'd flaunted Yuri at him without intending to. She might not want to be with the man, but she should be more considerate of his feelings.

"Again, I'm sorry about that."

Angelo raised his head and looked at her. She could see the question clearly and was relieved that he had the decency not to ask. So, she answered it anyway.

"Yuri is a business acquaintance who thought he was more than that. I disabused him of that misconception last night, much to his distress. He should be back in Alaska by now."

"Oh. Good." He slid a hand across his mouth as if to erase the last word. "Uh, I am sorry about the meal."

"That's okay. It made a point of Yuri's shortcomings, a matter I might not have noticed otherwise."

"If you need any assistance in that, you know, getting some guy to show their shortcomings, just bring him by. I'll be glad to ruin another meal for you."

"I'll keep that in mind," she made her tone as dry as possible.

Angelo laughed and she joined in. It felt good. It felt friendly as if they'd each managed to apologize for last night without having to apologize.

He struggled to his feet and she helped him up. He didn't sway much, any more than anyone else who'd rapped their head hard.

"I'm fine. Just need some aspirin. Then I'll be fine."

Jo dug into her gym bag and found her emergency stash and a water bottle.

Angelo took them gratefully.

"Thanks, Jo. And again, I'm sorry about last night."

"Me too. You sure you're okay to drive?"

He nodded and only winced a little at the unwarranted motion. He started to reach for his bag and keys, but she got them before he had to bend over. He'd have a screaming headache by now at the very least.

"Thanks." He had his van's door open.

"Do you want to work out together sometime this weekend?" Now where had that come from? Was she really so needy for company? No, she was simply that desperate for anything familiar in a world that contained something as crazy as Renée's offer.

Angelo looked as surprised as she felt.

"I, uh, usually go for a bike ride on Saturday morning. My sous chef does lunch and we both do dinner. Do you ride?"

"Sure. Loop of the lake?"

"That sounds great."

Jo felt a little manipulative. It was her standard training ride, but it was also a long ride. Yes, she had an ulterior motive, that somewhere along the way they'd be able to discuss Renée's offer to take over the management of Pike Place Market. She needed a sounding board so badly.

But it wasn't just an ulterior motive, it would also be nice to have someone to ride with. Cassidy was a runner and Perrin looked at exercise as a disease contracted by the undeserving as punishment for a wicked former life.

"I'm done shopping for the restaurant by seven."

"Perfect. We can start the ride while the day's still cool. Meet on the trail under the Fremont Bridge at half past?"

With a shared smile and nod they climbed into their cars.

ANGELO BUZZED through the morning shopping.

Or he tried to.

But his mother had insisted on coming along. When he was selecting a long side of swordfish from the iced counter at the Pike Place Market fish vendor, his mother was chatting with Henry.

As he chose only the most perfect avocados and artichokes, she'd found out that Uli had two children and a third one on the way though it wasn't showing yet. At least not that he could politely see.

Maria Amelia greeted the bread baker in passable French, and she stopped them for a cup of espresso and to split a morning baklava at Mister D's Greek Delicacies even though he wasn't really open and serving yet.

Angelo barely tasted it and seared his mouth on the hot coffee.

It was past seven, almost seven thirty by the time he got back to the apartment and changed. Then Russell's cat, Nutcase, still thinking she was kitten-sized, had decided Angelo's hand was an invader from deep space resulting in a long bloody scratch that Angelo had wiped on his bike shorts without thinking, so he'd had to change again and get a Band-Aid.

His mother stopped him in the hallway and he almost exploded with frustration.

"You go have a nice ride. She must be very pretty."

That stopped him cold.

She patted his cheek. "I am only retired. It does not make me blind, *mio figlio*. I hope she is as pretty as that nice girl at the wedding. I see you later at the ristorante." She held the door open and shooed him out with his bike before he could respond.

Angelo had planned to ride the couple miles to meet Jo, now he tossed his bicycle and helmet into the van and sped through the early-morning streets. His nerves may have made him squeeze a couple of red lights on the way.

He found a spot only a few blocks away and almost worked up a sweat sprinting down to where the Burke-Gilman Trail cut under the Fremont Bridge. He was worried that she'd have given up and gone without him, but saw her right away.

He'd thought she looked amazing in workout clothes at the gym. In the warm morning, she wore shorts and a cycling jersey made of the most amazing, brilliant crimson form-fitting Lycra. These clothes covered more, but hid not the least little curve. The dark, wrap-around Oakley shades only served to make her look even more fearsome.

You will speak to her normally. Like a normal person. Angelo admonished himself as he rolled up to where she was stretching her hamstrings with a heel resting on the back of a park bench. A little park was all that separated the paved bike-and-running trail from the Fremont Cut where Lake Union flowed down to the sea.

Already, pleasure boats were working their way along the cut. They were heading for the Chittenden Locks which would let them out onto Puget Sound. He and Jo would be heading the other way. Along north Lake Union, through the University of Washington, and then north beside Lake Washington they'd follow the Burke-Gilman for fifteen miles before turning south.

"Sorry I'm late," Angelo managed against a dry throat. Also glad that he hadn't missed her, which would just give him a new offense to worry about. "My mother..." He cut himself off.

"Is she okay?"

"Sure." She was fine. He was the one going quietly mad.

Jo faced him with those power glasses. "You ready to ride or do you need to warm up a bit?"

"I'm good to go." He'd take his morning shopping at Pike Place Market as his warmup. A slow start and he'd be fine.

Then he looked at her bike and whistled in appreciation. It

was an electric-red Rodriguez custom-built road bike with Dura-ace shifters and a lay-down bar. There was no way in hell he was going to keep up with her. The machine was almost as hot as its owner.

"I know. I know. The bike is ridiculous for a rider like me, but it feels amazing. I feel fast just looking at it, even if I'm not. A friend told me it was the best, so Cassidy insisted that's what I should buy. I don't like buying things twice."

After the few miles of weaving at an easy pace among the local joggers, they rode clear of the city foot traffic. *Okay, I can do this without making a complete idiot of myself.*

From there, Jo shifted up and led the first half mile at an impressive clip. Following just a bike length behind Jo was immensely distracting. Her hair flew behind her like a banner from underneath her helmet. Her fine figure was only accentuated by the cycling position and her long legs spun quickly with the evidence of long practice and training. It was enough to make him overheated even without the exercise.

There was the steadiness of a practiced rider about her. Clean strokes, fast spin, and a quiet body position on the long flats of the Burke-Gilman.

At the half-mile mark, she swung to the center of the trail, letting him zip past her on the right side. In his peripheral vision he could see her tuck in close behind him. Now it was his turn to take on the extra work of breaking the wind, letting her rest in the slipstream of his draft. Drafting wasn't a skill for beginners, but she held her position perfectly, her own front tire perhaps a foot behind his rear one.

He almost took a full mile, but that could look as if he was trying to impress her. He thought of it as being gentlemanly but decided that discretion was the better part of valor and swung aside and let her pass after he'd led a half-mile matching hers.

They rapidly fell into an easy rhythm of alternating lead and draft, spinning along the shore of Lake Washington and its stately homes. The trail, dappled with cool shade and warm sun passed by more easily than it ever had before.

PAST JUANITA PARK, Jo had the lead when they hit the hill. She downshifted and began the grind up. It was a long slog. At this speed there was no advantage to drafting, it was steep enough that this was just about low gears and a lot of spinning. Angelo dropped back a bit and they each focused on their own climb.

She'd woken so sore this morning that she'd almost called Angelo to cancel. Might have, if she'd had his number. She'd arrived only moments before he did, and she half hoped she'd missed him. But now with the miles rolling beneath them, she was glad she'd come. The ride had loosened her muscles and been beautiful so far.

Though, her muscles reminded her as she climbed, the ride was barely half over. A loop around Lake Washington ran forty-five to fifty miles depending on which exact route you took.

And now, for the two miles of the longest climb in the route, she'd just hunker down and think of something else while her legs earned their keep and knocked off the excess calories from yesterday's lunch, and the cheese, salami, and wine dinner she'd fixed from the depths of the Pike Place Market basket.

Her mind had shifted to a place of denial. Even if she had heard the unstated offer correctly and Renée was offering her the position at Pike Place Market, why on Earth would Jo be interested? The last big Alaska case had made her partner in one of the country's elite maritime law firms. That had earned her not only a rather astonishing salary, but also a significant share of the law firm's yearly profits. She wasn't the most junior partner in some thousand-attorney firm, she was the fourth partner in an elite, extremely specialized, astronomically expensive boutique firm. The fisheries case had already set her up

49

nicely. The North Slope case could easily cover her for many years to come, assuming she won and didn't go off buying jet planes or something equally stupid.

Yes, it would be several years of every waking minute, but she could do that. Her father had just cruised through life, the perfect counterexample. If the weather was rough, he stayed in his shack, at least until the bar opened. If he didn't feel like fishing that week, he left the boat tied up. Yes, it had probably extended his existence, but was it worth extending? He was lazy, his wife had left him before Jo's first memory, and his daughter had *run* from Ketchikan at the first chance.

Executive Director of Pike Place Market couldn't pay a quarter of what she was making now, or a tenth of what she would make. It wasn't even a reasonable offer. It made no sense.

So clearly, she shifted down another gear as her legs tired, she had misunderstood Renée Linden's unspoken message. Perhaps she was asking Jo to help her select the next Executive Director, maybe head up the search committee which would have good prestige and connections in its own right.

Or maybe Renée wanted to make sure she'd be willing to work for the new director on legal issues despite her high-profile cases. She'd be glad to, if she had the time. Her offices were at the edge of the Market, she ate most lunches there, and enjoyed doing part of her shopping in the various stalls.

She heard Angelo puffing up beside her. She shifted to the right edge of the shoulder, if he wanted to pass her on a hill climb she had no ego about it. At least not until the moment his wheel edged one inch past even, then she'd upshift and dust his behind if she could find the reserves.

Jo glanced over as he pulled up beside her. She knew she was perspiring, the band inside her helmet was barely holding back the tidal wave of sweat from her eyes.

Angelo looked positively fresh, as if they'd just spent the ten minutes on the flat, or coasting downhill. He'd be extremely easy to hate in this moment.

"I'll meet you in the park at the foot of the hill. I'll catch up with you."

Before she could even nod, he dropped back and was gone. She twisted her head and saw him turn into the parking lot of a grocery store right before the crest of the hill.

She considered circling back, but then she'd be stopping with the last hundred yards uphill still to go. Screw that. She wasn't going to intimate that she needed a rest in order to beat this hill.

Jo rolled over the highest point of the whole ride and began adding back gears.

She hit the downhill slope going fifteen miles an hour. By mid-descent, she was in a high gear, spinning hard in a full racing tuck, and going fifteen over the twenty-five mile-an-hour speed limit; maybe twenty. Praying for no police, she hammered down the hill. Fifteen minutes of grinding work uphill, turned into a three-minute flash down into the heart of Kirkland and straight on into the park.

At nine on a Saturday morning the waterfront park was already busy with couples and families. The small park jutted out into Lake Washington so that it was surrounded on three sides by water. Early cyclists and joggers packed the park. The customers for the boutique shops which wrapped around the bay wouldn't be hitting for another couple of hours.

She rolled out to the very point, past the gazebo, and dropped to the grass.

A quick check on her cycle computer made her do a double take. They'd chopped fifteen minutes off her best previous time. She wouldn't admit it to Angelo, but she'd driven herself up the climb from Juanita Beach like never before. The cardio settings said that she'd killed off the worst of yesterday's excesses and was making a good dent in whatever ones she'd find for today.

"Chocolate or vanilla?"

She looked up at Angelo as he pulled two supermarket-freezer ice cream cones from the back pocket of his shirt and presented them with a flourish for her consideration. She didn't ask, she just snatched the chocolate one.

He settled beside her as they both peeled the paper wrappers.

When she sank her teeth into it, the cold smacked her over-heated body. This wasn't some healthy, demure dish of frozen yogurt. This was a high calorie, fat-turbocharged treat of chocolate and nuts on cheap chocolate ice cream in a really crappy wafer cone, just like all pre-wrapped freezer cones.

It tasted fantastically good.

"Oh. My. God!" Her mouth still half full of ice cream. She turned and kissed Angelo right on the lips. "This is wonderful."

It was only as she faced back out over the lake and took a second bite, despite the possible risk of serious brain freeze from eating it too fast, that she realized what she'd done.

Two ways to deal with it. Ignore it or risk a sly look from behind her dark sunglasses to gauge his reaction.

Her brain chose a third. She turned and shot him a chocolate-laced grin, then stuck her tongue out at him.

He laughed and, much to her relief, did the same through vanilla-covered lips.

CHAPTER 6

*a*ngelo's legs were shaking by the time he got back to his condo in Pioneer Square. A hot shower, a high-carb lunch, and then he'd have some chance of surviving Saturday night service. He'd never ridden the Loop of the Lake so fast, or had so much fun doing it. He felt simultaneously hammered and supercharged.

They'd barely spoken during the three-hour ride, no way to really do it while riding. But it was as if they didn't need to. He never knew what to say to someone as smart and beautiful as Jo Thompson anyway, but doing the ride together had been easy and fun.

In the park they had eaten their cones and laughed about the Thursday night disaster. Who knew he'd ever be able to find the least morsel of humor in the situation, but Jo somehow made the impossible possible.

His mother wasn't at the condo, maybe she was out exploring Seattle. He'd have to remember to take fresh clothes into the bathroom with him. Thankfully his new place had two baths, so they could each have their own. There'd be at last some privacy.

He was halfway through his shower when he remembered where his van was parked. At the Fremont Bridge.

Angelo stuck his head out of shower to check the clock on the bathroom counter.

Great. Just great.

Not only did it mean getting back on his bike, but by the time he got there, if the Seattle Police were operating at their usual level of efficiency, he'd have a parking ticket as well.

FORTY-SEVEN DOLLARS.

Angelo was out the cost of a good bottle of wine and now, as he tried to park behind his restaurant, the one space reserved for his own use had been taken by some useless tourist. Well, he was going to get their behind towed and cost them a serious chunk of change and irritation. Perhaps it would mitigate some of his own.

But it wasn't some tourist. It was his own car, parked in the van's space.

This was Pike Place Market on a Saturday afternoon. There'd be nowhere to park for blocks around that didn't cost at least half as much as his parking ticket. The traffic was suicidal and it took him forever to escape.

He drove down to Pioneer Square and pulled into the secure garage, hauled his bike upstairs, and then set out on his usual walk back up the hill. By the time he was done, it had taken him almost two hours to reach his own restaurant just six blocks from his condo.

Okay, the bike ride had been good. He'd stay focused on that. He had finally found an interest in common with Jo and they'd had a fun time. That ranked as a good date. Didn't it?

He'd like to have discussed his mother descending on him. It would be nice to talk it through with her. The thought surprised him a little. He would have liked to hear Jo's opinion. Angelo wagered that it would have been well considered and thought-ful. But the subject hadn't come up and then she'd blanked his brain.

He'd been too surprised to react to the chocolaty kiss, and was glad she'd given him an excuse to not do so by sticking out her tongue at him. If he'd had a moment to think about it, he'd have found some way to screw it up. Instead, he'd laughed at the momentary image of the ever so proper attorney Ms. Thompson sticking her tongue out at a jury if she didn't like their decision.

Angelo walked down the half block of Pike Street that led from First Avenue into the heart of the Market. The uneven brick was as packed with people as the sidewalks. Woe to a tourist stupid enough to attempt to drive on this street. He ignored the fact that he'd fallen into just that trap an hour before while attempting to park his van.

It was warm and sunny. The gelato merchant's success was evident in dozens of people's hands, bright globes of pure, glis-tening color perched on thin cones stood out among the kalei-doscope of summer attire. Bags held everything from fish and produce to soaps and trinkets. A woman wearing strike-you-dead-with-lust perfume brushed by him, her arm full of dahlias, her hair a bright chop of blonde and chartreuse.

Left Hand Books was so crowded that the people visible through the window could be seen doing the awkwardly slow shuffle step among the shelves. Henry shot him a friendly salute from the big fish stall right before flinging a twelve-pound salmon through the air toward the cashier for wrapping and sale.

Angelo tossed a couple of dollars to Uli at Frank's Quality Produce and snagged a basket of strawberries to eat as he headed along.

At Mr. D's he gave the rest of the strawberries to Demetrios and his family and turned up Post Alley careful not to look in the Sur La Table display windows. He always heard tourists complaining that they, "really didn't need anything more for the kitchen, but how could they resist" as they staggered out with the overstuffed trademark brown and maroon bags. For a chef, the place was a nightmare. Add on the commercial restaurant and Pike Place Market vendor discounts, and the place was beyond dangerous and often downright lethal to his budget.

He was, despite his best efforts, being drawn by the glistening copper Zabaglione pot in the window. His were getting pretty battered with use and some nights having only two caused timing problems.

That's when he noticed the snarl of people up near his restaurant. At first he hoped it was the Perennial Tea Room across Post Alley, but it wasn't. He hustled along and almost got clipped by a car as he crossed Stewart Street.

The day, delightful and warm a moment before, slapped him with a latent heat that had him sweating. People were milling around beneath the discreet Angelo's Tuscan Hearth sign. Oh God, another disaster.

He'd apparently dodged the first crisis. No bad reviews had come of the Notorious Thursday Night Fiasco, as Jo had named it. But by the size of this crowd he was too late to recover from whatever was happening this time. They were between services, yet the crowd was massive. Kitchen fire. Or worse.

He resisted the urge to shove his way through the crowd, instead nudging and begging-his-pardon through the claustrophobic horde toward his own door. He'd almost made it inside when he spotted his mother.

She stood with a great smile on her face. Clad in a floppy sunhat, she wore a floaty blue summer dress with a deep cleavage that would have been totally inappropriate on a woman of her age if it didn't look so good on her. A shawl of nearly transparent floral chiffon graced her shoulders. Daisies, she'd always had a soft spot for daisies. Her dark hair flowed to her shoulders and a tray of bruschetta balanced on one of her hands.

His avocados and artichokes.

He slid up beside her and gauged the crowd. They weren't upset. They were smiling. Laughing, chatting, bantering with his mother, and enjoying themselves. They formed a line into the restaurant.

That was it. Service had crashed and was far too slow, and his mother was taking care of entertaining the crowd while they waited.

"Oh, there you are honey. Everyone!" She called out to the crowd and conversations hushed. "This here, he is my son. This food, it is his. Isn't it wonderful?"

A round of applause burst forth that didn't make any sense for people stuck waiting in line. Why would there be a line at two in the afternoon anyway? There were always some patrons in the restaurant even on Saturday afternoons, but never a line out the door between the two main services.

"I think," Maria Amelia leaned close to him and spoke softly, "that perhaps Manuel would like it to have you in his kitchen." She stuffed a bruschetta in his open mouth. "Close your mouth, chew like a good boy, now *tu vai!*"

He went.

EVEN AS ANGELO chewed and went, the flavors began to bloom in his mouth. The lush richness of the avocado, the smooth balance of artichoke heart, a sliver of lemon-cooked swordfish and a chiffonade of fresh basil on toasted, thin-sliced Ciabatta bread was remarkable. It unfolded and unraveled, revealing layer upon layer, leaving him desperate for more.

"Angelo!" Manuel called out as he entered the kitchen. The

man practically wept with joy. "Hurry, an apron, three orders of the Cioppino and I will marry you and bear your children."

Angelo grabbed an apron and three bowls. With a rescue operation underway, you didn't ask questions. After five orders of the Cinghiale, braised boar meat over pasta, and a half dozen more of the Stuffed Chicken Picatta al modo di Angelo's, he began being able to see the flow of orders. There were no holdups. In fact, he'd rarely seen the team move food more quickly.

"What's the problem?" He tossed some more pasta with olive oil as a bed for his Braised Venison in Marmora Red Sauce.

"The problem is your mother," Manuel gasped out between commands to the grillardin to refire the duck breast and start another three orders of swordfish.

Angelo really didn't need this. Was his mother going to destroy him?

"She saw the lunch rush fading," Manuel talked between plating orders and yelling for Graziella to put some hustle on it even though she already was. "It was a good one for June, especially on a day when most people want to stay outside in the fine weather instead of sitting in a gourmet restaurant. Next thing I know, she takes a tureen of that chowder we were making for dinner, and a couple dozen spoons out the door. Before I can breathe, the restaurant, she is packed solid. When that ran out, she makes this bruschetta. You tasted it? *Estupendo,* eh? And she is gone out on the street again giving that away too. We've never had a Saturday like this one."

Chowder gone. He needed to start a soup base for dinner service to replace that. He yelled for Marko. The boy came running, wiping the soap suds from his hands. Angelo dug into his wallet and pulled out whatever cash he had.

"Go. Buy green beans, baby ones, none bigger around than a chopstick, more artichokes, fresh parsley, and another thirty pounds of swordfish. Go, don't gawk at me, *tu vai.*" It felt good to order someone else to jump on it.

Marko went at a dead run.

"If they're out of swordfish," Angelo yelled after him, "tell Henry you need twice that in fresh tuna."

"Hope he heard you," Manuel muttered. "Now I need at least a dozen more batches of fresh pasta dough. Go." Angelo knew better than to mess with the flow sliding through and around Manuel's station.

He went.

CHAPTER 7

*J*o answered the pounding on her door. Only one person ever pounded on her door, and never like this. She found herself near to running across the charcoal deep-pile carpet of her condo and yanking the door open.

Perrin practically collapsed into her arms. She looked as if she'd been in a battle and lost badly.

"What happened? Are you okay? Should I call the police?"

"Oh," Perrin leaned on her and allowed herself to be led into the apartment. "Thank God you're home. Take off your clothes."

From anyone other than Perrin, Jo would have been offended and made a sharp riposte. But with Perrin things always made sense, eventually.

"You look awful. Can I get you some food or something?" Her slender frame was actually weaving with the effort to remain standing. Her hair was a frantic mess and she wore no makeup, revealing an abnormally sallow complexion. Both were so unusual for Perrin that Jo again checked her friend for cuts and bruises. Perrin was always immaculate in how she presented herself to the world. Outrageous, often, but always perfectly presented and attired.

Perrin braced herself against Jo's cherrywood coat rack almost taking herself and Jo's coats to the floor. "I'll be fine once you try this on." She wiggled a white dress bag she held slung over one shoulder that Jo hadn't noticed.

"When was the last time you slept?"

Perrin waved one of her fine-fingered hands. "I dunno. Cassie's wedding? Maybe a couple nights ago? What day is this? Never mind, don't care." She shoved Jo toward her bedroom. "Now go get naked and try this on. And if you look in the mirror before I tell you, you're dead."

Jo started down the hall toward her bedroom. Perrin followed close behind leaving palm prints in the middle of the glass of more than one of the framed pictures as she stumbled into walls. When Jo reached out to steady her, Perrin simply slapped her hands aside and nudged her along.

Once in the bedroom, Perrin hung the dress bag on the back of the door and collapsed onto the quilted white bedspread. But in seconds she was back on her feet and vibrating with energy as she opened the bag.

"Turn around and get undressed."

Jo moved to close the curtains.

"Forget the curtains. You're like a gazillion stories up in the air. No one can see you unless they have a monster telescope like on top of one of those mountains, and if they do, all they're going to see is how gorgeous you are."

Jo closed the curtains anyway, she had her standards, no matter how much Perrin enjoyed pushing them. Once they were closed, she shed the sweatshirt and pants.

Perrin rolled her eyes. "The woman is home alone and she wears a bra. You're crazy, you know that? Lose it."

Normally Jo would have argued at least for form's sake, but

Perrin looked so wound up and simultaneously so fragile, that Jo simply obeyed.

"Damn but it sucks that we're both straight."

Jo refused to blush at Perrin's catty remark.

"Okay, close your eyes."

"You're kidding."

"Jo-o!" Perrin stamped her foot.

Jo closed her eyes and heard the zipper on the bag open the rest of the way. It was hard to resist peeking but she managed by thinking instead of the map of the North Slope continental shelf and the implications of melting ice access to oil and mineral resources.

"Arms out."

She held them out and cool fabric slid over them, the sensual slickness of silk.

"Okay, now up."

She raised her arms and the fabric slid down over her face and shoulders. She'd worn a lot of Perrin's creations over the years. Back in college the results could only occasionally be conferred with a label better than "interesting." But a decade later, "good" was a low standard and "exceptional" had almost become the norm with the occasional "sensational" like Cassidy's wedding dress and the two bridesmaid dresses.

Jo did her best to ignore the way the fabric wrapped around her like a full-body kiss. She hadn't been made so aware of every inch of her skin in a long time.

Perrin began tugging and adjusting, settling the dress into place.

"Can I look yet?"

"Don't you dare!" Perrin's voice was half shout, half mumble as though her mouth was full. Jo would bet it was, at least partly. She'd seen Perrin dozens of times, radiating near-mad intensity during a fitting, with her fingers flying deftly over the fabric, and a bunch of pins clamped in the corner of her mouth.

"Okay," more of a mumble. Then her voice cleared as she stuck the spare pins back into a cushion, or perhaps into Jo's bedspread. She'd best check before lying down tonight. "I'm almost there. I got the idea when I saw that celery green on you last weekend."

Jo typically wore black power suits, but it had been nice to wear such a pretty dress for the wedding. It had been so pretty that it had made her feel almost confident as a woman—an unfamiliar side of herself, as though she herself was an acquaintance she only met on rare and slightly uncomfortable occasions.

"There, okay," Perrin turned her slightly and pulled her half a step sideways. "You really should be wearing heels, but you hate them so I designed it so that I can make it work without. I'll do that later, though your legs in heels would be positively amazing. Open your eyes."

Jo did. Perrin had placed her directly in front of the full-length, beveled mirror that covered her closet door. But she didn't recognize the woman reflected there.

Perrin came up beside her, scooped up a handful of Jo's hair and held it up before turning to inspect the result in the mirror.

"I thought your hair should be up, but now I'm not sure." She let it down again and brushed it back off Jo's bare shoulders.

"What's this?" the far away voice was all Jo could manage. The floor-length dress started at her feet like the palest blue sea foam, with a thousand tiny overlaps of fabric. The pattern built and strengthened as it flowed around her hips, somehow accenting their womanly curves while making them appear trim. From there it bloomed upward, wrapping her breasts in the palest-blue waves, as gentle as they were bountiful. A slit did indeed reveal some leg, but ended just above the knee allowing the dress to cling, but allowing the wearer to move about freely and look dazzling as well.

Perrin was rummaging through the jewelry on Jo's dressing

table, probably turning it into a hopeless tangle. She returned with the strand of Jo's mother's pearls, the only thing she had from the woman she couldn't remember. Her dad claimed that she'd left them behind by accident, but she doubted that once she learned it had been his wedding gift to her mother. Perrin scoffed after a moment and tossed them carelessly onto the bedspread.

Next the gold chain and dangling orca she'd worn for the date with Yuri.

"Almost." Perrin tossed that on the bed as well.

She finally held a silver chain bearing a sparkling silver filigree medallion with an amethyst-colored backing that Jo had loved and bought, but never found anything to wear it with.

"Oh my God." Jo was finally able to see the breathtaking woman in the mirror. "You made…my wedding dress?"

Perrin's reflection finished fastening the chain then peeked over Jo's shoulder. Her face was pixie bright.

"Am I good, or am I good?"

Jo could only gaze in amazement. "No, you're way better than good."

"Wait until you see the back."

Perrin spun her around and grabbed a hand mirror from the table scattering a couple of necklaces and an earring to the carpet.

It felt as if nothing were there and Jo was worried about having to let Perrin down gently. She wasn't the sort to wear a risqué dress, especially not to a wedding, most certainly not to her own, and Perrin should know that by now.

But when she had the hand mirror aligned with the one behind her, Jo could only shake her head in amazement. The line of the dress followed the line of her hair. With her hair down, there would be constant flashes of bare shoulder and glimpses of skin, but it was somehow, impossibly, demure as well. The conservative shape of the rest of the back balanced the piece perfectly and made her look impossibly enticing.

In profile, well, her chest was too big, but it didn't look like it in this dress. The dress design accented without embellishing.

She turned to hug Perrin, "It's incredible!"

With their arms around each other, they turned to look back in the mirror.

"It's just incredible. I've never looked so beautiful." She rose up on her toes and considered. Maybe she'd wear heels on this one occasion.

Perrin looked simply radiant. "I've also got ideas for Cassie's and my dress to go with it."

That brought Jo back to reality, which was an almost crushing blow. For an instant, she'd felt giddy. As if she was flying. And had now crash-landed in a gloomy swamp.

"Uh, Perrin. There's just one problem."

"What? What is it?" she began inspecting the perfect dress for some hidden flaw.

"Perrin," she had to take her friend by her shoulders to stop her and make her to focus on Jo's face.

"What?"

"I'm not getting married."

"Oh," Perrin shrugged that away as being of no consequence. "Is that all? That's not a problem."

Jo stared at her. "Not a problem? You give me the absolutely perfect wedding dress and now I have no reason to wear it? That's a big problem in my book."

"Phft," Perrin waved a hand again and turned them both back to admire the dazzling woman in the mirror. "With a dress like this in your closet? No worries. You'll find someone to fall madly in love with you, just so you get to wear it."

"Years, Perrin. I've still got years of my career before I'm ready. I'm going to be commuting to northern Alaska for at least two years on my next case for goodness sake."

"Never underestimate the power of a really good dress," her friend insisted cheerfully.

As always, it was pointless to argue with Perrin. Jo looked in the mirror again. One thing Perrin had right, it was a really, really good dress.

PERRIN SLEPT through breakfast and lunch. Jo had stuffed her into the shower and then tucked her into bed in the guest room. She'd only allowed herself to sneak in twice to make sure her friend was actually still breathing.

It felt like being back in college, back when Perrin was so wild that she and Cassidy had often taken shifts making sure she'd be okay after her latest escapade. This time, thankfully, it was just exhaustion. Perrin had stayed straight and sober since she and Cassidy did an intervention during freshman year, except for the occasional gal's night out, but that was nothing compared to the bouts with alcohol poisoning Perrin had been habitually pursuing.

By late afternoon Jo sat in the living room doing her best to pretend she was interested in the latest Grisham novel. Normally his legal thrillers kept her riveted, she had every one in hardback, a few of them even signed, but not now.

The problem was that everything was in churn. And the dress was not the least of her problems. Last night, after she'd made sure Perrin was finally settled, she had returned to her bedroom and locked the door. She'd carefully brushed out her hair, knowing it was her best feature, and slipped back into the dress. This time she selected a pair of dark-blue Kate Spade heels making her several inches taller.

She'd studied the woman in the mirror carefully. She remained a mystery. Jo could still smell the stench of fish that had permeated the home of her youth. It had seemed to waft down the high school hallways behind her and no matter how she scrubbed in the shower, she'd never been clear of it.

Her early physical development had drawn the boys, but she'd built up a barrier knowing that the smell followed her. She'd heard the whispers of "arrogant" and "stuck up" and each time they had cut out a piece of her soul.

But she simply couldn't stand what someone would think if they really knew, so she did her best to never let the pain show. She trusted no boys and very few girls and had instead dedicated her every waking minute to getting out of Ketchikan High and Ketchikan, Alaska. Valedictorian, straight four-point-oh student, Native American heritage, a cakewalk for scholarships. She'd left and never looked back. When the call came from Debby Rowe for the tenth-year reunion, Jo had asked her as a personal favor to please lose Jo's contact information somewhere dark and obscure.

By the time she'd arrived at Vassar in Poughkeepsie, New York, she'd built a barrier so high that none could pierce it. Or so she'd thought. Her roommate, Cassidy Knowles, had been the perfect match, both of them quiet and both dying to get away from somewhere.

What would have happened to them if Perrin Williams hadn't entered their lives was anyone's guess.

She and Cassidy had still been gently probing each other as new roommates by comparing favorite high school classes, when a wild girl had stumbled into their room. "I'm Perrin! Right across the hall!" She had hair in five colors and a henna tattoo that ran up one arm and down the other, "and right over my left breast. Wanna see?" she'd cheerfully begun hauling the hem of her blouse out of her skirt's waistband. Despite her awful background, that she'd shared much more reluctantly, she'd consciously chosen to be a positive person, albeit with an often-manic intensity.

For reasons Jo had never been able to unravel, the three of

them had been inseparable for the four years following that moment.

Without Cassidy and Perrin in her life, would the woman in the mirror, wearing the dress made of pale blue ocean waves and passion, be staring back at her? Probably not.

Without Cassidy's heart and Perrin's deep-seated joy, Jo would have continued on some perfect track and married some New York stockbroker who would never be as smart as she was.

The woman in the mirror didn't look like Jo. She had a confidence that Counselor Thompson only found in the courtroom wearing black power suits. She didn't recognize the feminine form that stood before her, constantly running her hands over the fine stitching and soft shapes that encircled her form.

Who was this woman?

What decisions would she make that the Counselor would never even consider?

Jo had no idea, but she watched the woman in the mirror for a long time before taking off the dress and putting it away again.

She'd been careful not to look in the mirror before going to bed.

PERRIN STUMBLED out of the guest bedroom in the early evening as the sun headed toward the Olympic Mountains.

It filled Jo's apartment with the warm oranges and reds that had sold Jo on it the first time she'd walked through the door. She'd decorated with her west-facing view and this time of day in mind, white walls and neutral carpets so that the changing light of outdoors would fill the room.

Perrin had clearly raided Jo's closet with what should be amusing results but were fetching instead. She'd folded over one of Jo's billowing floral skirts and trapped it about her trim waist with a belt leaving the waistband to flop over the belt. The Vassar college t-shirt, rather than being grossly too large, slid off both of her shoulders leaving a broad expanse of bare skin that made her look cute instead of slutty.

Her hair was still dyed as black as Jo's, making her pale skin and blue eyes even more startling. She'd finished it with Jo's mother's pearls and a pair of bright green and red woolen Christmas socks despite the evening's warmth. On Perrin the outfit looked ludicrous and wonderful.

Jo sighed. Once again Perrin proved that a woman with a thirty-two-inch chest could get away with wearing anything and still look charming.

"What day is it?" Perrin collapsed onto the other end of the red leather sofa at perfect ease. Like a cat waking from a long nap in the sun.

"Sunday. You've been asleep for almost twenty hours."

"Good. Guess I needed it. Do you have any food?"

"How about pizza?"

"Yum!"

Jo dialed downstairs. One advantage of living in a condo built on top of prime downtown retail space, there were a dozen restaurants in her building and they all delivered.

Perrin propped her feet up on the glass coffee table and admired Jo's Christmas socks as she wiggled her toes.

"Now, we need to figure out who you're going to wear that dress for."

"Perrin."

"What happened to that banker you were seeing?" Perrin rolled right over Jo's admonishment.

"That ended months ago."

"Too bad. How about Russell's dad? He was really cute, in an older guy sort of way, seriously rich too, but he seemed pretty attached to his wife."

"Have you heard from Cassidy?" Jo shot for a subject change.

"All I've been doing is your dress. I couldn't stop until it was done. Even Cassidy's didn't attack me like that. I just saw this one in my head and I had to do it. Tell me again you think it's amazing." There. That was why she loved Perrin. Beneath all of that bravado and flair and extrovert assuredness, was a woman cautious, uncertain, and impossibly real.

"Beyond amazing, Perrin. You keep outdoing yourself, but this time you really did."

Perrin nodded. Jo could see that she still had trouble accepting she was any good.

"I need to check in with Raquel," Perrin offered her own subject change. "I left the shop to her all week."

Jo didn't really want to pay for a wedding dress without a wedding, but Perrin had invested so much of herself in it that she'd have to. Even without a major designer label, a dress like that was worth thousands. Even worse than figuring out how much to pay, would be figuring out how to pay Perrin without paying her. Perrin didn't care about money, especially didn't want it from friends, which was one of the reasons she and Cassidy had practically forced Raquel upon her. The woman possessed immense business sense. Maybe Jo would just pay Raquel and tell her not to mention it to Perrin.

"Did she send any pictures?"

"Raqu—" Jo started then cut herself off. They were back to the subject of Cassidy. Even with a decade of practice, it was still hard to keep up with Perrin's mercurial subject changes. Jo again wondered, as she had from time to time, if Perrin wasn't the smartest of the three of them. Probably the most screwed up, which was saying something, but astonishingly intelligent in her own way.

Jo pulled out her iPad and tapped for the last three e-mails from Italy. She checked, yes, they'd been copied to Perrin.

Then she held it out.

Instead, Perrin scooted over so that sat shoulder to shoulder.

Jo tapped for the first image. It was an airplane bathroom shot through a partly open door.

Cassidy's caption on the picture was, "So not!"

"So much for the mile-high club," was all Perrin had to say to that.

CHAPTER 8

"*H*ow's the head?"

Angelo looked up from the bench-press machine to see Jo towering over him. Again she wore little enough to reveal exactly how amazing her conditioning was. Cyclists' legs of strong thighs, a workout-flat stomach, and arms with just that womanly hint of muscle that did nothing to mar the illusion of smooth skin but hinted at lurking power beneath.

"Uh, fine." He lowered and released the handles then sat up. That brought his face level with her breasts, dark green sports bra this time. He struggled to his feet.

"Barely a lump anymore."

"Sore from the ride?"

"Not particularly." He'd been teased throughout dinner service for hobbling like an old man. "You?"

"Plenty. Clearly we need to do that more often."

That he liked the sound of. "Anytime."

"Well, I should finish my workout and leave you to yours."

Angelo scrambled for some way to keep her close, even for a few moments.

"I'm off today, the restaurant is closed Mondays. We could go for another ride."

"This is my work week. I have to be in the office soon." She glanced down at the slightly scary wristwatch, heart monitor, exercise thing she wore. "Actually, I'm done and headed for the showers or my assistant will beat me up for being late. She's fierce."

They shared a smile over that. Angelo remembered the sweaty years working for one chef after another in New York, and several summers in Italy. The former had cared about time, the latter about flavor. However, both had busted his ass enough on both points that he could really appreciate being his own master. And the fact that he drove his staff as hard as his mentors had, and himself harder, was only par for the course.

Angelo eyed the wall clock. It was barely seven-thirty. Right, that's when they'd gone riding too. Jo was clearly a morning person. He was a night owl who'd learned to be awake for two hours every morning to do the restaurant shopping and a workout before sleeping three more hours.

"After work?"

She'd started to turn for the locker room, but turned back and did that appraising thing.

Then she smiled, "Do you run?"

"Sure."

"I'm training for the Hagg Lake triathlon next month in Forest Grove, Oregon. Meet at five o'clock by your restaurant?"

"Sounds great."

Angelo watched her head off, damn that woman could walk. Then he pictured her in a sleek one-piece swimsuit and decided he'd better look into that triathlon himself and see if it was too late to sign up.

HE WAS ALREADY WELL STRETCHED and warmed up as she trotted up to him. Again those legs killed him. She wore a loose black t-shirt and bright, fluorescent orange running shorts. The wrap-around shades and her hair back in a ponytail swinging easily side to side completed the picture. But she had legs of bloody iron.

He fell in easily beside her. They dropped down Stewart Street and, after a little judicious zigzagging around tourists, they followed Western Avenue toward Broad Street.

"You enter many tri's?" He'd signed up for the Oregon event online. He'd been lucky enough to catch the last day of registration. Thankfully it was a short one: a mile swim, twenty-five-mile bike ride, and a ten-K run. There'd also been a shorter sprint tri, but he figured he could, depending on which Jo was doing, more easily choose to drop down to the shorter one than climb up to the higher one on race day.

"No." They jogged in place waiting for a light change where Alaskan Way cut uphill as Broad Street. "This is my first. Figured I'd embarrass myself where no one else would ever see me."

Whoops! Well, he could always just lose the entry fee.

"Let me know if you want some company."

Again those impenetrable glasses inspected him.

"Green," he noted the light and trotted across the street.

They dropped down through Myrtle Edwards Park and turned north along the shore of Elliot Bay. The water was busy with ferries and sailboats, a pair of container ships, and a ridiculously tall cruise ship. The wind off the water tasted of the ocean and the mountains beyond, crisp and fresh on the warm afternoon. The sun beat down on them from high in the west, heating his back.

They ran in silence and Angelo worked on finding his rhythm. He used to run a lot, but this last year had been so crazy with the success of the restaurant that he hadn't been out much.

He knew that he'd have to push to be ready in a month, even for just a ten-K.

At Roy Street, Jo turned and cut uphill. A dozen blocks later they were winding through the mansions that covered the western slope of Queen Anne Hill. The narrow twisting streets wound and climbed in a maze-inspired array and he was quickly as lost as the dumbest rat.

"Wow! There's some serious money here," he managed to gasp out. He'd seen enough of that, growing up in Russell's house. These places weren't as big as the East Coast mansions owned by the New York magnates. The Morgan estate sat on a small island in Old Greenwich, Connecticut with only three other homes across the short causeway that separated them from shore. Their house had been a modest one by Old Greenwich standards, and would be a major one here, but not the biggest or best.

Jo drove up the hills at a steady pace, and he had to struggle to keep up without dying on the slopes. At long last, they crested the hill and ran down along Queen Anne Avenue itself. He could feel his legs unknotting, though his lungs didn't recover as she upped the pace.

Either she was in as amazing shape as she looked, or she was trying to run him into the ground. Or maybe both. She ran as if a demon dogged her heels but as if winged Mercury, the Greek messenger god himself, had blessed her feet.

They pummeled down the hill on Fourth Avenue. Only the one street clung to the steep north face of Queen Anne Hill, and it dropped straight down. At the bottom of the descent they crossed the Fremont Bridge and hit the Burke-Gilman Trail where they'd started their bike ride, this time on foot.

"This is like the Oregon terrain."

"I knew it." Jo ground to halt and Angelo doubled back to her. He kept jogging in place though she'd stopped.

"Knew what?"

"You signed up for the Hagg Lake Tri today, didn't you?"

Shit! Well, time to be a man about it. He shrugged a, "Yes."

"Are you stalking me, Angelo? What's really going on here?" She was shaking out her legs. He knew they'd be vibrating with the interrupted run. He stopped running and gestured helplessly as his own legs began to vibrate with the sudden break.

Should he try the truth? What the hell did he have to lose? He'd met her barely a half dozen times and she was all he could think about. Fat lot of good it did him.

"SINCE THE FIRST moment I saw you, I don't see anyone else." Angelo traced his hands through the air as if tracing her face.

Jo loved watching his hands as he spoke, it was so, she searched for the right word. It was so Italian.

"A pretty girl goes by," he waved to indicate a long, lean, blonde running by them on the Burke-Gilman path with a graceful, gazelle-like stride. "I don't even see her."

"But you just did." She had to bite the inside of her cheek to not laugh at him.

"I..." He turned to look, but the runner had already passed out of sight under the bridge. "She..." He smacked a palm against his forehead. He looked so perplexed.

"Let me guess," Jo put on her Counselor Thompson tone as Angelo seemed to find it so daunting. "If you were alone, you would have perhaps jogged up to that woman, greeted her in Italian, pretended you were new in town and only knew a little English. And then...let's see...you'd have asked if she knew a 'great gelato place' somewhere nearby."

"Sure," then he blushed a brilliant red, then shrugged in that eloquent way of his. "Probably."

He hedged, but she wasn't buying it. He was too handsome to not know his power over women.

"Last year, before I met you, no problem. Of course I would. She wore no ring, either." He slapped a hand over his mouth. Then shrugged again and uncovered a boyish smile.

"Okay, so I still notice. But since the first time I see you," he flicked a finger against his own temple. "Nothing. I watch them run by and I don't even think, 'Angelo, you should chase that one.' They just go by and I wonder when is the next time I will see Jo Thompson."

His voice was rising and Jo was having trouble swallowing. No one ever talked about her like that. And the faster he spoke, the more an Italian rhythm slipped in, making his voice even more engaging.

"I just can't win with you, can I? No matter what I do, I just screw it all up. I can't sweep you away with the best food at the most romantic wedding I've ever been to. I can't go running with you with not making myself an *idiota*."

"You can't cook dinner for me, you proved that," she couldn't resist the tease. He was past hearing the tone. It struck home and his dark eyes flashed.

"You come by without some *bastardo*, out-sized, 'I'm so gorgeous' Russian and I'll show you what I can cook." His anger rolled louder still. "Hell! Bring him along and I'll show you both what I can do. I'll cook that...that... whatever he is right under the damn table!" He made as if to hurl down a gauntlet.

He took her breath away. No one had ever seen her as he did. Outside of her legal expertise, all men ever saw was her body, but Angelo hadn't glanced down once in his entire tirade.

And he was so impossibly cute about it. So wound up that she could only think of one thing to stop him as he launched into a description of exactly what he would cook to show that Russian what was what.

She clamped his face in her hands and kissed him, hard.

If he hesitated even a second, she didn't notice it go by. He didn't drag her against him. He didn't clutch or grab. He barely moved.

In an instant he went from raging Italian to leaning ever so gently into the kiss. It floated through her like...

She was so good with words. She should be able to attach some words to how she felt as he tipped his head in her hands and deepened the kiss.

It floated through her like...a kiss. It sounded stupid inside her head, but it was all she had at the moment.

He slid his hands over hers. Caressing them, then holding them in his, and finally sliding them from his face, then rocking back just enough for their lips to part.

"Breathe, *bella signora*. Before you pass out." His dark eyes sparkled so close.

"I'd better take my own advice." He stepped back, dropping her hands after a final gentle squeeze, and made a show of taking a deep breath that ended on a soft chuckle.

Jo managed to drag in some much-needed air and shared his laugh for a moment.

"Okay," his voice was a caress. "I expected that kiss to be strong, like a spicy Sicilian sauce, but..." He whooshed out another breath and scrubbed his hands over his face.

She still couldn't respond. Couldn't quite tell if he was happy or upset. Couldn't quite tell how *she* felt about it either.

"Next time we try that," Angelo grinned at her, "I want to be somewhere we won't injure ourselves when our knees give out."

Jo looked down at the hard pavement of the trail then back up at Angelo.

"Please tell me there will be a next time, Jo. Please tell me there will be."

Jo's wits finally came back to her. She'd just received the best kiss of her life from one of the most handsome men she'd ever met.

"Damn straight there's going to be another chance," she assured both of them.

CHAPTER 9

*A*ngelo and his mother arrived at the airport just before midnight. Cassidy's somewhat frantic e-mail had popped up while Angelo had been out running with Jo. They were on a direct flight home and could Angelo or someone pick them up?

She'd been less than clear about why they were aborting their honeymoon after only a week and Angelo feared the worst. Their first trip to Italy had been a four-alarm relationship disaster, but Russell had assured him that everything that had caused that was resolved. After all, he'd married her rather than setting off to sail alone around the world in anger and misery, which was a good thing. Angelo wondered if he should have hidden Russell's boat.

Mama had insisted on coming with him to the airport even though the plane was arriving near midnight. She'd known Russell as long as Angelo had and was just as worried. They'd driven the car down as the van had no back seats.

Now they waited at the head of the escalator for international arrivals. It was a leftover from the days when you could meet arriving flights at the gate, and no one had ever updated it. International flights landed at the secure southern terminal. After people wended their way through customs, they boarded the underground train to the main terminal and rode up the escalator at the end of the secure zone.

That was all well and good. But the escalator popped out in the middle of baggage claim where a total of three uncomfortable seats had been bolted to a gray wall well off to the side. Other than that, you just had to stand in the busiest and narrowest corridor of the whole airport, among a vast array of baggage claim carousels, and wait.

Angelo sucked at waiting.

He'd settled into pacing down past the first couple baggage claim conveyors and back while his mother settled in one of the three awkward seats. Some installation artist had mounted dozens of pieces of abandoned luggage with a massive iron pipe rammed through their centers. Suspended above the baggage conveyor were skewered leather suitcases, punctured nylon carry-ons, a guitar hard-shell case pithed like a giant black beetle, a garment bag bullet-shot through the heart, and many more. Like this was supposed to instill confidence in the airlines? He was halfway down the art piece wondering if any of these was the suitcase that had never followed him back from his last trip to California to teach, when he heard the twin cries of "Mrs. Parrano!"

He spun to see his mother embracing Jo and Perrin. Cassidy's plea for help must have gone to them as well.

Damn! He kept forgetting to tell Jo about his mother's moving in with him, never mind that she was making him insane at the restaurant. Already the three of them were talking so fast he couldn't begin to follow. How in the world did women all talk at once and still hear everything? He'd never understood that.

Jo barely broke the flow as she shot him her hotshot attorney look with one raised eyebrow. Well, the news of his mother's move had just come out, probably the retirement would be only seconds behind it.

He tried a shrug to say, "Okay, you caught me. I screwed up. I'll never do it again. Trust me."

Her laugh informed him that she'd read right through his bullshit of best intentions.

The woman made him crazy. All he'd been able to think about was when he'd get a chance to kiss her again. And more. But she'd gone shy at the end of their run, leaving him quickly when they reached his restaurant. He didn't even know where she lived, though by the direction and that she'd walked rather than jogged away without looking back, he figured it was some-where downtown.

He'd managed not to follow her, but had broken down and Googled her. All he got back was her law offices two blocks from his restaurant and a daunting list of lawsuits. He didn't even understand what most of them were about, corporate craziness of some breed or other, but he poked through them enough to learn that she never lost a case, at least not that he could tell.

He was lusting after one of the top corporate lawyers in the city, one who could slice and dice a corporation or a govern-ment lawsuit before breakfast without breaking a sweat. He usually went for the simplicity of a vapid, no-strings-sex kind of women.

Workout girls were a nice bonus, though he'd learned the hard way to never pick up a woman at the gym he used. It made things awkward after the breakups.

He'd tried dating other chefs, but between their mutually workaholic schedules and his generally superior cooking skills, those never lasted.

Now he was chasing a woman who was probably smarter than most of the people on the planet. He should be running full tilt the other direction.

Then why had her kiss rooted him to the ground? One moment he'd been raging against something he still couldn't quite recall and the next his world had gone quiet. All he'd known were the cool touch of her hands and the burning heat of her lips. He'd always been the one in calm control and he wasn't liking the change.

Jo continued to chat with his mother as if they were long lost friends.

Oh God! His mother hadn't only become friends with his butcher and his seafood supplier. She was also charming the woman he wanted to date. If she did become his girlfriend... Maybe he should just leave quietly, go back to his restaurant, and throw himself on a chef's knife. Then he'd be comfortably dead and the craziness in his head would stop. *Bene!*

Another train must have unloaded downstairs as a fresh flood of passengers flowed up the escalator. That's when he spotted the friendly face. A friendly male face.

"Sanctuary!" He hustled past the three women, through the crowd streaming off the escalator, and over to the elevator where he'd spotted Russell Morgan.

He stopped, put his hands on his hips, and looked down at him.

"And what the hell happened to you?"

CHAPTER 10

The three women enveloped Cassidy and it was left to Angelo to keep a level head and roll his friend's wheelchair to the side, freeing a blockage in the flow of traffic when the next elevator load spilled out. He considered trying to also move the four women, now catching up on news, out of the way, but decided that his long-term survival would be improved if he left them to their own devices.

He rapped his knuckles sharply on Russell's leg cast, noted the slight wince and rapped it once more with a little more force.

"How in the hell did you break that?"

"It was Cassidy's idea."

"Was not." Somehow she'd heard despite the half-dozen paces and stream of tired tourists that separated them. She came over to stand beside her husband's wheelchair. The hand she stroked over his head and down his neck was gentle and told Angelo that at least the relationship hadn't blown up unlike their last trip to Italy.

"Mr. Athlete here decided he just had to try parasailing behind a power boat."

"You said it looked like fun."

"No," Cassidy rested a hand on his shoulder. "I said it looked like stupid fun."

Russell just harrumphed.

Angelo rapped his knuckles on the cast again and would have received a sharp jab in the ribs if he hadn't dodged quickly.

"How long?"

"Damn thing itches. It's already too long."

"Six weeks," Cassidy kissed him on top of the head. "And he's already got three weeks of complaining in during the first forty-eight hours. I can't begin to tell you how much fun this is going to be."

"That does it. I'm never going back to that stupid country."

This time Angelo's mother rapped her knuckles sharply on Russell's cast and he caught his breath sharply.

"You no say that about my country or I no make you my special biscotti."

Russell looked up at her, "Yes, Nana. What are you doing in Seattle?"

"Good boy," she leaned down and kissed him on top of the head just as Cassidy had. "And no making Cassidy crazy. I know you."

She turned to Cassidy, "I warn you. He is even a worse patient than my boy Angelo."

"Baggage." Angelo grabbed the handles to the wheelchair and pushed he and Russell clear of the group. "We definitely need to find baggage."

"And a bar," Russell put in.

"Definitely a bar," Angelo agreed.

ANGELO HAD OVERRULED the women's vote to head straight home in a quite simple way. He'd settled Russell into his car and gotten behind the driver's wheel. Then he drove them out of SeaTac airport, across Highway 99, and right into the 13 Coins Restaurant parking lot. It was their traditional stop after crazy trips. The place offered twenty-four-hour fine dining and alcohol from six in the morning until two the next morning.

He'd dragged Russell here after his ill-fated first trip to Italy with Cassidy and let him drink himself straight through oblivion and into passed out. Russell had made sure Angelo got good and loose, though stopped him short of plastered, after he'd returned from his first time as a guest instructor at the Culinary Institute of America last fall. Cassidy had kept telling him what fun it was to teach there, and he'd fallen for it like a babe in the woods. He still shivered at the memory of it. The CIA wanted him back this fall, but he had never been one to get up in front of a room full of people. Just let him hide in the kitchen and cook. Besides, he'd need to buy a new suitcase.

The 13 Coins had deep booths with high, dark leather backs and soft lighting. You could crawl into a booth and not be seen for hours. The waitresses were discrete, understood the necessity for speed on drink orders, and always offered to keep track of your flight time if you were outbound to make sure you didn't miss your plane. Even the stools in front of the bar were tall, cozy, and wrapped around you shutting out the rest of the world.

In the middle of the room were low tables and comfortable chairs scattered about like someone's living room. They found a table with room for six plus Russell's extended leg.

"I came down wrong is all."

"Yes. Right on top of a jet skier's head, then got tangled in the controls as it rolled over."

"You thought those looked like fun too."

"Suicidal stupid fun? Yes. Something any rational, thinking human would actually do? Not so much. Don't you hear adjectives?" She turned to face everyone else. "I took a nap on the beach and next thing I know a polite Italian ambulance driver is waking me up. The guy he landed on was the cameraman and his camera is now deep in the Mediterranean Sea, so we, thank God, don't have video of it. Though if we did, I could lord it over him whenever he got out of line." Cassidy was clearly enjoying herself. Quite happy with being right, she did nothing to halt the sharp rap Maria Amelia Avico Parrano landed on Russell's cast each time he whined.

"Are you trying to extend my lifespan or something?" Russell groused at his wife.

Angelo shook his head and whispered to his friend, "Still a crazy thought, you being married."

Russell nodded in agreement and he studied his beer while Cassidy kept going. She was having way too much fun at Russell's expense, which Angelo was trying not to laugh about in his friend's face.

"Hey, you're the one who showed me that I loved you. So if you die before I do, I'm going to have to kill you." Cassidy dipped up a cracker full of the Crab and Artichoke Dip clearly feeling she'd won the point.

Angelo would have to agree that she would have to kill Russell if he died first, so, out of loyalty he kept his mouth shut. All he really wanted to do was run everything by Russell, but he couldn't with his mother and Jo sitting right there. And he wasn't so sure he wanted to talk about Jo with him anyway. He could hear Russell's answer right now without asking.

"She's hot. You should go for her."

Not really helpful. The first part he couldn't argue with. The second part he already knew, it just scared the crap out of him.

Jo sat between his mother on one side and Cassidy and Perrin on the other. They were just far enough away that he couldn't make out their soft conversation.

"What happened to you?"

Angelo turned to face Russell. "What are you talking about?"

Russell rolled his eyes toward Jo.

So much for not bringing it up. "Uh, I hit my head. And we went for a bike ride together." Could he sound more stupid? "And a run." Yep, he could.

Russell studied him over his beer for a while before continuing his thought.

"You know, this whole being married thing is strange. It changes your outlook in some really interesting ways."

"Like what?" Angelo tried not to scoff, but it must have come out that way.

"Like being married to Cassidy makes me think of the other two as my sisters. I always thought they were beautiful and a lot of fun. But now it's more than that."

Angelo sipped his own beer in acknowledgment.

"I love you like a brother, but if you hurt one of them, I'm gonna be hurting you so much worse. Whether or not I'm still in this cast."

Angelo slumped in his chair. Okay, that was even less helpful than he'd expected.

"ANGELO DIDN'T TELL me you had moved here to Seattle." Jo had gone with ginger ale. She'd needed to be awake in under five hours and headed to the gym before work. She really needed to be home in bed, not chatting with Angelo's mother in some all-night in-crowd airport bar.

"Ah, I was more than right. You are the girl who rides the bicycles. That is good."

Jo eyed her carefully, but the smile was genuine. A quick glance showed Cassidy's attention was with Perrin at the moment which, Jo decided, was a good thing.

"My Angelo's taste. Sometimes it is good, sometimes not so good. I tell him that he should find someone as pretty and nice as you, and now he has."

Jo glanced over at Angelo, slumped in his chair and pretending to ignore Russell. "So you told him to chase me and he does? Doesn't speak much for his initiative."

"No. No." Maria flapped Jo's words away. "He said he was going riding, and I tell him I hope she's as nice as the pretty one at the wedding. The boy, he doesn't say a word yes or no, not that I gave him the chance." Her smile was easy. "It does good to keep that one a little off his balance. He is too sure of himself. Men always are. Cassidy does it to Russell, I've never before seen him so fascinated, as if he is always waiting for the next act of the magic show to see what Cassidy will do next."

"It's true," Cassidy joined the conversation. "Around Russell I get all of these great ideas. It's like our thoughts spark off each other."

"And your bodies, I hope," Perrin leaned in from Cassidy's far side.

"Oh yeah," Cassidy smiled at her. "Seriously."

"Until he earned the cast," Jo noted.

"It ends mid-thigh," Angelo's mother offered a far-too-wise smile.

"It does," Cassidy sighed happily. "Indeed it does. You know, Italian hospital beds aren't all that narrow."

"I knew it!" Perrin flagged the waitress for another cosmopolitan. "Where else?"

"Well, we hadn't gotten to the sailboat yet. But we did stay with my friends at their villa in the Piedmont. In the middle of the vineyard they have a splendid little gazebo and a spread of grass open to the night sky."

Jo heard her sigh echoed by the other two women as well.

"Then there was this powerboat with a small, but well-appointed cabin on Lake Como. Let's just say that we spent a lot of time on the water, but didn't see the lake very much."

"Then the *idiota* broke his leg." Maria pulled Cassidy over across Jo's lap and kissed her cheek in sympathy before letting her go.

"Then the *idiota* broke his leg." Cassidy sipped her wine. "I'd be angrier if he didn't keep apologizing so much. He does feel really awful about ruining the honeymoon."

"Well," Jo thought about all that was going on in her life and felt guilty for saying it from such a selfish place of needing to talk to Cassidy, but it was true anyway. "We're really glad you're back safe. And had some fun."

"We did." Then Cassidy grinned a bit and blushed. She glanced sideways at Perrin who burst out laughing.

It only took Jo and Maria a moment to catch on.

"Of course Russell did need some help getting back and forth to the bathroom on the flight home," Perrin said right on the verge of one of her merry giggles.

"He did," Cassidy acknowledged, her smile deepening. "He did indeed."

CHAPTER 11

*J*o spent most of Tuesday inhaling international law. The UNCLOS, United Nations Convention on the Law of the Sea, had been ratified by all parties bordering the Arctic Ocean, except for the United States. As usual with international treaties, even ones the U.S. sponsored, it remained unapproved despite all common sense and decency.

That didn't stop the U.S. from claiming Territorial Waters to twelve miles offshore, the Exclusive Economic Zone to two hundred nautical miles and, in addition, trying to claim continental shelf out to three-hundred-and-fifty miles. They were attempting an undersea land grab much of the way to the North Pole. All of the countries were.

The U.S. government was also claiming some of the same territory as Canada. Oddly enough the border where the Russian claim neighbored Alaskan waters to the west was clear and undisputed. Of course the Russians and Norwegians couldn't agree on anything. And Canada was duking it out with Denmark over a tiny, useless uninhabited island. That made the whole thing a pretty typical international fiasco.

In addition, the melting of the polar ice was opening up the Northwest Passage for shipping for the first time in recorded history. No one could agree which law would take precedence in case of a disaster, like a wreck requiring rescue in the deep Arctic or an oil spill. As the Passage actually existed primarily among Canadian-owned islands and the Alaska seaway, the points of law should be clear, but they weren't. Canada's laws were much stricter than those in UNCLOS and no one could agree on any of it.

Jo had been brought in because, putatively, the fisherman were being chased out of the entire Beaufort Sea even though only a small wedge not much bigger than New Jersey was all that was under contention. Yet the oil companies had been granted six leases for exploration in the disputed region. The yelling had barely begun and because of her success fending off the madness in the last lawsuit, she'd been brought aboard to do so once again.

As to what fisherman was crazy enough to want to fish in the Arctic Ocean, she couldn't imagine. Or perhaps she could.

Jo pulled up the legal complaint that had started the whole cascade of suits and countersuits on her screen and scanned the signatories. Earnest J. Thompson had signed. The chance of her father ever striking a hundred miles beyond Ketchikan were so minimal as to be laughable. That he might make the insanely hazardous three-thousand-mile voyage simply to fish wasn't even a possibility. But he had signed, nonetheless.

It was so ludicrous that she could almost certainly use it against the small fishermen if needed. Probably one signatory in a hundred actually might fish the Arctic Ocean if given the chance. After all, she wasn't being paid to represent the fisherman. Or, it would give her a chance to recuse herself from the case based on conflict of interest that now existed, no matter how marginal.

Jo set that thought aside. First, it was a flimsy excuse to get out, and second she knew that to do so was always tempting in the first month or so of research on a new matter. In the beginning, lawsuits were terribly messy. The larger the lawsuit, the worse the mess. Relevant documentation could be spread across dozens of states or even countries and in multiple languages. The pertinent fifty-eight articles of UNCLOS had clearly been drafted by committee, worse, an international multi-lingual committee. Hundreds of pages of brilliantly impenetrable legalese that, once analyzed in the full sight of legal case precedents, probably signified little to nothing.

She closed her eyes and rubbed her forehead. The lack of sleep from Cassidy's midnight return was starting to tell on her and it was only two in the afternoon. Three more hours, plus she really should put in four or five more to make up for missing all of Friday afternoon for the lunch with Renée Linden.

Her whole body throbbed with the exhausted beating of her heart, as if it were pumping out tired blood with each stroke instead of the freshly oxygenated little red cells she so needed.

"You need a break, boss."

Jo hadn't heard Muriel come in. She didn't bother to open her eyes.

"No, I just need sleep. And maybe one of those big shots of adrenalin they punch into your heart with a foot-long needle."

"How about another piece of chocolate? I saved some."

"Anything would help." Jo held out a hand without bothering to look. Something cool and solid slid against her palm and she looked up.

A slim tube-style vase of pale-blue blown glass bore a single red rose.

She blinked again, but it remained in her hand. It really was there.

"Let me guess. No note again."

"Not even a 'PPM' one this time," Muriel simply smiled at her. "What am I doing wrong that I'm not getting gift baskets and beautiful red roses?"

"I'll get you one of each for Christmas."

"But then I'll know who it's from. Besides, that's over six months away."

Jo considered if another piece of chocolate with an aspirin chaser would avert the pending headache.

"I'm too tired to guess, just tell me."

Her assistant raised her hands palm out. "I don't know this time. Honest. I even grilled the delivery guy, a nice young boy named Marko. He claimed it was a phone-in order, no idea who sent it. Even gave him a nice tip from your petty cash, and he didn't give. Want me to hound the owner for the name on the credit card? Actually, I can't, I'm not sure what shop he was with. But I could call around."

Jo scowled at the rose. Renée? Not likely. Angelo? She'd left him less than a dozen hours earlier at the bar. He and Russell had been talking about speedboats and parasailing. Apparently, despite Russell's broken leg, his head was dense enough to think it had been a pretty cool experience. That left Yuri and she definitely didn't want to think about that.

She set the rose by her monitor. It was pretty after all and the vase was exquisite in its simplicity. Another Renée bribe she decided.

"That wasn't chocolate."

Muriel pulled out a bar of chocolate she'd tucked in her skirt pocket. She wore a close-fitting white angora sweater and an actual fifties' poodle skirt, except that it was black with pink poodles instead of the other way around. Knowing her assistant's attention to detail, she probably had on bobby socks and two-tone whatever they were called shoes. Jo sat up a bit straighter to see as she reached for the chocolate that

Muriel broke off and handed over, but the desk still blocked her view.

Without being asked, Muriel raised a foot for her to see. Black bobby socks topped with pink lace and those white-and-tan shoes.

"Saddle oxfords," Muriel informed her recognizing the blank moment.

Jo nodded. They'd long since stopped trying to figure out how they knew what the other was asking without, well, asking. It wasn't because they'd been working together for five years either. They'd done it since the first day Muriel had showed up, fresh from college with a resume in her hand.

Jo ate the chocolate, dark, candied ginger–chili pepper this time. She wanted to close her eyes and just lay her head on the desk, instead she focused on convincing her body that she'd just eaten some magic, high-energy candy rather than soothing dark cocoa.

"You also have a visitor. Or will in another two minutes."

"Who?" that straightened Jo back up a bit. Yuri had gone back to Alaska, hadn't he? She waved a hand toward her jacket.

Muriel took it from the hanger on the back of the office door and handed it over.

Jo pulled it on and checked the lie of it in Muriel's appraising look and quick nod. She was going to have her power armor in place in case it was Yuri.

A tap on her partly open door and Renée Linden stuck her head in.

"I'm not interrupting, am I? Oh, what a pretty rose. Who sent you that?"

"I THOUGHT you might like to see the shoot for my final ad campaign. They can be quite fun actually." Renée led Jo out of the office and toward the Market. "I still haven't had a chance to talk to the board, their next meeting isn't until tomorrow evening. I hate to impose, but I'd appreciate if we still kept it between us girls until then."

"Of course," Jo granted easily. What she hadn't found, despite two days of thinking about it, was a gracious way to inform the most influential female power broker on the Seattle scene that Jo's answer was a definitive, "No." Part of the problem was she didn't know if her guess was right, though she had circled back around to it being a job offer.

However, the answer was no even though Renée hadn't technically made the offer, at least not in as many words. It still made no sense why she would offer Jo the Executive Directorship—assuming Jo's guess was right.

Her first intention, of informing Renée of her decision while in her own office and on her own turf, had somehow failed. Perhaps on a stroll through the Market she'd find the right moment to acknowledge Renée's kind and subtle offer to suggest her for the Executive Directorship and to thank her kindly as she turned her down.

"We do a great deal of tourism marketing," Renée was telling her as they walked together down Pike Place and into the heart of the market. "We use websites, airplane magazines, participation in television cooking shows, and the like. I decided that it was time we expand that clientele. The Pike Place Market has long been a destination visit for travelers, but I think there is a high-end that we've been missing."

Jo nodded. It made sense. She'd seen the Market change and shift over the decade she'd been in Seattle. There were still the odd little kiosks at the north end where amateur artists rented six feet of table to display hand-crafted earrings or their latest knit fashions for toddlers. Cute and very good for what it was. But in the heart of the Market there were some true artists selling their wares. Clothing designers, high-end galleries, and antique stores specializing in rare collectibles had joined the food entrepreneurs which were the backbone of the Market's image.

There was no mistaking the photo shoot when they found it at The Glass Shoppe. There were two photographer's assistants adjusting umbrella flashes, one with a couple extra cameras dangling around her neck. A thin, young man sat next to an open makeup case of immense variety. A short rack on wheels waited outside the shop sporting a small but tasteful selection of high-end clothing to be ready when needed.

At the center of the bustling array were a photographer and his model.

Jo gasped. There was no mistaking her. She'd been on enough covers over the last year to be unmistakable.

"Melanie."

Renée simply nodded. "You see, I'm right. Everyone knows her. She's immensely marketable right now. I managed to find her when she was traveling through Seattle, so it was not too hideously expensive to hire her. We only have her for the day, but I think it will definitely be worth it."

Jo had seen her in person once, but she couldn't quite place where. A failing that she could only credit to how Renée was overloading her neural pathways. She absolutely couldn't afford to be out of the office, yet here they were, chatting pleasantly at an advertising shoot that had absolutely nothing to do with her.

They watched as the magnificent, six-foot tall supermodel swept her waist-length blonde hair over her shoulder and flirted, using her trademark ever-so-slight French accent, with the slightly shy vendor in his small shop. The photographer snapped away. Like most of the Market's spaces it was deceptively small but had been used incredibly well to display the blown glass art making it feel much larger.

Blown glass. She glanced around. There, behind one of the photographer's silvery umbrella flashes stood a display of exquisite little bud vases in all the shades of flowers. It only took a moment to note that there wasn't one to match the pale blue vase now holding a rose on Jo's desk.

A delivery boy named Marko, huh? From an unknown flower shop? And a vase purchased right here in the Market. She kept her smile to herself but placed a small wager with herself that Angelo had someone named Marko working in his restaurant. One who wouldn't reveal the sender despite a nice tip because he was protecting his boss and his job.

Neither Yuri nor Renée, Angelo had sent the rose. Well, that was awfully sweet of him. She knew this shop well enough to know that the vase hadn't been cheap either, she owned a couple of this artist's pieces herself.

But she had reconsidered their kiss during the rest of their run and only seen it reemphasized last night at the airport bar. Angelo was nice enough. And he would be too easy to get close to with his smooth accent and stunning looks. But he suffered from a problem similar to Yuri's. First, she wasn't ready to be involved with anyone for a couple more years and second, she wanted someone as serious about their career as she was.

That wasn't quite right, Angelo was serious about his cooking. Maybe even as ambitious in his own way. But her career was a whole different world than a single nice restaurant in Seattle. And his college had been cooking schools, not Vassar. Not University of Washington's School of Law.

He wasn't beneath her, that was too demeaning a thought. But neither was he what she was looking for, even if her body kept reacting as if he were.

"This is the last shoot of the day," Renée interrupted her spiraling thoughts as they watched a clothier offer Melanie a different jacket and a dark scarf that transformed her from casually elegant to delightfully urban.

"We did jewelry, antique cars, the little ones that were toys in the

1930s and '40s. I've been working here for almost two decades and had no idea they commanded such prices. And a number of others. The haute couture shop was to have followed this, but it closed last week. I always thought it was a tad silly myself. Simply too surreal for even an opening night at the opera. At least on this coast."

Jo inspected Renée's outfit and saw another reason the woman might feel that way. She was ruthlessly fit, as was probably only achieved with a personal trainer, and impeccably dressed in a simple maroon dress that shouted to take this woman seriously, without masking that she was a woman. It was an outfit that Jo herself would have selected if she could afford such tailoring. Her dark blonde hair had highlights and not a hint of gray, worn just long enough to reach her collar, and held back in a no-nonsense clasp that was simple enough to have come from Bartell Drug Store but perfect enough that it probably came from Nordstrom.

An image was forming in Jo mind's eye. It started with Melanie and filled out slowly like a camera pulling back to reveal the surroundings. An image of this beautiful, shining woman in a dusky, warm Italian kitchen.

"Did you shoot a restaurant?"

Renée shook her head. "We considered Maximilien's, but we frequently feature them in our ads and we wanted these to be different."

"Have you been in Angelo's Tuscan Hearth since they remodeled?"

Renée inspected her intensely for half a heartbeat then smiled radiantly.

Jo wondered at the meaning of those two emotions side by side.

"No, I haven't." Renée's smile didn't diminish, but it felt as if were part of another conversation that was again eluding Jo. "I do keep meaning to go in. Coming back into the city with

Nathaniel after we both finally get home from work is a very rare occurrence."

She looped a hand through Jo's arm. "That's a brilliant idea. Come."

Jo had intended to go back to work. Had to. But was making little progress in that direction.

CHAPTER 12

*J*o felt a bit like a scout leader as she led the troop down the old bricks of Pike Place and turned up Post Alley. Behind her followed Melanie and Renée talking about how charming the Market was on a summer day. Apparently Melanie had been here only once before and that had been a chill and spitting winter's day. Not a day when the smell of the sea was battled back by fresh flowers, sweet pastries, and rich coffee thick on the Seattle air.

Following them were the photographer, his laden assistants, the makeup guy, clothier, and several others apparently connected to the shoot that she hadn't noticed in the surrounding crowd.

As it was only a block away, they'd decided it was better to show up and ask forgiveness later rather than calling ahead.

She asked the others to wait outside, taking only Renée, Melanie, and the photographer in with her.

"Table for four?" The slender Italian woman greeted them. Jo remembered her as the hostess from last week's meal with Yuri. She'd been terribly gracious about Jo's request to see Angelo. Gracious. Graziella.

"Graziella. I was wondering if Angelo might be available."

The hostess' memory was clearly up to the challenge as well. "Ah, Miss Thompson. Table seven."

They were both careful not to look toward the offending piece of furniture.

"A moment please." And the woman was gone.

Angelo breezed into the room, his apron immaculate, his smile radiant.

"Why hello, Miss Thomp— Melanie!" He rushed forward and greeted the supermodel with a kiss on each cheek and then a profound hug though she towered several inches over him.

"Angelo!" They slid into the rapid speech that only close friends apart for too long shared.

They laughed together. A flirting kind of laugh. Angelo was flirting with a supermodel right in front of her. She'd been planning to thank him for the flower if they found a moment alone, but now he was holding hands with a super-model and they were talking excitedly over one another, just inches apart.

Jo's body flashed hot and then very, very cold. The power suit she'd put on in case her visitor was Yuri, which then looked appropriate beside Renée's perfect, understated attire, now did its job. Jo's clothes wrapped around her like armor. Sensible heels, navy blue slacks with a perfect crease that matched her wide-lapelled jacket. The dress white blouse with the muted-floral bow tie. She'd taken down federal cases in this exact outfit. She could deal with one lousy Italian restaurateur while wearing it.

Clearly the whole shooting plan had passed back and forth and been approved in moments. Graziella began escorting in those who had waited outside while Melanie toured the restau-rant on Angelo's arm.

Had the man been playing her? Simply wanting someone to amuse himself with while his supermodel lover was flitting about the world on her climb to fame and fortune? Melanie made Jo feel downright dowdy.

ANGELO COULDN'T STOP LAUGHING. Melanie kept going on about how she'd clearly fallen in love with the wrong man, because Angelo was so much more handsome. Then she told a rather racy story of how Zaia, Essence, and Stella Star had been found naked together in a bathroom at the Carlton. He hadn't heard that one about her fellow models, but Melanie told him he must search on it, as the person who found them had indeed had a smartphone that linked video directly to YouTube. It might not have been so bad if the three women hadn't been having a screaming match about sleeping with the same film director.

"You have made it so beautiful," she kept looking around the restaurant and he couldn't stop himself from grinning.

"This was the second try. The first one was pronounced 'butt ugly.'"

"Russell?" Her voice sounded a touch sad as she said his name, so he did his best to gloss over it as if he hadn't noticed the change.

"His words exactly. But he helped me do this."

"That man," she sighed lightly. "He does have an amazing eye. No one has ever made me as beautiful as he did with a camera. Not even Claude, though he is better than most." She flicked a long red fingernail in the direction of the photographer who was moving about the restaurant checking angles through one lens and then another.

"He still…"

"Angelo, buddy," Russell swung through the kitchen door on crutches. The few mid-afternoon diners startled at Russell's bull-in-china-shop shout. "You gotta save me. I'm bored to dea—"

He came to a halt when he spotted Melanie, all of his bluster gone. As far as Angelo knew, they'd never spoken since that awful day a year ago February.

Melanie had pulled back her hand from Angelo's arm and hunched her shoulders a bit. It didn't look good on her.

Though his heart ached, he didn't know how to help them. Melanie had fallen in love with Russell, who had neither understood nor returned the emotion, though they'd been lovers at the time. Involved. "The Season's Hot Item" according to the tabloids. The flashy heir to the Morganson shipping empire, and the molten supermodel. No one but Angelo knew that both their emotions had been caught up as well, that not only the glamour had kept them together as long as they were.

"Hey Russell," Angelo reached deep for some tiny bit of casual. "Melanie's in town for an ad shoot for the Market. They decided to drop in and use my restaurant for one of the ads."

All they did was stare stone-faced at each other and Angelo didn't know what to say. Couldn't figure out how to help them out of their mutual pain and embarrassment.

"It was my idea," Jo came up beside Russell and laid a friendly hand on his arm as if nothing were amiss.

Didn't the woman have any sensitivity in that severe suit of hers?

"You and Angelo did such a beautiful job of redecorating. And your art on the walls. It was irresistible."

"Uh, thanks."

She *was* doing it. By avoiding the subject of their mutual pain entirely, Jo had gotten Russell to relax a half-inch, though his hands still clamped around the crutch handles as if holding on for dear life. But that little bit of easing on his part had in turn removed some of the hunch from Melanie's shoulders. Angelo would have tried stepping straight into the breach, whereas Jo just circled around it as if it wasn't even there. It was as artful as the muted paintings and crystalline photographs on his walls.

"I thought over by that table, the one by the central hearth, would look really splendid." Claude had clearly recognized Russell, but his tone clearly said, this is my shoot, that is my choice.

Russell's gaze begrudgingly shifted from Melanie's face to the room about them.

"No."

Claude blinked and suddenly looked like a fish out of water.

Angelo could see Russell swallow hard, then it became a bit too obvious that he wasn't going to look back at Melanie now that he'd looked away, but there was nothing Angelo could do about that.

"No," Russell cleared his throat and tried again. "That's a four-topper. It's the right position, Claude, but for the photograph you'll want a two-person table even though she's the only one seated there. It's an ad. She's waiting. Waiting for the viewer of the ad to come join her." He swung off on his crutches to direct the change.

Melanie turned to Angelo and mouthed a "Thank you" before bending down to lean her cheek against his. He could feel her hands in his squeeze long and hard, then steadier. She stood, her shoulders back and nodded once.

Angelo turned to Jo to thank her as well, but she was no longer beside Melanie.

"None of these clothes are right," Russell was riffling through the rack by the front door.

"It's all I brought," the clothier was complaining.

Jo had moved over beside Russell. Angelo watched her turn that appraising attorney gaze on Melanie and slowly inspect her from shoes to hair. Her eyes didn't track over to Angelo even in the slightest flicker.

She pulled out her phone and dialed.

He moved closer to hear the conversation.

"Perrin? This is Jo, I'm at Angelo's and we have a bit of an emergency. Could you bring over your dress from last Saturday, the one you wore? A pair of heels, not platform, but spike. In," she glanced at Russell, "red."

Russell nodded.

"Fingernail red. Thanks."

"No lipstick. Only a little makeup," Russell told the man who'd set up his kit on a side table. "You shouldn't be able to see it at all."

Then the room kicked into action.

CHAPTER 13

"*J* fall for zis..." Melanie pointed an elegant finger negligently at Russell. "Zis fool and you are the one who marries him. How does this happen?"

Cassidy grinned at Jo and squeezed her hand beneath the dinner table. No one knew better than she how many potholes and pitfalls Cassidy had discovered along that particular road.

"Just my punishment, I suppose."

Melanie threw back her head and laughed. Any easy, joyous sound.

Jo marveled at how the tone of the room had changed over the last few hours.

First, it had all been a great rush of preparation. Part of it clearly to distract from the tension in the room.

Then Perrin had roared in from her design store a couple blocks up the hill. Not only with the green bridesmaid dress, but also with about a third of her shop on a long rolling rack, just in case, which added to the mayhem. They'd shot four different outfits, but Jo was pleased that her instincts had been right. Perrin's dress with its long lines and surprising reveals had fit Melanie perfectly with only a few minor adjustments, and had been the star of the shoot. Thankfully they were of a size, even if Melanie was taller. The height had revealed a little more arm and a fair amount more leg while hugging her body perfectly. Melanie still wore it and swore she was never giving it back, much to Perrin's vocal protests and obvious delight.

Russell had coaxed a camera from one of Claude's assistants and, somehow without offending the notoriously irritable photographer, had taken what everyone, including Claude, had agreed were the best shots.

Renée, on discovering Russell's previous ownership of one of the top boutique ad studios in New York, had somehow coaxed him into agreeing to build the ads based on his and Claude's photography. Claude, being a purist, photographer only, had managed to not be offended after only minimal coaxing on Jo's part.

Cassidy had arrived in search of her errant husband and soon they were all gathered around one of Angelo's exquisite meals.

Jo was relieved by that. She worried that she'd become a curse for him. But he produced amazing food in unbelievable quantities despite how shabbily she'd treated him earlier this afternoon. It was Cassidy who'd straightened her out over the appetizers.

"Remember the first time we saw them, that Valentine's Day?"

And now Jo did. She, Cassidy, and Perrin had been out drinking. Celebrating Jo's partnership in her new firm if she remembered correctly. And Cassidy breaking up with the drip she'd been seeing. Melanie and Russell had breezed through the bar on the way to the restaurant. Her back had been toward the entrance and she'd caught just a brief glimpse, no wonder she hadn't been able to place the moment.

"I got the story out of Angelo because Russell wouldn't tell me." Cassidy confided so that the others at the table wouldn't hear. "The three of them were close friends in New York. Can you believe that my husband used to date her but ended up with me? It makes no sense."

Jo thought it made perfect sense, at least as soon as you saw the way Russell looked at Cassidy. She was the center of his world, perhaps even more than he was the center of hers. If that were possible.

Jo had finally registered that it wasn't Angelo who was thrown by Melanie's sudden appearance, it was Russell. And something about it had hit him far deeper than "they used to date." Yet Russell had managed to move past that, even if he wasn't quite back to his usual blusterous self. He might sound it, but to Jo's trained ear the testimony of his bravura didn't quite ring true.

She had also overheard him at one point during a break in the shoot whispering to Melanie. Whispering that he was so sorry.

"I have a suggestion." Jo hugged Cassidy for a moment so that she could whisper in her friend's ear.

"What?"

Angelo hadn't been so much flirting with Melanie as trying to help his friends. And he'd done it so well that it had mostly worked. He was such a good man, it was hard to credit.

"I think," Jo told Cassidy, "that when you take Russell home tonight, you should be especially nice to him. He's an exceptionally good man."

Cassidy had smiled and nodded. And she hadn't looked the least bit upset by the burden.

———

"YOU ARE in rare form tonight, my son."

Angelo's mother patted his back as he fussed over the final plating of the desserts.

"I tried. I really tried."

"I quote that short thing to you, 'You no try, you do.'"

"Yoda," Angelo supplied.

"Yes, whatever. Finish that and you deliver it. Manuel and me, we finish the dinners. You go be with your friends and with the bicycle lady."

Angelo wiped the edge of a spotless plate and tried to calm his nerves.

Jo was pissed at him about something. He knew that much. When Russell had drifted through the kitchen at one point, he'd asked, but his friend had no idea. He'd tried to offer Angelo a warning scowl of poaching on his honorary sisters, but Angelo was too worried about what he might have done to care.

It was like whenever he was with Jo, she was the most amazing woman he'd ever met. And then the lawyer would appear and he felt like an undereducated slob who couldn't do anything right.

"Go. You fussing like an old woman. I'm an old woman, you are not. So you are not allowed to fuss like one."

"Yes, Mama." He kissed her cheek, then picked up the tray and tried to breeze through the door.

He served the dessert, describing it as he went around the table. Practiced diners like these would absolutely want to know what they were eating.

"This is my mother's Panna Cotta recipe, with a few twists. Atop her Italian cream, I floated Tarocco-blood-orange-infused eighty-five-percent dark cocoa sauce topped with honey-glazed strawberries. Rather than a grappa, I've paired it with espresso. Though I would suggest Marolo Barolo Grappa if you'd prefer that."

Only as he finished serving did he dare look at the people around the table. Russell, with his broken leg propped on a chair, and Claude were busy discussing ad composition at one end. Renée was listening closely, making occasional suggestions.

The four other women sat down the table, Melanie and Perrin on one side, Cassidy and Jo on the other.

He looked at Jo last, trying to be careful about gauging her temperature. He took the last Panna Cotta and espresso for himself and hesitated. Jo slid her chair slightly toward Cassidy and pulled her dessert over as well, opening just enough room for him at the end of the table.

He'd take that as a good sign.

He set his dessert in the cleared space and pulled over a chair from the next table as he fielded all of the compliments about the meal and the dessert that rippled up and down the table.

Jo was silent as she took one bite, then another.

He settled enough to try his own. It was the best he'd ever done. Even his mother had not tried to alter what he'd added to her old recipe. She'd simply tasted it then turned away to walk to the sink. At first he'd thought she was going to spit it out.

She'd run a little water over her fingertips then patted them dry on her apron and brushed them lightly over her eyes. If he didn't know better, he'd suspect her of blinking back tears before she turned clear-eyed to tell him how wonderful it was.

"Thank you for the rose. It's beautiful."

Jo wasn't looking at him. It was if she were speaking quietly to her dessert.

"You're welcome." The second word came out on a dry rasp despite the chocolate and cream coating his tongue.

Then she looked at him with those dark, amazing eyes and he almost fell forward. They were so clear that their depth felt infinite, and their gaze cut clear through him until his soul lay bare before them.

She looked back down at her dessert but didn't take another taste.

He waited, barely hearing the buzz of laughter over something that enveloped the rest of the table but left them alone together.

"I have to work late tomorrow." Again that quiet comment in the direction of her dessert.

"How late?" He held his breath not really daring to understand what he thought he understood.

"How late do you have to work?"

Angelo struggled to get his thoughts moving. "On a Wednesday, I can be done by nine."

Jo looked up at him again.

For the length of three breaths she said nothing, merely studying him.

"That sounds good," was all she said and returned to her dessert.

Angelo looked down at his own Panna Cotta, then up the table.

He was fairly sure that someone was asking him a question, but he couldn't hear it over the pounding in his ears.

CHAPTER 14

"*A*aaaaaaaaaahhhh!" Jo wanted to pound her head on the desk. Not that it would solve anything.

The whole discovery process had been completely screwed up. A dozen filings with the court would be necessary to straighten it out before she could even initiate a serious review of the key case documents. And she should really start writing those now. She'd need at least five interrogatories, and probably more. She already had a deposition list going and it was only the fifth or sixth day she'd been working on the case.

Muriel would know what else she needed to do to fix this mess. Jo hated it when they didn't bring her in right at the start of a case. This one had muddled along for months in the lower courts before anyone realized that it was going to become a major piece of litigation with ramifications easily reaching into the billions of dollars. Arctic Ocean mineral rights, oil reserves, fisheries, Northwest Passage navigation... The list was rapidly growing.

Some idiot in Juneau, with no actual knowledge of Maritime Law and apparently wholly unaware of the applicability of International Sea Law, had advanced the case to Alaska's

Supreme Court. It should have gone straight to Federal. Instead, there were now dozens of interest groups suing and counter-suing with no idea that most of their noise was meaningless but would take months of work to sweep aside.

Why had she sent Muriel home? Just because the woman had a date was no excuse. Muriel had remained uncomplainingly until Jo had used up very possible second, including her time to go home and change which was plain cruel on Jo's part. It was only in a fit of martyrdom that she'd told Muriel to finally go and have fun. What had Jo been thinking when she did that?

Then there was Renée Linden's parting comment last night still churning about in Jo's brain like a nasty little whirlwind wreaking destruction upon any line of reasoning.

Not once in all of yesterday afternoon and evening that they'd been together had Renée mentioned that she was recommending Jo for the position, making it especially hard for Jo to turn down something that hadn't been offered. Nor had Jo found a way to even once intimate that she'd discovered that is what the woman was planning. Because Jo would sound like a fool if her deductions had wandered astray.

Yet, at the end of the evening, Renée had rested a gentle hand on Jo's forearm and said, "I knew you would be wonderful at this. So many think it is about doing the job. You and I know that it is about finding the right people to do the job." And then she'd disappeared into the dark Seattle evening before Jo could get her verbal-acuity feet back under her and even consider forming an intelligent response.

And then there was Angelo.

Okay. Somewhere in the middle of the night she'd finally understood the ugly emotion that had swamped her at seeing Angelo and the beautiful Melanie together. Jealousy. What did she have to be jealous about? One kiss. Okay, two if you counted the ice cream kiss from the bike ride. Being a guy probably meant that he did, but being a sensible member of the female gender, she definitely didn't.

Yet she did.

Okay, damn it! Two kisses.

They'd shared two kisses totaling something on the order of ten seconds. Perhaps longer. She wasn't so sure about how long that second kiss had lasted. Hard to estimate time when your mind blanked beneath the electric-shock wave of sensation.

But none of it should be enough to justify jealousy.

And then once she'd absolved him from the crime of flirting with Melanie, beyond his being male and Italian and Melanie being drop-dead gorgeous and a close friend, what had she done? She'd invited him out on a date.

What kind of a date started at nine on a weeknight? When she wasn't working, she'd normally be in bed with a good book by nine. That supposedly gripping Grisham novel still sat there untouched. That wasn't like her either.

If she wasn't herself, who was she turning into?

She flashed momentarily on the opening of Alice in Wonderland. The part where Alice can't make sense of her world or remember her multiplication tables and decides she must not be Alice after all, but rather a sad little girl named Mabel and she weeps a pool of tears.

"I must be Mabel."

"Really? I thought you were Jo Thompson. Did I bring these to the wrong office?"

Jo jerked upright in her chair to see Angelo leaning against the doorjamb of her office holding a small white box.

"How long have you been there?"

"Long enough to find your office by your screams. Strange thing to do all alone in the night."

"How did you get in here? And what's in there?"

"One question at a time, counselor." He moved easily across the room to sit in one of the client chairs across from her desk.

He looked gorgeous. His faded jeans were tight fitting, not because they were tight, but because he had such good muscle under them. His shirt was unbuttoned only two buttons from the neck, but that was at least one too many as it hinted at his strong chest and raised her temperature in an unseemly fashion. She almost asked him to stand and turn around for a moment just to see that wonderful taper from shoulder to hip, then lectured herself sharply to behave.

They were just getting together for a date, which she was really too busy for anyway. She'd make them some tea in the office kitchen, they'd share whatever treat he'd brought and now set in her In Basket, then she'd send him on his way.

"I got in here because your building guard is Manuel's cousin, Manuel is my sous chef, and we feed her when she finds someone she wants to really impress."

"So you just bribe your way into any building you want?"

"Oh," he sat back and folded his hands behind his head looking perfectly relaxed. "We chefs have our ways. To answer the rest of your question, the outer door to your offices is unlocked and I found your office because it is the only one with the light on. And also, you know, the screams."

Jo fought the heat that rushed to her cheeks and reached for composure.

"The door was unlocked because it's a secure elevator so the last one to leave, tonight being me, actually usually being me, would lock up. But courtesy of Manuel's cousin, her master passcard to the elevator, and your relationship with her..."

"Don't go there," Angelo cut her off. "Won't do you any good. Dora's nineteen, good at her job, and a lesbian. Our relationship is purely caloric."

Jo would give good money to know how he looked so relaxed when she so wasn't.

IT WAS a good thing Dora had been the security guard on duty. If the guard had been a stranger, Angelo would have had no compunction about turning around and sprinting out the door when faced with the edifice that was the sixteenth-floor entrance to Stanley, Tu, Rolfmann, and Thompson. Every single thing about their offices had reeked of intimidation and power.

First, the thick glass doors with the four names in gold leaf, didn't open like doors, with handles. They shot aside with a soft, "whoosh!" like they were from Star Trek. Not some clunky supermarket door either. One moment the things were there blocking him out. The next moment they were gone, and the fittings were so seamless it was hard to tell where they'd gone into the sides of the ebony-marble archway that dared the intruder to pass beneath. He half expected a *Stargate* vortex to shimmer to life and swallow him whole.

Five feet into the office, they'd magically reappeared behind him like an invisible cage. He'd considered returning to the elevator just to make sure he could escape if needs be, but he knew if he started down that road there'd be no turning back.

The lobby was all dusky blues: the carpet, the leather furniture, the walls. Even when the lighting automatically came up, it was subtle and indirect. The ceiling appeared to be fathomless glass, as if you could look up into it forever and never find yourself. Behind the receptionist's desk, a wall of floor-to-ceiling windows threatened to spill you over a dozen stories down into Elliot Bay. Even at night, it looked precipitous. A bad place for anyone who feared heights.

Offices ranged right and left along the Sound-view face of the building.

The only light had been at the end of the left-hand corridor, which is how he had arrived at Jo's equally intimidating corner office. The walls were dark-smoked glass. The photographs of wilderness sunsets and morning vistas were framed in bright stainless steel which appeared to float off the glass walls like magic in some futuristic art gallery. They offered the only color other than the dark wood of Jo's desk which was covered with a large, ocean-blue map. That had been pinned down by deep stacks of files that appeared to have been deposited in stages like layers of stone. There was no clock, but rather a projection of one from somewhere behind the glass. The clock face, similar to the giant one looming over Pike Place Market that he could see many stories below through her window, simply shown deep red on the smoky glass.

And in the middle of all the futuristic reek of power had been Jo with her head down in her hands.

That's when he'd found his equilibrium. No matter how high-powered she might be, no matter the trappings around her, she was a woman obviously deeply tired and frustrated.

Somehow, her heartless office made her, by contrast, so much more human. A human Jo Thompson he could deal with.

The power-suited Counselor Thompson, a named partner of an elite law firm? That one scared the shit out of him.

So, he would just pretend that one wasn't present. He glanced down at a glass coffee table and spotted a copy of something called the ABA Journal and the cover had a picture of Jo and three guys grouped around her but a half-step behind. They were probably Stanley, Tu, and Rolfmann. Angelo absolutely was going to pretend that he hadn't seen that.

And she looked so distressed that he reset his agenda even as he watched her. Tonight she didn't need an eager lover, he hoped that's what she'd been suggesting. Tonight she looked as if she needed a friend.

"So, what's going on?" He'd just ignore her question about how he looked so relaxed, because if he thought about it, he wouldn't be.

"Everything. Nothing. It's… I'm…" Then she scrubbed her face for a moment and flipped a fistful of hair back over her shoulder. "I'm a mess."

"But such a beautiful mess."

"You're so Italian."

"Sue me," he grinned at her.

"Don't tempt me, Angelo. At this point that might just cheer me up."

"So if you sue me, do I get to see more of you, or less?"

She slipped a bright pink pen behind her left ear which held her hair back on that side, leaving the other side free to spill strand by strand forward over her right shoulder. He had to blink to resist the mesmerizing movement of sliding hair like liquid midnight.

"I'd see you more because of depositions," she tapped a stack of notes, "and discovery," she slapped a tall stack of files then had to grab and re-center them to keep them from falling.

"Sounds good. Let's do it."

"But also much less socially, and never without opposing counsel in attendance to protect your rights."

"Ah, well. Now that doesn't sound so good. Not unless she's extremely cute."

Jo laughed then scowled at him. He'd ignore that as well.

"So what is all this mess?" He'd had Russell look over his restaurant lease renewal agreement a few weeks ago, because he didn't understand such things. They'd made a few minor tweaks, but Russell had declared the thing really fair, so Angelo had signed. What Jo had ranged across her desk looked utterly meaningless. Overlong pages of paper had numbers running down the left side and strange blocky headings on the first page. The equally long, yellow legal pad already had a dozen pages folded under and the exposed page was mostly full of tightly spaced notes.

"It was supposed to be the next year of my life, but I'm afraid it's going to be the next five. I really don't want to spend the next five years commuting to Alaska."

"Alaska?" Angelo did his best to hide his distress at the idea of her being so far away. Especially for so long.

"North Slope mineral and oil exploration rights," she patted one pile of files. Then another, "Fishing rights." And a third, "International agreements. And disagreements." A fourth.

"All controlled by international law, superseded by case law, governmental protests, diplomatic letters, and U.N. negotiations." She aimed a finger at various piles.

"U.N.? As in the United Nations?" Angelo could feel his cool slipping once again and struggled to find it and pull it over him like the cloak of baked mozzarella on an Eggplant Parmigiana.

"Yes. It's pretty exciting actually. I might get my first chance to argue a case in front of the U.N. Maritime Court."

She couldn't have named anything more impossible. The White House made more sense than the U.N. The U.N. was the place he'd gone on a high school class trip, had a toured lecture while hovered over by a dozen security guards. It wasn't technically in New York. It was in some weird International Zone that wasn't even a part of the United States.

"Whoa! We're talking about that big building on the Eastside mid-town Manhattan? The one with the hundred and something flags around it?" He blew out a breath. "That's too unreal. Let's get you back down to Earth." He nudged the white box still sitting in her In Basket.

She glanced at it without reaching across the piles to pick it up.

"If it's more of your Panna Cotta I will charge you with malfeasance and criminal intent regarding the condition of my waistline."

"Mal what? And you have an amazingly attractive waistline."

"Intentional wrongdoing." The waistline comment appeared to fluster her. He'd have to remember that. It was as if she'd shed a little bit more of the lawyer when he said it.

"Oh. No, it's not Panna Cotta." He was starting to like the

way she spoke. At first it had put him off, but it was simply a different world than his own. They were both specialists, just vastly different specialists. The Alaska thing worried him though.

He nudged the box again and she finally gave in.

She took it and peered inside. "What are they?"

"Very decadent."

"I guessed that much. How decadent?"

He smiled when she looked up at him with those dark eyes of hers.

"Very."

CHAPTER 15

*D*ecadent? Jo really needed something to be decadent right at the moment. Not Alaska, not case law, not Pike Place Market, not even a triathlon. She needed something that was wholly for her. And she knew exactly what it was, but it was so outrageous she didn't want to risk even speaking in case that somehow ruined it.

She closed the little white box and rose without a word. She left some part of herself in that leather office chair. If she'd been less tired, she might have returned to gather it back up, but at the moment she just didn't care. She tapped the control embedded in the desk's surface and the tight-focused overhead desk lamp faded to darkness leaving only the soft glow of the walls and the city lights from the windows. Angelo found her jacket on the back of the door and held it out for her.

Past the lobby and through the doors. She hit the button on her keyring remote. The doors snicked shut and locked, then the lobby lights dimmed to a soft glow. Nineteen stories down to the parking garage and into her BMW Z4 roadster.

Angelo whistled appreciatively, but when he would have

spoken, she shook her head. She'd had way too many words today. And yesterday. And the damned day before.

He bowed his acquiescence as if he were a butler in full tails rather than a chef in jeans, a loose button-down shirt, and scuffed sneakers. He held the door for her until she was settled in her seat, then closed it gently. Climbing in beside her, he took the small white box and she fired off the car and flipped the switch to open the convertible top.

She loved this car. It had been a bonus the day she made partner and had her name added to the Stanley, Tu, and Rolf-mann letterhead. The stunning magazine ad for the BMW had been her screensaver for six months and the partners had noticed and purchased it for her as a bonus for the big win she'd pulled off on behalf of the fishing corporations last year. She liked working for this firm. She truly did. But she wasn't going to think about them anymore tonight.

The BMW ad had been a hell of an ad, the long-legged blonde in thigh-high red leather boots and a single red rose contrasted with the jet-black car with black leather upholstery. She almost missed a gear shift when she connected that Melanie must have been the model in the ad. Cassidy had found out that Russell had shot and composed it, and Jo now knew that the supermodel had been his favored subject while he was still a professional ad photographer in New York. Was it because they'd been lovers, or because she was so beautiful? Well, it was interesting either way.

The car tires screamed along the coiled ramp leading upward from deep underground, the engine humming as if eager for the open road, and they almost launched onto the city streets. Angelo reached a hand over and slid his fingertips just once along her thigh. Like an electric shock, her pulse rate jumped up by a third.

Ten blocks. She could make it ten blocks. Besides, tackling

him in the tight confines of the car wasn't terribly practical on well-lit city streets. Not that it wouldn't be interesting to try.

She whirled down into the condo's underground parking and rolled into her spot.

They took hands as they approached the elevator.

Once the elevator passed the lobby floor with no one else getting on, she pushed him against the cool steel wall and threw herself at him.

He was more than up to the challenge. His kiss crushed against hers. His arms, those splendid, chef-strong arms, wrapped her so tightly against his chest that she'd probably have trouble breathing, if she'd cared to.

It was the last concern on her mind.

She nipped his ear, ran a tongue along his neck and bit the base of his throat. This wasn't the Jo she knew and maybe that was a good thing. She could hear Muriel in the background somewhere telling her to drag the man into her lair.

Damn straight!

Jo ran her curled fingers down his chest, her short, practical nails making a slick sound over his linen shirt. She dug them into his pecs and he groaned in her ear.

That groan reached right down inside her. She had the power to make a beautiful man groan with need. Her last concerns about Angelo as a lover dissipated. For tonight she didn't care about past or future, education or ambition. She deepened the kiss until the heat raged over her skin.

The elevator dinged her floor. She grabbed him by the belt at the front of his pants and dragged him into the hall and down to her condo door.

She opened the door, but didn't waste time placing her keys in their little bowl. She tossed them aside and heard them plink off a picture.

"Not one word," she growled as she slammed the door to her lair and shoved Angelo back against it. "Just make me feel.

That's all I want. I just want to feel. Don't make me think. Don't let me think."

She dug her hands into his hair and tasted his lips again. She felt the smile and growled. He grunted as she shoved him against the door again driving their hips together hard.

His hands were on her. Rather than clawing her breast, he leaned down to take it in his teeth through blouse and bra.

Jo tried to strip off her jacket, but he stopped her.

In moments she stood with her skirt pooled around her feet, her blouse and bra open, but still dressed in the power jacket.

She shoved his shirt up in her need to feel flesh on flesh.

Trapped by the shirt bunched around his armpits while she rubbed against that beautiful chest, he flexed and clawed at it until he could get it off.

Jo drove his pants down until she could cradle him in her hands.

"God, I just want to feel."

He recovered protection from his pocket as his pants fell to the floor and slid it on even as she nipped at his chest.

They drove against each other with a mutual cry of relief and finished the job right there against the door.

ANGELO WAS BLIND. It was the only explanation. He was blind and his wildest fantasy, that now lay draped against him gasping for each breath, must be in his mind's eye. That dusky skin of Jo's face and arms had driven his dreams wild. He now knew it ran all the way down the length of her body unbroken by tan lines of lighter skin. Her entire body shone lustrous.

Jo lay against his shoulder and all he could think was how much he needed to do that exact same thing again right now, if only his body was ready. Well, even if his wasn't, hers was.

Before she could recover, he lay her back on the charcoal

carpet and did something he'd been fantasizing about since the first time he'd seen her. He might be physically spent for the moment, but he was dying to taste her, wondering if she tasted as good as she looked.

She tasted better.

As the dim lights of the city shone into the darkened apartment through the tall windows, he reveled in her body. The side of her breasts had the light salt of a sweaty sheen. The tips themselves throbbed sweetly against his tongue when he scraped them with his teeth. That soft line where hip met leg harkened to the entertaining savory of a fine meal. But when he ran his tongue along her and she arched against his mouth with intense need, he knew he had found the main course and drove her until she cried out and dug her fingers into his shoulders to hold on.

When the last shudder had rippled beneath her flesh and his own need was climbing once again, he scooped her up in his arms and carried her into the bedroom.

It was several maddening, body-aching hours before their mutual needs wound down enough for his head to stop spinning. He'd had entertaining little amuse bouche, one-bite taste, relationships. He'd had women who were a nice appetizer or even a fine meal. Counselor Jo Thompson was a full five-course banquet. Every time he thought he'd sated her, or himself, she had proved him splendidly wrong.

They laughed, they clung, more than once she whimpered and he may well have done the same, but they didn't speak a word.

When at last they collapsed from exhaustion, he fetched her a warm washcloth and a dry towel. When she would have cleaned herself, he did it for her, driving her up again, making himself mad with touching her.

Afterward, when he figured that neither of them could take

any more, he fetched the little white box which had somehow survived their frantic entry into the condo.

He tucked Jo in under the quilt and then slid in beside her.

Opening the box, he held one of the dark chocolates out to her mouth.

She took it from his fingers leaving a small nibble on his fingertips.

She fed him the other, he sucked on her fingertips as he took it until she actually moaned. Or perhaps it was because of how he stroked the glorious bounty of her breast beneath the covers.

He tasted the richness of the dark chocolate as it melted in his mouth. When he broke through to the interior, the flavors exploded into his mouth. Layers began with a wash of sweet Courvoisier liqueur and orange zest. At the very last, he bit into the dark fruit and the cherry built into a heady denouement. Then the surprise, the tiny burst of the lemon and carob chocolate chip he'd slipped into the cherry where the pit had been.

"Oh my God," Jo sighed and curled into his arms. "Now that is very, very decadent."

CHAPTER 16

"Where are you going?" Jo's voice was warm and slurred with sleep.

Angelo had been trying to leave without waking her, managed pants and socks, but couldn't quite figure out what to do with his torn shirt. Maybe a stapler. He'd torn it himself as the only way to get it off fast enough. Even that idle thought had his body responding.

He came back to the bed and looked down at her. The white quilt was tucked up around her chin and her dark hair spilled over the pale green pillowcase. The city lights did little to light the room in the predawn darkness, just enough for him to admire the picture she made. He leaned down to kiss her but she stopped him with a long bare arm that snaked out from beneath the covers and planted in the middle of his chest.

"Trying to slip off in the middle of the night?"

"It's almost five."

"Still. You're one of those men who doesn't want to wake up next to a woman." Her tone had gone accusatory and was heading toward counselor.

He brushed his fingers along her cheek.

"I have to go shopping for the restaurant. The fish monger will be opening shortly and I like having the first pick."

"Oh."

"Oh?" he did his best to hide his smile but it wasn't working. She looked so amazingly good all curled up and warm beneath the covers.

"Oh." Her hand shifted from warding him off to pressed against his bare chest for a moment. Then she pulled her arm back beneath the covers which she used to pull the covers up even tighter beneath her chin.

He settled beside her and brushed the backs of his fingers on her impossibly soft cheek. This time when he leaned in, she allowed the kiss, a soft lingering moment that refired his blood.

"I, uh…" she protested. "I don't know what happened."

"We made wild passionate love all night, how could you forget?" He did his best to sound mortally offended.

"I remember that part." She raised her head from the pillow enough to brush her lips on his. "Trust me, I remember that part. I'm just not sure who you were with. It didn't seem like me."

"Oh, I don't know," Angelo traced the line of her body through the quilt, down over breast, waist, and hip. "I found the contrast, ah, invigorating." At one point last night after he'd gotten her naked, he'd had her put the power jacket back on. Just the power jacket. It was the sexiest thing he'd ever seen, cleavage almost to her belly button, better than sheer cotton or intricate lace. It had been a while before he'd allowed her to remove it again.

"Invigorating?" She practically shouted in his face. "Invigorating?"

He brushed down the quilt and attacked her breast with his tongue as he slid his hand down her body.

In moments, her arms had wrapped around the back of his head dragging him into that lovely softness deeper and harder than he'd have dared on his own. He didn't let her go until she arched against his hand and cried out when she came, curling against him and holding on as her body let go like an explosion.

He'd never been with a woman who so responded to his every touch. It was as if he unleashed a whole different person from the sophisticated Jo Thompson every time he touched her. He'd also never met a woman who he responded to so deeply. Whatever he'd thought about his physical attraction to Jo Thompson had been a gross underestimate.

"Invigorating?" he tried not to crow in triumph as she giggled at his question. Who would ever have thought that Jo Thompson could giggle?

"Okay. Yes. I'll give you that point."

When she at last relaxed, she tried to drag him back into bed by the remains of his tattered shirt.

He protested that he had to leave. "Mama will be waiting to go to the Market."

"That's a new one." Her voice was little more than a whisper.

It was. He suddenly felt sixteen again, slipping back into the house hoping his mama wouldn't know what he'd been out doing in the night. He really needed to figure out what was going on there.

He glanced at the bedside clock. And he really needed to get going, period. All he wanted to do was crawl back in with Jo, but that simply couldn't happen right now.

"I have to go. I'm sorry."

She nodded and stretched languidly, back on her way to sleep. Rather than jumping on that incredible body, he pulled the covers up around her neck and tucked her in.

"Russell left a windbreaker when he was here right before the wedding," her voice softened toward a sleepy mumble. "It's on the coat rack."

The jacket was too long for Angelo. Russell was enough

taller that it almost fit Angelo like a mini dress. But it was better than going through Pike Place Market in a shredded shirt.

He slipped out of the condo and hurried downstairs to begin the ten-block walk to the Market.

ANGELO'S MAMA was already flirting with Henry the fishmonger when he arrived out of breath; he'd jogged much of the way trying to make up time. He didn't want anyone else getting the scoop on him. But Charlene from Maximilien's was already there, he usually beat her to the day's best catch.

Not today, she had some incredible looking mahi-mahi set aside and about thirty pounds of steamers in from Penn Cove.

He couldn't regret the cause for delay, but it wasn't good.

His mother continued to chat with Henry, then she winked at him.

Perfetto! Now his mother was going to tease him about not coming home last night.

He poked through the various proteins and was considering the shark, but wasn't feeling terribly inspired by it. Charlene headed off, giving him a cocky salute obviously pleased with her coup.

"Is she gone?" Maria Amelia appeared at his shoulder and looked down the long tiled corridor of the Market to make sure Charlene wasn't stopping at the produce vendor or the cured meats counter.

"She's gone, Mama."

"Good. She's pretty, Angelo. But not as pretty as your lawyer friend."

She *was* pretty. But she'd never done anything to fire his blood. She was also married to her pastry chef and had been for years. However, even thinking of Jo for a moment turned his thoughts to mush. He had to get moving. Turning back to

Henry, he pointed toward the shark, but his mother slapped his hand aside.

She led him around behind the counter and waved a negligent hand. Out of sight at Henry's feet were three huge mesh bags of the most perfect sea scallops still in the shell that he'd ever seen. Beside them, a tub of ice sported some beautiful squid, perfect for side dishes of fried calamari rings.

She patted Henry on the cheek, "He's such a good man. So sweet."

Henry beamed.

His mother might make him crazy, but his menu was really going to shine tonight.

CHAPTER 17

"*F*ive o'clock at Cutters." Jo didn't even greet Cassidy when she answered the phone. Just issued the order.

"Uh. O-kay." Cassidy's voice was hazed with sleep.

Jo looked at the clock floating on the glass wall of her office. It was barely seven. The morning light was bright enough that the overhead lights were faded down to almost nothing. "Oh, sorry. I didn't realize the time."

Cassidy was usually awake by now, but she certainly didn't sound it at the moment.

"S'okay. Russell and I, we were just, sort of, uh, continuing the honeymoon."

Great, now she felt even worse. Unable to sleep after Angelo left, she'd skipped her morning workout and come straight to work. She hadn't even stopped for a bagel and cream cheese or anything else fattening and satisfying. She'd had her usual taste-less power drink and driven to the office. She had to drive to work most days now because she didn't want to be walking home on the city streets after dark, which is when she was typically departing. Even though it would be the longest day of the

133

year soon, she'd wager it would be a long time before she walked home during daylight hours again.

Muriel would be arriving shortly and the next round of case files would follow not long after. She wasn't up to facing this day.

Jo rubbed at her gritty eyes and apologized again for rousing Cassidy from her marriage bed.

"Sounds major," Cassidy's voice was a little more coherent.

"I...," Muriel rolled in on cue and dropped a to-go cup of coffee off on her desk. "Yes, it is." She dragged the words out until Muriel had drifted to her own office across the hall. "But I can't get into it at the moment."

"Okay."

"It's you I need to speak to." She felt crappy for saying it that way, but knew Cassidy would get the message. Jo didn't need Russell or Perrin, it was Cassidy's level-headed thinking she needed at the moment. And, most of all, it was her former roommate's reaction she was worried about.

After only the briefest of pauses, Cassidy replied, her voice fully awake. "See you at five."

Muriel brought in the first stack of the morning and looked for a space to set it on Jo's desk.

"Someone looks as if they had great sex last night."

"That is an assumption that I will neither confirm nor deny." Jo groaned to herself. That was the problem with working with Muriel for five years, she couldn't hide a single thing from her.

"Totally confirmed." Muriel swept out.

Jo took the first file of the day and began slogging her way through it.

JO HADN'T SHOWN up at the gym, not that he'd really expected her to, so Angelo had made his workout short. He'd started with lots of energy, but within ten minutes his body was dragging, within twenty it was stopped. Trying to function on two or three hours of sleep wasn't cutting it.

He needed to rethink his need for personal masochism. Of course she had the good sense to sleep while she could. She was a sensible woman. But not as sensible as she wanted you to think.

There was a wild streak hidden deep inside Jo Thompson that had startled, aroused, and fascinated Angelo. Brilliant, beautiful, and lethal. When he'd coaxed her back into that power jacket, and just that power jacket, she'd taken absolute control. It was a role reversal he wasn't used to. He didn't object, but he'd found most women wanted to abandon themselves to his control.

Not Counselor Thompson.

In that jacket, she'd climbed atop him and used him until his mind blanked and his body ached. Or had his body blanked and his mind ached? Whatever it was, it had been incredible. Out of the jacket, she'd gone soft and gentle, wrapping herself about him to welcome him in. He couldn't imagine ever getting enough of her.

After shopping and the lame excuse for a workout, he'd crawled home and sacked out until it was time to go to the restaurant for lunch service. A shower and shave did little to restore his equilibrium and nothing to erase the self-satisfied smile in the mirror. He practically floated up the six blocks to work.

"I hear she's at it again," Mr. D warned him when he stopped by to share a morning espresso.

Angelo didn't need to ask who, nor did he pause to finish his shot before running up Post Alley behind Mr. D's, dodging cars and slow-moving pedestrians who were plodding up the steep hill, so steep that the sidewalk had bumps built into the concrete to keep you from slipping back downhill.

Once again, a line, thankfully shorter this time, had formed in front of the restaurant. They didn't open for another hour, what was Maria Amelia doing this time?

Angelo slowed in order to appear calm when he arrived, though his heart was pounding far harder than the mere block-and-a-half run justified.

The patrons weren't lined up at the door, they were lined up at the kitchen window. He'd sometimes left it cracked open to let the cooking scents spill out into the alley as an advertisement. Now, someone had installed a small counter that stuck out from the windowsill and the window sash itself was slid all of the way up.

He stumbled to a halt at the edge of the crowd and stared.

Inside the window sat his mother. She wore a deep purple dress that clung to her curves and exposed a cleavage worthy of Sophia Loren. Her laugh sparkled out.

A smiling customer left the line and passed Angelo. She bore a tiny cup of espresso and a flaky cornetto, an Italian croissant filled with, he didn't need to lean in close to see, he could smell the sweet Italian sausage and pepper.

There was no posted menu, just a sign that said, "$3" next to a jar. He noticed that most people slipped in a five anyway and left happy. His mother's charm was apparently sufficient for the two-dollar tip. Even at five dollars, it was a bargain. The cornetti were large, flaky, and still steaming. The espresso was dark, rich, and served in an amount a little bigger than an Italian portion but not so big as an American one.

He slipped into the restaurant. There she sat, perched on her stool by the window. Her bare legs casually crossed and exposed by a knee-length skirt that rode just up on her thighs. She wasn't racy, but she was a fair amount too attractive, for even an Italian mother, and especially for his mother. He slipped up across from her and leaned against the window's wall, pretty much out of view of the customers.

"You're not going to make much money that way, Mama," he whispered just loud enough for her to hear in between customers.

"Sweetheart, I am losing you money." She smiled as if that were the goal.

But Angelo knew better. He left Maria Amelia to charm the next early morning patron after taking a cornetto and espresso for himself and leaving an, "I love you, Mama," behind. He strolled over to Manuel as he enjoyed the rich sausage in the almost painfully warm pastry.

"Better gear up, Manuel. We've got another lunch rush coming."

Manuel just smiled at him, took a bite of his own, almost-finished cornetto, and went back to work. Angelo pulled on an apron. He'd spent the night with a woman who presented more mystery and fascination after being with her, rather than less as usually seemed to be the case.

And his mouth was watering for the next bite of his second breakfast. His mother was actually fitting in at his restaurant. And they were about to get hammered by a massive lunch rush.

It was an incredibly good day.

CHAPTER 18

*C*utters Crabhouse was their go-to bar when they needed to talk. Jo and Perrin had met here on and off for years. Then when Cassidy had returned to Seattle to be with her ailing father and purchased a condo practically next door, it had become a fixture in their lives. Whenever someone had a crisis or a triumph, commiseration and celebration were handed out in equal shares at Cutter's.

The outer bar was lively, as it was one of those places that urban professionals went to see and be seen, which could be fun. But it also allowed them to slip into the anonymity of the crowd and gain a pleasant level of privacy. Good cocktails, great appetizers, and what Cassidy acknowledged as an acceptable wine cellar certainly helped.

It also sat a block from both Jo's office and Cassidy's condo and only three from Perrin's Glorious Garb in Belltown with her apartment above her store.

Jo scanned the room as she came in the front door, waiting for a couple who didn't quite understand that they had to keep going down a barely labeled side hall to reach the entry to the restaurant. Despite it having tasty food and some of the best views in Seattle, Jo and her friends rarely went for a meal, opting instead for the more relaxed community of the bar.

Cutter's trademark focaccia scented the air with rosemary and olive oil. Garlic of steamed clams and the bright bite of lemon for oysters wrapped around her and welcomed her in. The bright afternoon light shining in from the long wall of windows facing the Seattle waterfront actually left the bar feeling warm and friendly by contrast.

Jo could feel her shoulders easing even as she spotted Cassidy. Perrin sat close beside her, looking much better than the last time Jo had seen her. Though her hair was now bleach-white rather than the Jo-Thompson-black that it had been.

Cassidy spotted Jo and offered a near invisible shrug. It said, "I know what you asked for, but tough."

And Cassidy, as usual, was right.

Jo did need to talk to her college roommate, but whatever else might be going on, Perrin was a devoted friend and would do anything for her.

Cassidy had snagged them three tall stools at a small table by the window. Only about a third of the tables were occupied, leaving a bit of a hush in the bar. But it was barely five o'clock, give it half an hour and the place would be humming.

Cassidy had worn a simple silk blouse and designer jeans with flats, a serious dress down for her. She really was still on her honeymoon, which made Jo feel all the more guilty for dragging her away from it.

Perrin wore one of her own designs, again in the pale green of the bridesmaid gowns, but this time as a peasant blouse fallen off one shoulder. The floral skirt showed a long flash of her fine legs and looked great with her simple sandals. Jo had to stare at it for several moments before she recognized it as her own skirt, stolen from her closet, and redesigned to be more updated. She'd liked that skirt, but there was little point complaining about it to Perrin.

Jo searched wildly for some safe topic to start with as she joined them, and landed nowhere near one.

"Did Perrin tell you about the dress she made for me?" Jo needed to cut her tongue out now. She knew it was going to be going straight downhill from this point on.

JO RARELY DRANK, and almost never finished the first drink when she did, but when the second Honey Citrus Martini disappeared and a third one replaced it without her quite figuring out how it happened, she knew she was in trouble. The Dungeness Crab Cakes, Buffalo Wings, and Steamed Manila Clams in a sauce so luscious they were still dipping it up with another round of focaccia, had slid by just as easily over the last hour.

Thankfully, the dress turned out to be the right topic after all. It ended up that Perrin hadn't mentioned it to Cassidy. She wanted to drag them all off to Jo's apartment to see it right away, but she and Cassidy had vetoed that. Then Perrin rescued Jo's poor lead-in by starting on her idea for a line of custom wedding dresses, not designed as dresses, but designed for individuals.

"You'll be the Howard Roarke of fashion." Jo wondered blearily what neuron had remembered that tidbit of information.

"No. First, in case you haven't noticed because they're so small, I actually do have breasts. So I can't be anyone named Howard."

"You do," Jo acknowledged. "They look good on you too. Better than they would on Gary Cooper."

Perrin tipped her head sideways. "You're drunk. You aren't making sense any longer."

"Gary Cooper played Howard Roarke in the movie *The*

Fountainhead." Cassidy took up the gauntlet and tried to carry it down the field or across the polo ground or whatever one did with a gauntlet. "It's about an architect who believes that every design must be unique to the place and the materials."

Perrin stared down at her Cosmo for several long seconds before replying. "But I'm not building buildings. I'm designing wedding dresses. And I'm saying that they need to be unique for each woman. Jo's dress would look stupid on you."

"Because I don't have Jo's amazing breasts."

"Exactly!" Perrin flagged down a waitress with a loud, "Hey cutie!" Which turned a dozen or so heads at their end of the lounge.

The waitress was cute in a brunette, clingy-top clad way though Jo would never have thought of her that way. Let alone shouted it out for the whole bar to hear.

"Is it me," Perrin studied the table, "or did we run out of food?"

"I can fix that," the waitress was unflappable.

"Cool, thanks!" Perrin turned back to Jo. "What was I talking about?"

The waitress didn't even blink before wandering away. Jo wondered what would be coming next.

"Wedding dresses," Jo supplied.

"No. No, that wasn't it." Perrin searched the table again, this time apparently looking for her last topic rather than the next appetizer.

"Jo's breasts?" Cassidy offered as she sipped her wine.

"Bingo!" Perrin nudged Cassidy's arm almost tipping them both off their stools.

"So. What happened from, 'I have no one to wear a wedding dress for' to an hemergency meeting?" Perrin blinked hard then repeated more slowly and clearly. "E-mer-gen-cy meeting. Nope, not that drunk yet. He-emergency meeting. Hey! That must be it."

Perrin nudged Cassidy again but harder. Cassidy was better braced this time.

"Jo got laid. That's the problem." Then she turned to Jo. "Why is that a problem?"

Jo did her best not to groan. Somehow Perrin always found her way back to the topic, even when Jo no longer wanted her to. Over the first two drinks, she'd come to terms with just having to figure it out herself. It would be safer, easier that way. What part of her had thought that Cassidy, being Angelo's best friend's wife, was the proper confessor for Jo's sins?

"Because it was with Angelo."

Jo slapped her hand over her mouth, but she'd said it and now it was out in the world. She should have opened with the job offer that Renée was using to make her crazy. That had to be safer than this. Anything would have been safer.

She gauged her friends' reactions.

Cassidy had gone quiet. She looked like she did when tasting a new wine. Rolling the idea around on her tongue, letting it build and flow to see how it tasted.

Perrin practically shouted, "Shrimp and crab cocktail!" Her attempt to drunkenly hug the waitress while she still bore the next appetizer almost caused the woman to bobble the plate, but she was good enough to save the moment.

"Cute and smart! Too bad I'm straight. Are you?"

The waitress shook her head no.

"Bummer. Any takers?" Perrin asked Jo and Cassidy. Cassidy rolled her eyes and Jo just shook her head.

"Oh well," Perrin addressed the waitress. "No luck here, sorry about that. Girls, we have to remember to tip her extra nice." The waitress smiled easily and drifted off at a call to the next table. Another reason Jo liked Cutter's, the waitresses could deal with Perrin. Other places she tended to blow them out of the water and they never recovered.

Jo thought that maybe at least on one front, she might have dodged the bullet. Cassidy was still testing the idea and edging up on her opinion.

"Well, I knew he was attracted to you. But that was last year before I started dating Russell."

"You didn't date Russell," Perrin corrected her. She held up a finger and began counting. "First you despised his very existence. Then second, you fell head over heels in love with him. After that, third, you couldn't figure out what to do about it."

"I married him."

"Okay, that's fourth. But it took you long enough."

Jo considered that this might be an opportunity for her to quietly slip away but rather than rising to Perrin's tease, Cassidy turned back to face Jo, trapping her on her stool.

"And now, with no buildup, you, ah..."

"Jumped his bones," Perrin filled in when Cassidy hesitated.

"Well," Jo thought of trying to explain the wedding and the way Angelo looked at her and how uncomfortable that had made her feel. But it had also made her feel feminine.

When she thought of herself as a woman, it was the power suit one who came to mind. The lawyer feared far and wide, feared even more because she was a female and had kicked ass every time she'd entered a courtroom since her first mock trial in college.

But Angelo kept seeing a different Jo, one she didn't know, and, much to her dismay it was a version of Jo that she was finding she wasn't much comfortable with.

She thought of trying to explain the disastrous meal, his banged head, and how he'd been so cute about it. And their working out together. And...

It was impossible to wrap her mind around what had happened, never mind her tongue. Though she'd never behaved in such a fashion with any lover before Angelo, "jumped his bones" was also alarmingly accurate.

"Sort of did that," was the best response she could muster for Perrin. She reached for her martini to slake her dry throat, but it was already half gone and she really needed to slow down. Instead she dipped some crab in the cocktail sauce to buy herself a moment.

"When?"

"Last night!" Perrin answered for her. "That's why we're having the he-mergency meeting today." She pulled one sleeve onto her shoulder causing the other one to fall off.

Perrin leaned in. "Was it good? Yep, that blush nails that part of it."

Jo did her best to use sheer willpower to fight the heat rising in her face, which only made her cheeks burn hotter.

"Did he stay the night?"

This time Jo gulped some of her martini. When she recovered her breath from the scorch of alcohol sliding down her throat and the citrus twang had cleared her head a bit, she nodded.

"He stayed until it was time to go shopping for the restaurant."

"Yes!" Perrin did a fist pump and almost elbowed a passing guy in the crotch. "Damn good sign. And he's so awfully pretty. Is he prettier naked?"

"How do you do that?" Jo's voice had drifted out of her control and it came out half in anger but got snarled up in a laugh on the way out.

"Do what?" Perrin did her best to look all innocent, sitting up extra straight. This caused her blouse to slide off both shoulders making her look even more elfin than she usually did.

"Make me tell you things I never intended to say?"

"You're avoiding the question, counselor. All I want to know is, is Angelo Parrano as pretty naked as you'd expect?" She said it in a voice declarative enough that the women at two nearby tables paused and listened for the answer.

Jo ground her teeth and fought back the urge to scream.

"Yes, curse you. He's fucking gorgeous." That made two of the women at other tables look away. Two others sighed in what sounded like envy before they turned back to their own tables.

"Jo swore," Perrin dropped her jaw in mock horror. "He must look really amazing."

"Look, feel, made me feel... Beyond amazing." Now that she'd started, she couldn't shut up. But he had. There'd been a heat, a need, a yearning, that would have been unnerving if it hadn't been so completely mutual. He'd opened up whole new worlds of sensation that she hadn't known existed.

She wasn't a prude, or inexperienced.

But Angelo's body had simply been made for her. Every shape, every muscle, every texture had fit her perfectly. And while she'd had good lovers before, she'd never had one who made it so much fun. She'd found ways to tease him to madness, until his breath came in short, hot gasps, and he'd begged her to finish him off or just kill him now.

"It was," her voice sounded soft and dreamy even to herself, "the most incredible sex I've ever had."

"Then why are we having a he-mergency meeting?" Perrin placed an elbow on the table and propped her chin in her hand as if that were the only thing keeping her head off the table.

"Because," Cassidy still spoke in that slow analytic voice of hers. "Because she's afraid I'll be upset."

"Why?"

"Because I'm married to Russell."

Jo nodded, but Perrin simply looked more confused.

"She isn't sleeping with Russell. You are. She is sleeping with Angelo."

"Actually we didn't sleep much." The gin was talking. That

was definitely the gin and not Jo Thompson. She really hoped that was true.

"Now she's bragging," Perrin poked at the cocktail sauce with another shrimp.

"She is," Cassidy agreed. Cassidy straightened and only wobbled a little in her chair.

"We'll just all be adult about this. We're all grown and, uh, you know, worldly sorts of people. We'll just make sure that we all end up being friends."

"Or lovers," Perrin never missed.

"Or lovers." Cassidy acknowledged.

"Or married." This time Perrin positively smirked at Jo. "Told you not to underestimate the power of a good dress."

"I'm not marrying Angelo, I'm only sleeping with him."

"Except you said you weren't sleeping with him. Just having lots of sex."

Cassidy held out her hands to stop the conversation. Taking a deep breath, she tried to steer the conversation back to the point.

"We'll just be adult about this."

Jo nodded, thinking about she and Angelo groaning together in the shower somewhere in the middle of the night until it had echoed off the walls.

"We weren't very adult about it."

Perrin cocked her head to one side, still held up only by her chin on her palm. "You were juvenile about sex?"

"No, more animal."

"Now we're getting somewhere! Cassidy, we need to get Jo drunk far more often. This is way too much fun. Waitress, where did that cute butch gal go? We need another round."

Jo looked down, but her martini was empty. Yup, she really was in trouble now.

CHAPTER 19

"*M*y girlfriend is moving to Hawaii."

The phrase sent chills up Angelo's back.

First, it struck him as far too reminiscent of Jo's statement about heading to Alaska for the next three-to-five years. Second, it was coming from his patissier, Eugene, at the end of another brutal shift. Angelo didn't need him to be distracted when they were so busy they could barely breathe.

They sat around the stainless prep table.

Graziella lay with her head on her arms as if someone had shot her. Marlys the grillardin had kicked ass on the grill tonight and now she looked like the kicking had been the other way around. Vic and Valerie who'd done such yeoman service on the fryer and the soups were still upright and Angelo couldn't imagine how. Marko was still finishing the last of the dishes. Angelo would go over there and drag him to the table in a headlock as soon as their late dinner was ready.

Manuel was throwing together a batch of his No-Knife Pasta. He'd shredded fresh tomatoes by tearing them apart with his fingers, then added a liberal sprinkling of torn basil and fresh oregano, some smashed garlic that already spiked the air, and a fistful of Kalamata olives, all sprinkled with red pepper flakes and olive oil. He'd mixed together the last of the day's fresh pasta, mainly fettuccini and penne. And if Angelo had the energy, he'd bless the man because otherwise he would have felt obligated to do it himself.

He wouldn't trade last night with Jo for anything, though eight hours extra sleep sounded awfully good right now.

But exhaustion wasn't the real problem.

The real problem was his mother, who he'd finally forced to go home an hour ago.

Running Angelo's Tuscan Hearth had evolved into a science. Open at eleven thirty and be three-quarters full for lunch, an afternoon dribble, and two seatings at dinner. Close the doors at eight, finish the second service by nine, done and clean by ten. With the shopping and prep it was only twelve to fourteen hours a day, with everyone getting a couple hours off in the afternoon or perhaps an early leave on a quiet night.

That was about the easiest restaurant job Angelo had ever had, or at least the fewest hours. Add on the two days closed every week and it was downright cushy. It also, he knew, would make his staff insanely loyal by keeping such an easy schedule.

But Maria Amelia Avico Parrano had thrown a hatchet into that the last several days. There was now a line sufficient to fill half the restaurant the very moment they opened the doors, and the tables were packed solid by noon. Afternoon was the staff's time to shift over to dinner prep, cook the staff dinner, often they could even eat together, or run some personal errands. Now they stayed at busy-lunch levels right to the five o'clock start of dinner for theater goers. And when he'd locked the outer doors tonight, he'd still had two parties of six and three of five that hadn't even been seated yet. They'd been more than happy to wait, especially as his mother had served them wine and complimentary hors d'oeuvres while they waited.

His mother was just too pleasantly charming and too incredibly beautiful. She flitted between the cookline and the table service. When Graziella and her two assistant waiters were swamped, his mother showed up on the floor with the black pepper grinder for the patron's salad or the parmesan shaver for their pasta. When Valerie was seasoning the soup, his mother was there to taste and give her an opinion.

Angelo himself had agreed with Maria Amelia so many times that he was beginning to sound like a parrot. Even when it was his idea in the first place, her agreement with him somehow instead sounded like his agreement with her. Just trying to figure out how that happened made his head hurt all over again.

Manuel dumped the pasta into a massive colander, flipped the pasta right back into the pot and tossed in all of the ingredients. A couple fistfuls of mozzarella and Asiago then he dropped the pot in the middle of the table.

"Hey Marko!" Angelo didn't have the energy to go and grab the kid. So he'd be both lazy and devious, killing two noodles with one fork. "Bring over some bowls and forks."

"We gotta get some more help on the line." Manuel dropped onto a stool.

"That's not the problem." He took the dishwasher-hot bowl from Marko, which would have singed his fingers if he didn't have a cook's calluses. "Okay that's not the only problem."

He nudged Graziella from her nap. "Food, Grazie."

"You're welcome," she mumbled.

"Not thanking you. Eat, *per favore*." He nudged her again and she came fully awake, shook her head to clear it, and tried to serve herself from the big pot. She almost lost it all to the table.

"Then what is the problem?" Manuel took the bowl from her fumbling hands, filled it, and handed it back before she noticed it was gone. Then he filled another and slid it down the table to Angelo. Angelo skidded his empty one back.

He dug in and took his first real bite of food in over eight hours, perhaps twelve hours since he'd had his mother's cornetto. He couldn't be sure anymore.

"Oh, Manuel," the flavors bloomed in his mouth. Simple, fresh, clean. Three spices, perfectly ripe tomatoes, and olives for depth. "Damn, you're good, my friend."

Manuel was a dark Mexican from Oaxaca in the south, squat, broad-shouldered, and quiet.

"Did I ever tell you how I met this guy?"

Graziella had been there, with him since before he opened the restaurant, but the others simply shook their heads.

"This guy," Angelo took a mouthful of pasta and then aimed his empty fork at Manuel's chest and spoke around his food a bit. "He shows up at my kitchen door. It was the same day I installed the grill and thought I was finally getting somewhere. He stood silhouetted in the back door of the kitchen."

"'Italian?' is all I say to him." Manuel joined in his own story.

"That was it, one word. When I said it was, he just nodded and walked away. I didn't think anything more of it."

Manuel just grinned at him.

"You were a little spooky," Graziella told him then turned to the others. "Half an hour later he walks back into the kitchen with a couple of shopping bags from the Market. Without a word he pulls out a knife, a beautiful piece of chicken, some sherry, and three other ingredients. He just walked in and started cooking as if he owned the damn place."

"That basil-mustard-lemon chicken poached in sherry was truly spectacular," Angelo told him. "Simpler even than this, nowhere to hide any mistakes. I'd had this whole plan of interviewing and training my sous chef. Had to have at least culinary school and ten years' experience. Manuel took the job that afternoon. A crazy Mexican who cooks Italian."

"Want to try my Chinese?"

"Don't even think it!" Angelo knew he'd be a goner the day Manuel left.

He laughed quietly. "Thanks boss. It's been great. But we need help. Why you say that *no hay problema?*"

Angelo dug into his pasta one more time hoping to find another answer.

It was a problem and Angelo knew it. But it wasn't the only problem. Hiring more people didn't scare him, he had the cash flow to do that. It was the other idea that was worrying him spitless.

They all ate in silence for a minute or two while he tried to collect his thoughts. They were drooping, every last one of them.

"The problem," he went to the walk-in cooler and found himself a beer to balance the heat of the red peppers and tang of the garlic. "The problem."

Shit! He was already in over his head, might as well go the rest of the way. He got back to the table and faced his team, they deserved to know.

"The problem is that we don't have enough seats in this restaurant. Between the amazing cooking and service we've been doing, and what my mother has taught us about marketing ourselves better these last few days, there just aren't enough seats here."

"Well," Valerie looked up at the ceiling. That's where she and Vic lived, right over the restaurant. "I guess we could move."

Manuel was shaking his head. "No! The kitchen, she matches the restaurant. If we go up, we need bigger kitchen. That fix nothing."

"Right. What we need," Angelo knew he was going to hate himself in the morning. "What we need is to open a second restaurant."

The collective groan was exactly the answer he'd expected.

"BUT MY GIRLFRIEND is moving to Hawaii," Eugene repeated his news as if it were a protest.

"That'll give youse more time to make fine Italian desserts." Marlys, the grillardin, used her fake Brooklyn mobster accent and slapped her drinking buddy on the back almost making him snort his pasta.

No one quite knew how the two of them got along. Marlys hailed from a good Italian family in Brooklyn. She and Angelo had met when he was working a restaurant in Brooklyn Heights, he'd been the master of the grill then, and she'd been in charge of the fryer. When he'd started the restaurant, she'd been one of his first calls. Her lover had just dumped her and she leapt at the chance to move out of the city.

Eugene, was, well, to put it kindly, a slightly annoying kid from Colorado. But he made exquisite pastries.

Angelo knew they double dated on several occasions, Eugene and Audrey, Marlys and whatever woman she was seeing at the time. On the cookline they were always talking movies or the latest hot television series that Angelo had never heard of, they were seriously into media. Eugene was also into online gaming, though not in a deep fanatic kind of way, and Marlys kept teasing him about not living in the real world. As if performing detailed analyses of this week's shape-shifting-vampire-British-spy episode placed her on such superior footing.

"No," Eugene planted his fork in his pasta as if for emphasis. "I'm going with her."

That shocked the table to silence. For two years the core team had remained inviolate, except for Marko joining them just six months ago when Ricky had decided to go to college, in astrophysics of all unlikely things. To lose their patissier was unimaginable. There was no position harder to replace. Angelo was the only one who could possibly fill in, but he'd need to work full time at just pastry and he had a restaurant to run.

"Are you, uh," Angelo struggled to find his voice and keep calm. "Are you sure?" It was also hard to imagine the sallow-faced boy in the land of sea and sun. Boy. He was four years younger than Angelo, but he always seemed to be eighteen going on sixteen.

"I was going to tell you today, but service never stopped."

Angelo glanced at Marlys. She looked surprised and worried. Neither of them had missed the way he'd phrased it. Not, "My girlfriend and I are moving to Hawaii," but rather "My girlfriend is moving." Did he know Eugene well enough to point out that maybe she didn't want him to follow her and was being too nice to say so?

He remembered Heather at the CIA. She never said, "No, we're done." She simply kept not finding time to be with him. It had taken him a while to learn that while some women said no and weren't listened to by the jerks, there were some women who simply didn't know how to say no in the first place.

He opened his mouth and shut it again when Marlys shook her head. He'd leave her to delve into it. In the meantime, he'd start hunting for a new pastry chef, two of them if he was going to open another restaurant. Gods but his head hurt. Maybe he'd be better off if Jo went to Alaska, because whether or not Eugene remained, he wasn't going to have time to breathe, never mind sleep or fall in love.

That shocked him bolt upright.

He never fell in love. He fell in lust. Lust was fun, healthy, and made the passage of time exceedingly pleasant.

That's all he had with Jo. She was beautiful, enticing, and did really wonderful things to his hormone balance.

Counselor Jo Thompson was the one, again, causing him trouble. That woman was interesting, intense, brilliant, and had him near-enough hypnotized. He was definitely under her spell.

He took a bite of the now-tasteless pasta as the others began probing Eugene about what he would be doing in Hawaii, but he couldn't hear their words.

What in hell had Counselor Thompson done to him?

CHAPTER 20

"*You're a witch!*"

Jo burst out laughing and completely lost her rhythm on the rowing machine. Her legs stretched at full extension, but her hands lost the handle which retracted with a sharp snap. Without the tension of the rower handle, it was hard to sit back up.

Angelo leaned over and placed a warm, solid palm on the center of her back and provided the leverage for her to sit easily upright.

She looked up at him standing beside her, a towel over his shoulder. They'd missed each other for three days in a row. First she hadn't gone to the gym, then he hadn't. She'd drifted by the restaurant on her way through the lunchtime Market, but the long lines told her not to risk disturbing him. At night, all she was doing was working crazy hours, then plummeting into bed.

Now they were together in the Eastlake gym.

She looked up at him and everything that she'd told herself she wasn't feeling burst through her body in a flash of animal heat. She hoped the flush of her workout would hide the flush rising to her cheeks.

"Yes, a proud member of the order of..." she tried to come up with something witty. "The raw need for your body," came to mind but she discarded it. "The order of legalus witchcraftia." It was the best she had off the cuff.

He looked *so* good standing there. His hands casually holding the ends of the towel looped behind his neck. Sweat shone on his chest above the line of the black tank top. His arms were flexing in a way that told her he'd just finished with the weight machines.

"How did you discover my secret membership?" She felt goofy around him. He was looking at her as if he'd devour her right there in the middle of the gym floor. She was lousy at flirting with men, much better at staring them down into silence until they slunk away. But somehow she was flirting with Angelo. She tasted the salt of sweat when she licked her upper lip only afterward realizing that too could be a flirtatious gesture.

"Well," he dropped down to sit sideways on a recumbent-cycle machine next to her rower. "My first suspicion was Cassidy."

"Cassidy?" What did she have to do with the nice flirt they had going?

"Cassidy. When she bewitched a confirmed bachelor like Russell, I knew something was suspicious about you three."

"The three witches of Eastlake?" She reached for her own towel and wiped at her face before draping it around her own shoulders in such a way that it hid most of the exposed skin above her sports bra.

"Something like that. At the wedding Josh Harper described you three as beauty, truth, and joy."

Cassidy was the great beauty of their threesome and Perrin had to be joy. That left her as truth. While accurate, she could wish for a somewhat sexier label.

"But I think he missed the mark."

"Oh?" What was she besides truth? Hard working lawyer, no social life, no personal activities except her solo pursuit of a triathlon simply to provide focus for the one thing she ever did for herself, working out. She found a peace in wearing her body toward exhaustion, and exhilaration in discovering what she could do, but no more.

"Yes," Angelo clearly hadn't been distracted by her reverie. "I think that my problem with you is that you embody all three elements."

Beauty. Truth. Joy. No one had ever called her joyous before. And while she was often labeled pretty, none of those who did so had been interested by the deep 'truth' that was far more a part of who she was.

"All three?" She could become deeply attached to being seen that way. "Does that make me the head witch?"

"More the goddess template of which all others are but pale copies."

"That does it," she burst out laughing. "That is so over the top, Angelo. How do you come up with these lines?" She pushed to her feet and he did the same bringing them closer together. But even as he shrugged it off with a laugh, his eyes did not change. If it wasn't a line... That possibility was not one she'd ever consider.

She stroked fingertips down his cheek.

"That's sweet, but I am a real woman, Angelo. Flesh and blood. Not worthy of any pedestal."

"I'd argue the point, but I'd rather see you again."

Jo checked her watch. "I have phone conferences to Washington and Alaska this morning and this is Friday and you're open late."

His eyes clouded for a moment with worry, but the look was fleeting.

"We could ride together again tomorrow? I don't want to get in the way of your training."

Damn the man for being so considerate. Yes, she needed to ride, but what she wanted was to feel even half of what Angelo had made her feel their first night together.

"Sure, a ride sounds great." Then the Evil Jo took over, the one with too much lust and sex on her mind. "If you meet me on the other side of the locker rooms, I'll give you my spare key and the code for the elevator. Maybe you can bring your bike over after work tonight, then we can ride in the morning." She'd never been so forward in her life and found that she was holding her breath to see his reaction. Consciously ordering herself to breathe didn't work, so she held on and waited, hoping he'd answer before she passed out.

He didn't make her wait too long.

"And how in the world am I not supposed to put you on a pedestal? You're bloody glorious."

CHAPTER 21

*A*ngelo risked the front hall light to help him navigate inside the unfamiliar apartment. Bike, helmet, and shoes he left against the wall and crept through the entryway.

The kitchen was immaculate, so immaculate that he wondered if she used it much. A quick peek in the refrigerator revealed the answer of, "not much." Leftover containers roughly equaled number of food products.

The combined dining and living room was almost Spartan except for one wall which was a solid, tight-packed bookshelf. Half law books and half thrillers. He looked closer, most of them legal thrillers. Clearly she was interested in nothing other than law. So what the hell was she doing with him? A woman like her should be with—

Angelo cut himself off. Don't go there. She should be with *him*, that's who. For every second she'd allow.

The room was female, but in an odd way it wasn't feminine. Or maybe he had that backwards. It was feminine in the perfect taste that had been applied to the selection of furnishings and art. It wasn't female in its lack of what he would typically expect: brightly colored pillows, knick-knacks, or a knit throw over the couch.

Of course his own décor was primarily a wall of cookbooks. So he wasn't one to talk.

The perfect control of her entire world revealed yet another facet of Jo Thompson. Her car was incredible, her apartment exquisite, her personal conditioning exceptional. As a matter of fact, the only thing that didn't fit her was that disaster she called a desk in that terrifyingly powerful office. It had looked as if a bomb had gone off there and he'd bet it was far worse by now. He hadn't seen it in three days but he'd wager it had begun breeding on its own.

He turned off the hall light and slipped into the master bedroom. She'd left a soft blue nightlight on for him. Without it, the heavy curtains would have left the room pitch black. Again, the perfect feminine. Dusky carpet, white walls, white-stained oak furniture, and floor-to-ceiling white curtains. He wondered what lay beyond those. He'd gotten turned around in the building and certainly hadn't bothered to consider the view his first time here. A quick peek revealed a sweeping panorama of Seattle, Puget Sound, and moonlight on the Olympic Mountains. He could get to like this. He let the curtain slip shut.

The room smelled like Jo. Not some strong floral or citrus scent, as far as he knew she didn't wear perfume. But it smelled of her nonetheless. A scent, a flavor that he hadn't been able to erase from his mind since their first ice-creamed kiss.

She reminded him of sky and sunlight and, with all apologies to his history teacher, the deep richness he'd always imagined surrounding the Greek Fates, the three women who measured and cut the time of a man's life.

Or better yet, Gaia, wasn't she the mother of the Three Fates, or something like that? Jo really did remind him of a mother goddess. The incredible beauty, the perfect posture as if she were dancer rather than lawyer, the groundedness in who she was. Didn't the woman have any doubts about anything?

In the soft light, he could just make out her hair spread across the white pillow and the deeply embroidered white bed quilt. She lay on her side and the scattered hair hid her face leaving only a dark sheen upon the pillow.

That's when he remembered her in her office, the dark hair spilling over her face, right after she'd screamed in frustration.

No. He had to keep reminding himself. This wasn't Counselor Jo Thompson, not in this room. Here was his lover. That sounded awesomely good. It sent a shiver and a heat washing the length of his body.

Strictly human, he reminded himself. No pedestals allowed, no matter how he wished to place her upon one. He undressed and slipped in beside her appreciating the softness of the flannel sheets and the warmth and scent of Jo Thompson that pervaded the bed.

As gently as he could, he brushed the hair back from her face.

She sighed as he did so.

"Angelo." It was barely a whisper.

"Right here, Jo."

She slid up against him, draping an arm over his ribs and curling to bury her face against his chest. Then, with another sigh, she fell back asleep.

His body thrummed with need. Her face on his chest placed her hair where he could nuzzle it and inhale even more deeply of sky, sun, and Mother Earth. Her hair, long and thick, was also soft and smelled of a light shampoo.

He considered waking her, but didn't have the heart to do so. She must be as exhausted as he felt. Eugene still insisted he was departing at the end of the month. Barely two weeks' notice. Even in a foodie-town like Seattle, there was no way to find a good patissier so quickly. He would put out notices for several positions, hoping to find his way through the current madness as well as begin staffing the new restaurant.

No! He had to stop his whirling mind. He wouldn't bring work into this place. He didn't care what Jo said or didn't, he'd declare this a sanctuary, even if it was one without pedestals. He simply wouldn't tell her that he'd done so. In this place at least, it would only be about the two of them, the overwhelmed Italian and the woman who filled his senses as if she were indeed born of heaven.

Then he thought of something that calmed his nerves.

Even mostly asleep, she'd called him by his name as if he filled her thoughts as much as she did his.

Jo woke slowly to the smell of coffee and bacon. Coffee! Her body woke faster simply for knowing caffeine would be consumed shortly. She opened one eye and saw the empty pillow beside hers. It was dented. But she'd gone to bed alone and woken alone.

To the smell of coffee her body reminded her.

So, she'd apparently been alone at either end, but not in the middle? Had he held her in the night? She thought so, felt as if she had been held, but couldn't be sure.

Unravished. Held or not, her body was distinctly unravished. The man tells her she is beautiful like a goddess and then doesn't touch her. It was enough to make a girl downright irritable.

Coffee. Right, she was always irritable before coffee.

She slid from beneath the covers wearing the extra-large gray t-shirt with the arched maroon "Vassar" fading over her chest.

Angelo stood at the stove cooking, his back mostly toward her. He wore only his jeans riding low enough on his hips to reveal that his underwear probably was still somewhere in her bedroom. His bare back rippled slightly as he tended the bacon. God he was beautiful. She was about to slip up behind him when she noticed the cloth-covered cookie sheet on the counter. It had been set with napkins, silverware, and a large stoneware mug that steamed thickly of caffeine and French roast. An impromptu breakfast tray.

Breakfast in bed! She'd never had that except when she'd made it for herself. Well, she certainly wasn't going to spoil being spoiled for a morning, and scooted back to the bedroom slipping between the covers. Be awake? Feign sleep? Jump him the moment he got through the door and to hell with the consequences? No, that was too high a risk to the precious caffeine.

Jo went for the second option, burying her face in the pillow that smelled of Angelo, how she'd missed that when she woke up was beyond her. There she listened to the song of her pulse gaining tempo rapidly.

She ignored the first whispered, "Jo?"

At the second, closer call of her name, she made a show of waking slowly. Then she had an idea, but she'd have to be fast if she wanted to hide the smile.

"Jacob?" She dragged aside a fistful of hair and looked at Angelo confusedly through a curtain of what remained.

He stood balancing the improvised tray and revealed that breathtaking chest of his on full display.

"I was expecting Jacob," she shot for a pout and thought she did pretty well.

"And why were you expecting Jacob?" Rather than looking put-out, Angelo's smile was radiant. Oh well, so the tease hadn't really worked. Or had it?

"Because Jacob would have ravaged me in the night rather than leaving me to sleep."

"Well, I could ravage you right now, but your omelet would be cold. And your coffee."

"Coffee!"

Angelo made a pout in return as he rested the tray at the foot of the bed. "Well, I now know where I rank. Below coffee. And Jacob."

"Well, Jacob is pretty special." Jo sat the rest of the way up in bed. "Now shed those jeans and get back in here under the covers."

He dropped his jeans and her attention went sideways without her.

"Ooo, come to Jo." She reached out.

Angelo took a step back. "You'll spill the coffee."

"No," Jo slid off the edge of the bed careful not to jostle the tray and slid her hand around him. "No, I'll take you right here on the carpet."

"But your breakf—" His breath cut off as she ran both her hands over him. When she slid them up between his legs and grabbed his buttocks then pulled him forward between her breasts, his knees let go and he half eased and half collapsed to the floor.

There, still wearing her t-shirt, Jo straddled atop and settled down over him. They set about ravaging each other.

CHAPTER 22

*J*o lay on Angelo's chest and hummed. Her entire body hummed, there was no other word for it. If she were a musician, she'd say she felt like a string vibrating ever so softly and perfectly in tune. What the hell, she'd use the metaphor even if she wasn't a musician, it certainly fit.

Angelo stroked the hum forth by running his hands from her shoulders down over her buttocks and back along her thighs to the knees where she knelt over him. Then returning by the same route.

"Breakfast shouldn't be that much colder." His tone was wry. They had certainly sparked their need off each other and it had burst forth fast and hot.

"That was barely a ravage."

"Consider it a deposit on a ravage."

Jo clung to his glorious shoulders and nuzzled his chest for a moment longer.

"Okay, I'll try to work with that. I should demand a signed and notarized letter of further intent to ravage, but I'll trust you this one time." Jo climbed off him and scooted back onto the bed.

Angelo continued to lie there on the floor looking all handsome and content.

"Your omelet is congealing, Master Chef Parrano."

He smiled but didn't move. "Too late for that, Counselor Thompson."

She took a forkful. Barely warm, but still light and fluffy with the nicest hint of oregano.

"Still yummy."

Then Angelo pushed to his feet. "Do you have a pen and paper?"

She pointed at the nightstand. She kept them in the top drawer for when she thought of a good case argument or line of research and didn't want to lose the thought in the middle of the night.

He scrawled on the pad quickly, tore off the page and folded it in half, and handed it to her. Then he bowed formally and joined her cross-legged on the bed.

She opened the note as he took his coffee.

I, Angelo Parrano, being of weak mind but sound body, do hereby intend, promise, swear, vow, affirm, and otherwise commit that I shall hereafter happily ravage one Jo Thompson at every opportunity.

Signed, Angelo Parrano

Addendum: Ravaging also available by special request.

"I don't have a notary handy. I hope that's okay."

She couldn't meet his eyes. She'd hugged the note to her chest without realizing it. She held it out and read it again.

It wasn't the promise to ravage that had set her heart stuttering. It was that he'd done it in her language. She'd received plenty of mash notes over the years, though most of them had been back in Schoenbar Middle School when she'd been among the first of the girls to develop a chest. But even the couple that she'd received as an adult had never so thoroughly acknowledged who she was. They'd always been about her body, not about her. The fact that he'd used the "sound mind" quote from a standard will, probably without intending to evoke death and estate law, only made it more charming.

He offered her a forkful of omelet that she dutifully took and chewed, though she barely tasted it. There was another taste on her tongue. One she didn't know, couldn't identify. No, not a taste.

Rather there was a flavor running all through her insides. It was good, but unfamiliar. It was as if it *came* from the inside rather than the outside, but she still couldn't define it. But she knew how it made her feel. It made her feel desired. It made her feel alive.

She climbed from the bed and carefully tucked the precious note under her alarm clock. Then she shifted the tray to the top of the dresser, and, facing Angelo, stripped the t-shirt off over her head, dropped it behind her, and climbed back into bed.

His eyes were transfixed upon her, the coffee mug frozen halfway to his lips. She'd never had such an effect on a man and it made her feel freer than she could have imagined possible.

She lay back on the pillow atop the covers, "By special request."

He set his coffee on the coaster on the nightstand.

Then he slid over her and whispered in her ear, "By special request."

CHAPTER 23

"*M*ama. We need to talk."

Angelo and his mother were walking in the sun together, moseying along First Avenue from the apartment up to the restaurant. The Saturday morning traffic was busy with some tourists, some locals, and monstrous city buses jockeying for position like sumo wrestlers amidst a stampede of Chihuahuas. Seattle was always busy during the day. Thankfully, unlike New York, the city did sleep at night. He liked that, felt it added some character that the Big Apple had somehow lost.

Men kept turning to look at them. No. To look at his mother and he didn't like it a bit. She wore her hair loose, with a bright floral scarf over it. The powder blue sweater swept low across her chest and clung in all of the right places. She wore a dark skirt that wrapped tight about her hips and revealed good legs.

He wanted to buy her a trench coat.

"Is it about this girl, this Jo? When does she come by? When do I get to sit and share a meal with her?"

"No, it's not about Jo." They'd never made their bike ride. Hell, they'd barely made it through breakfast.

"What I see, my son, is a most happy man. But he confuses me. It also looks as if you slept last night. That is not a kind thing to do to a new girlfriend. You are not supposed to sleep a wink together."

"Mama!" He really couldn't be having this conversation with her. And she agreed with Jo that he should have just ravaged her though she'd been sleeping so sweetly. What the hell did he know anyway, he was just a guy.

"What? I don't get to be glad for my boy? Sex is good for you. You should marry her."

"We are so not having this conversation."

"Why not? You marry her and we can all live happy together."

Angelo caught his shoe on a shifted block in the sidewalk and almost planted his face on Madison Street. The cars were bolting down the steep Seattle hills as if the waterfront shops would float away before they got to visit every one. Or, perhaps more realistically, as if the last available parking spot on the full length of Alaskan Way was about to be filled.

His mother grabbed his arm to keep him on the sidewalk and burst out laughing. It was such a merry sound. He was being sassed by his mother. What was up with that?

"It was the restaurant I wanted to talk about." And he definitely didn't want to talk about Jo or marriage or married life with his mother in the apartment or…

She harrumphed at him as they waited for the red light at Spring Street.

"Okay, so talk."

"You shopped with Manuel this morning, like I asked?"

"Of course I did. I take care of things so that you can not sleep with this Jo, but instead you—"

"Mama!"

She offered an elaborate shrug that only an Italian mother could achieve which told him, "Fine, change the topic if you want but I gave birth to you and cleaned your bottom and you still need someone much smarter than you to take care of you and this topic is not even a little bit done with."

Angelo inspected the blue sky between the towering buildings, searching for patience. William was just unlocking McCormick and Schmick's as they passed by. Angelo waved at him as he put out the "Lunch Specials" sign, a classy chalkboard sign with cheerful yellow chalk. Angelo's Hearth didn't do "specials" but he was considering it. The board did catch the eye.

"Hey, Angelo," they knew each other by name, but not much more. Then he turned to his mother, "Hello, Mrs. Parrano. When are you going to leave your son and come live with me in sin?"

She patted his cheek as if he were a little boy rather than a man her own age, "Just as soon as your wife stops choosing your clothes for you. You are dressed far too nicely to have chosen that yourself." They traded air kisses.

William did look sharp, even if Angelo couldn't quite identify why. He looked at his own comfortable clothes and knew his mother had not been talking to William alone.

Angelo rolled his eyes at her back.

William just winked at him over her shoulder.

Once they'd left William behind, Angelo opened his mouth and then closed it sharply. Had she charmed every male in the whole city while he wasn't watching? If he started down the path of that topic, he'd never find his way to where he wanted to go.

"Mama," he tried again. "I'm going to have a problem at the restaurant and I was hoping you could help me." What on Earth was he doing? Jo. This was Jo's fault. She'd cooked up the idea this morning when they'd finally pulled on handy clothes and then taken their cold breakfast and reheated coffee out onto her umpteenth floor balcony. The egg and bacon flavors had still been good, but retoasting the toast hadn't helped the texture of it. He'd told her about Eugene leaving and the complications his mother was causing the restaurant.

"It's perfect, Angelo," Jo had assured him as she glowed in the morning light and ate cold eggs. "It sounds as if she's doing wonderful things for you, but I would conjecture that retired life is not sitting well with her. I'll bet she's bored. She wants to help you, which is so sweet. I wish I'd had parents, or even one parent like that."

When he'd asked her about that, the subject had changed without his really noticing, at least not until just now.

"My pastry chef, Eugene, is following his girlfriend to Hawaii," he told his mother.

"Is he sure that she wants to be followed?" She didn't even miss a pulse beat before jumping to the question that had taken Angelo some time to arrive at. And that Marlys had been unable to answer when Angelo had gotten her aside.

Angelo gave her a shrug that felt both uncomfortable and made it clear that in the end it was none of his business.

"The problem is, Mama, I need a pastry chef, at least until I can hire another one."

"And what does this have to do with my shopping with Manuel?"

"That's different. Last night I decided that you have made us too successful. So," he took a deep breath because it was still too huge to really comprehend. "I'm going to open another restaurant."

"Just like that?" She stopped in front of a storefront window and posed with her hands on her hips. Not realizing that she'd taken exactly the pose of the anorexic, aqua-clad mannequin in the clothing store window behind her. He started to smile until he saw the fire on her face.

"Just like that you go and decide to open another restaurant and you don't even consult your mother?"

"Ah..."

A businessman in smart Saturday attire, but still swinging his briefcase on the way to work, cut right between them without a glance either way.

"Ah. Mama, I'm sorry. I didn't think—"

"No! You no think!" She began ticking points off on her fingers. "You no think about little treats to advertise your food. You no think that Manuel can shop just as good as can you." As her ire rose, her English frayed even more than usual around the edges.

"This Eugene," she flicked her fingers. "You are so worried about losing him. Well, his Panna Cotta is not one-half so good as mine. His Zabaglione is a disgrace. And his Lemon Olive-Oil Cake is so sad that little girl Graziella could make better. You no understand why you, the head chef, the owner, spend so much time at the desserts. Let him go, that boy is why you waste so much time with them. Oh," she continued her rant as more people passed close by eyeing him curiously as to why the beautiful Italian matron was yelling at him.

Angelo stepped across the flow of people through a gap until they at least stood side-by-side without blocking the sidewalk, but her tone did not soften in volume or ire, despite their now standing barely a foot apart.

"Oh, he is a good enough cook. But he has no heart," she thumped the center of his chest hard enough to sting while making her point. "No heart in his chest!" Thumping him again. "And no heart in his food. Let him go. Let him find out how fickle love can be. Let him learn like your father never learn—"

She stopped herself, her expression shifting abruptly to one of deep distress.

"My father what, Mama?"

She looked away down the street, turned back when he rested a hand on her arm. Tears were welling in her eyes.

"Mama?" the sinking in his stomach left a bitter taste in his mouth.

"I should have told you." Her gaze veered away from his. She never did that. Maria Amelia always looked right at you with those wide, dark eyes.

"Told me what?" He had to ask, yet would bet that he didn't want to know. He could see something in her eyes.

"He's still alive, isn't he?"

She nodded then shrugged a "maybe."

Angelo couldn't think of how to react to that. His mother continued before he could react.

"Your father," then a flash of that heat came back into her eyes even as she blinked against the tears, "he had no heart. I tell him I'm pregnant and I never see him again. My family was very Catholic. So, I was sent to America to have my baby, to have you. But my Julia and John, they take me in and I cook for them. They love you like their own son when you are born and I stay. I never hear from your father again. I'm sorry. I should have found a better and sooner way to tell you, but I never could."

Angelo leaned against the cool window so that his knees did not let go. His father hadn't died, he'd left a pregnant single mother.

"You told me he was dead." He'd never felt so lost. Nor had he ever wanted to kill a man before. Leaving his mother? If he ever met the man, he'd murder him.

"He was dead to me. That is what I tell you. The half truth." Again that impossible strength and undeniable truth. She had that in common with Jo, an ability to speak from perfect truth. How scared she must have been, but she had come through it and he'd wanted for nothing. His mother had pampered and punished him with equal amounts of Italian passion. And loved him no matter what he'd done.

"Did you love him?" That felt intensely important, as if he might cease to exist if the answer was no.

But his mother nodded and sniffled.

"What was his name?"

At that she smiled softly and brushed a hand down his cheek. "His name was Angelo."

ANGELO AND MARIA sat in the little coffee shop at the corner and held hands across the table. Little potted palm trees scattered about the shop offered a feeling of privacy, even though their table sat close against the glass with the First Avenue crowds just beyond. The coffee was good enough to justify the price.

"Is he still alive?"

She shrugged again.

"Are you still married to him?"

At that she blushed for a moment and inspected her coffee.

"Mama?"

"I was young. He was so beautiful; you look much like him. He too was a chef. He taught me to cook and he taught me to make love."

"But you weren't married?"

Again the eloquent shrug.

Angelo looked around as if someone else had the answer among the people waiting for coffee or walking the trek from the Market to Pioneer Square. He was a bastard, born out of wedlock. He probed the feeling, like you might a sore tooth, with great care. Every memory of his mother was a fond one, he had not suffered. His mother had seen to that. Fine. He'd often wondered about the man, and now, surprisingly, found that he didn't care about him anymore. It didn't matter that his father was useless, his mother was only all that much more amazing for it.

"I just hate to think of you having been alone all these years, Mama."

"Who said I was alone? Did I say I was alone?"

Again they were abruptly in a territory Angelo really didn't wish to tread. Mothers weren't supposed to have sex and lovers, not even beautiful Italian mothers.

"I was not so foolish as to flaunt my men in front of my teenage son no matter how many empty-headed girls my son flaunted in front of me."

"They weren't empty-head—"

"Feh! The only boy in this whole world with worse taste in women than my son is Russell Morgan."

She held up her hand to stop his protest before he even made it.

"It took a good woman with good sense like our Cassidy to see what was there beneath all of the dirty clothes."

Okay, but it wasn't just Cassidy. "Melanie was good for hi—"

"No!" She stopped him again. "She wasn't."

"But she—"

"Yes. She is nice lady, I know that. But all she did for Russell was stroke his ego. She did no hold his heart even if he so *stupido* he almost break hers." She placed a hand over her heart in sympathy. "That one, she is so pretty and so lost."

Lost? Melanie was about the least lost person Angelo had ever met. Successful supermodel, her own manager, as sharp a businesswoman as he'd ever met, and still a fun lady. Before he could form a coherent protest, she pinned him again with her dark gaze.

"Who holds your heart, my Angelo?"

How in the world had they looped back around to Jo?

"See," his mother aimed a neatly trimmed nail at his heart. "I see even if you are too *stupido*. So, I ask again, when do I see this girl my son is sleeping with? Sleeping with." She smacked her hand to her chest again as if mortally offended. "I can no believe you are so *stupido*."

"Fine, Mama. You win. Monday. The restaurant is closed Monday. I'll see if she is available Monday." Oh, God. He'd just agreed to "bring Jo home for approval." First, Jo just might kill him for doing that. Second, was it possible he was actually serious about her? Serious enough to bring her home?

He was.

Angelo took a deep breath and tried the thought again. From the first time he'd seen Jo Thompson, his ability to be seriously intrigued by other women had been swept away. Had he even gotten to a second date with anyone since then? Not that he could recall. All he could think of was Jo Thompson. God above! He really was gone on her.

Bring her home for approval? Bring her home for keeps was more what he was feeling. He'd never felt that before. He knew almost nothing about her, but in some ways he knew her better than he knew himself. He could read her moods easily and enjoyed every one of them. She'd gotten all the way under his skin. Russell was right, he was in so much trouble. Who knew it would feel so good when it happened?

"Good," his mother must have read something in his expression that she acknowledged with a very satisfied nod. "I cook a wonderful dinner. You have such a nice kitchen in your condo. You have not such good taste in decorating, but you are smart, the kitchen is good. The location too I like very much. It is such a pleasant change from the Morgan mansion. So much happens in Pioneer Square. You are such a good boy to let your Mama live there."

As if he'd had a choice. Angelo buried his face in his hands. His head ached. This had started as such a simple conversation. At least Jo had told him it would be simple.

At the warm touch of his mother's hand, he looked up into her eyes.

"Of course, I would love to be your pastry chef. Though you must hire at least two more in the kitchen and another for front of house and do it very fast. They must be good people, I will help you pick them out. You will train them right." She brushed her hands together as if dusting them clear of all of the impossibly complex problems which she now declared resolved.

"Now, tell me about your new restaurant," she took a sip of her coffee.

He eyed her carefully, wondering where the trap lay.

"I thought you were angry I didn't consult you first?"

"Surprise? Yes. Angry? With my Angelo?" A brush of her hand over his hand again. "I am so proud I could die. I'm only angry I did not think of it first. So tell me."

So Angelo did.

CHAPTER 24

*J*o was just returning from a half-hour swim in her condo building's lapless, jet-current pool. She still preferred to work out at the gym on Eastlake rather than the fifth-floor gym here. Eastlake had more machines, on-site trainers, and classes whenever she needed the extra motivation.

But they didn't have a swimming pool, and the condo had three of the powered tanks where you could swim in place against a driven current. She wore a light robe over her damp swimsuit and flipflops as she headed down the hall to her condo. Cassidy and Perrin were coming back down the hall, clearly not finding her home.

"You're all wet," Perrin observed as they hugged. Today she wore a simple summer dress that looked shockingly normal when compared to the other clothes she usually wore.

"I know. I know." Perrin looked down at herself. "It's so... pedestrian. But I wanted to remind myself of how it felt. Streetwear rather than fashionwear. I'm playing with some ideas. We came to see the dress."

The dress. Jo had managed not to think about the dress.

Cassidy simply smiled at her. No, she wasn't humoring Perrin, she'd come to see the dress as well.

What the hell. Jo led them back down to her condo.

In the bedroom, Perrin stooped and pulled something from under the edge where the quilt brushed the floor.

"What's this?" Dangling from her finger by its elastic band was a pair of dark red men's briefs, Angelo's underwear that they'd been unable to find as he was leaving. It must have slipped free as she was making the bed before her swim. Thank God she'd done at least that much.

She took it quickly, "Nothing." Though she imagined it felt warm against her palm.

Perrin grinned wickedly even as Jo stuffed it in her robe's pocket.

"Gee," she placed a red-painted nail to her lips and turned to Cassidy. "I wonder if a certain Mr. Parrano is walking the streets of Seattle commando this morning."

Cassidy smiled back at Perrin conspiratorially but winked at Jo, "Oh, I hope so. I really hope so."

Jo fought the desire to stare down at the rug and hide her face behind a fall of hair. Instead, she faced it head on.

"I am pleased to report to this court of inquiry, that he is indeed walking the streets without underwear." She clenched her hand on them in her pocket. Nor would he be getting them back anytime soon. Like a scalper's prize, they were hers now, though she had no idea why she'd want them.

"And is he well sated?" Perrin always wanted details.

"If he isn't, it's not for lack of trying."

She held her pride for a moment longer and then the three of them burst out laughing together.

Then she went into the bathroom to dry her hair before she tried on the dress.

"Oh, Jo." Cassidy's sigh said it all.

Perrin looked so pleased when Jo had put on the high-heeled shoes. She fussed with the hem a bit.

"I'll change it just a little so that you can wear these down the aisle, but dance in low heels."

"You won't change a single thing on this dress," Cassidy brushed Perrin's hands away. "You don't mess with perfection. Jo can take dance lessons."

Jo didn't know when she'd ever find time for a class, but Cassidy was right. It would be worth learning to dance in these so that she could look this good. She considered the woman in the mirror. This time, rather than the dark of night with closed curtains, the room was flooded with sunlight. The fabric revealed another facet that hadn't been visible before. Its pale blue material was ever so slightly iridescent as if Jo herself was glowing.

If Angelo could only see her now, he'd maybe keel over dead and need that "weak mind and sound body" phrase for his will.

Had she really just had that thought? Had she really just thought of Angelo while wearing a wedding dress?

Of course she had. They'd just spent a whole night and morning together. And true to his promise, he had thoroughly ravaged her leaving her head spinning and her body buzzing. So, of course she was thinking of him.

But that's all it meant.

She was merely thinking of him. And she was wearing a wedding dress. It didn't mean the two were related in any way other than a coincidence of timing.

The phone rang. She swished over to the nightstand to pick it up. She'd never swished before in her life.

"Oh. Hi, Angelo."

She glanced back at Cassidy and Perrin who weren't even for a moment considering leaving the room. Perrin grabbed Jo's robe from where it draped on the bed and fished out Angelo's underwear then began waving them at her.

"I found something you lost." Oh, no. She hadn't said that. She really needed to cut her own tongue out. Maybe she'd just kill Perrin as soon as she got off the phone. She turned away to concentrate.

"Oh thanks. I'll have to get those."

"Just like that? Just 'get those'?"

Angelo spluttered for a moment.

"I'm at the restaurant."

"And..." she teased him, knowing she had him trapped. "That's no excuse. What is it worth to get them back?"

"Go, Jo!" Perrin was giggling in the background. Jo closed her eyes to block out her friends. This was a very private conversation and they both were having it in public.

"Well," she could hear dishes clattering over the phone which must be the only reason he hadn't heard Perrin.

His voice went soft.

"I did have this one idea. If we ever have a day off together. There's a very private spot atop a mountain on one of the San Juan Islands that a friend showed me."

"And would this friend have been female?"

"Crap!" she could imagine him flushing red and looking around to try and find a way out of the hole he'd just dug. She let him dangle for several seconds before deciding to rescue him.

"Consider it a date."

"Really? Uh, really? That's wonderful." His voice went smooth for a moment as if someone was passing close by. He dragged out the start of the next sentence until whoever had finally passed out of earshot.

Jo would bet he wasn't fooling a single person on his staff except himself.

"I'll make it worth your while," he finally continued. "After all, I like my underwear."

"I like it better when it's off you."

Perrin cheered again and Jo wanted to slap herself.

"Okay. Whew. That took my breath away."

They appreciated the mutual images of being unclothed together in silence for several moments.

"Was there a reason you called?"

"Oh, yes," Angelo's voice shifted from smooth and warm to practically businesslike, as if he were suddenly afraid of her or something.

"My mother wants you to come to dinner on Monday."

"She what?" Jo's skin flashed cold.

"She's a great cook, as you know, and she wants to make a dinner for you. Get to know you and so on."

Her shock was so deep that all she could mumble was an, "Okay, I guess."

"Wonderful. I'll call later with details. Gotta run. Bye." And he was gone.

Jo set the phone back very slowly and stared out at the view trying to collect her thoughts into some semblance of order.

"So, what's the date? You said, 'Consider it a date.' We heard you. You can't lie to us." Perrin came around in front of her still waving Angelo's underwear. Jo took them, but having no pocket in the dress, simply tossed them back on the bed.

"Oh," Jo tried again to picture a dinner with Mrs. Parrano and failed. "There's a mountain in the San Juans. He wants to make love on top of it."

"Ooo. Starlight. Go at night. There's nothing like making love by starlight."

Jo had never done such a thing, though she'd take it under consideration.

She really should stop trying to avoid Perrin's questions, it never worked anyway.

Cassidy came up beside her and placed a hand around Jo's waist.

"What is it, Jo? There's something else."

Jo could only nod.

Perrin came up on her other side. Jo held onto both of them for support as she stared out the window, unable to see anything.

"He, ah, his mother, Angelo's mother, ah, Mrs. Parrano." Jo had turned into a babbling idiot.

She clamped her tongue hard enough between her teeth that she thought she could taste enamel.

"She wants to meet me."

"But that makes no sense," Perrin protested. "You already know her."

"She wants to have me over for dinner. Angelo's mother wants to cook a meal for me."

"Yes!" Perrin pumped a fist in the air. "The power of the dress! Yes!" She began dancing about the room, the skirt of her sun dress swirling and bouncing.

"Oh, Cassidy," Jo said quietly. It came out frightfully close to a moan.

"It'll be okay," Cassidy tightened her arm around Jo's waist as Perrin danced around them in the tiny circles that Jo's bedroom furniture barely allowed. "It'll be okay."

All Jo could think was that he was a chef and hadn't even known to sugar coat it.

The phone rang again. She almost didn't answer, but Cassidy nudged her.

"Yes, Angelo? What now?"

CHAPTER 25

*J*o kept her hands clenched on the wheel of her rental car. If she squeezed it any tighter, the wheel might snap. She already didn't have any blood in her fingers. Ordering her fingers to relax their death grip didn't ease them in the slightest. They weren't stupid, they knew they were holding on for dear life.

The car rocked lightly as the ferry from the Ketchikan Airport lurched through a wave. Ketchikan Airport hadn't fit on the same shore as the small fishing town backed by steep hills that had called gold-rushers to their doom or fortune. So, they'd built the airport on the island on the other side of Tongass Narrows. The airport ferry only took a few minutes. Would these few minutes be enough to bribe the ferry captain to turn left and just see how far they could get? Anchorage? Dutch Harbor? Russia?

The phone call had been just before lunch on Saturday and now Jo was going to be having dinner in Ketchikan, Alaska. Assuming she could keep anything down. Her single least favorite place on the planet. She didn't hold it against the state, the town, or the people in it. Well, not as much as she held it against one person in particular.

But he was no longer in it and that was the problem.

Earnest Jack Thompson was dead. And it was now up to his only child to deal with whatever mess he'd left behind.

MURIEL HAD a reservation waiting for her by the time Jo landed and called to check in. Jo couldn't remember what Muriel had said about it, so she would just head for her usual retreat up on the hill at the edge of town and hope for the best.

She hated to impose on Muriel on a Saturday morning, as they were supposed to be working that afternoon and Sunday. But when she'd received the phone call, her brain had muddled and she'd become wholly incompetent. Any court in the land would have declared her so, including a jury of her friends.

Perrin and Cassidy had removed the wedding dress while she'd stood like a lifeless mannequin. They'd given her clothes and she'd put them on.

Now, looking down as she waited for the ferry to carry her across the Tongass Narrows, Jo saw that she wore hiking boots, her Calvin jeans, and an REI rain jacket. Under that, her blue blouse and a dark gray flannel shirt. She didn't even know she still owned a flannel shirt. Well, her friends had dressed her appropriately for this adventure.

Her friends. They'd taken care of her. Packed for her. Muriel had found the flight and Cassidy had delivered Jo's mortal remains to the airport. She'd wrap that support around her and be strong.

Deep breath.

Another.

It was jolted from her by the ferry jarring hard against the dock pilings. The dock pilings in Ketchikan, Alaska.

She was so screwed.

She kicked on the windshield wiper to clear the heavy mist and ducked her head down.

She didn't wave at the deckhand, doing her best not to look at Dave Garvey as she rolled by inches away from his toes. The years had been hard on the former star wide receiver and king of auto shop class. Jo shouldn't be so mean about him; he'd always been decent to her—by never noticing she existed.

This was going to kill her. She was turning back into her fifteen-year-old worst self. She was a lawyer of national and soon-to-be international repute, God damn it.

She sat up straighter and eased her grip on the wheel. Just in time to come face-to-face with the ferry's Captain, Steven Lancaster. He hadn't added the thirty-pound beer gut which now weighed down Dave. He looked great.

"Hey, Jo!" He shouted it loud enough to be heard through the tightly closed windows. Loud enough to be heard throughout the town. Well, it would be out soon enough anyway. The locals weren't that big a community. Her graduating class had been a hundred-and-forty-six strong, and in all likelihood about a hundred-and-forty-five of them still lived in town. Ketchikan was the sort of town that everyone talked about leaving, but no one actually did.

She'd run into this the few times in the past when she'd been forced to fly in here for meetings. She actually scheduled dinners with her father when she was in town only partly as a reason to see him. Mostly it had been to avoid her former schoolmates as much as possible.

Her meetings here were typically all-day ones and much livelier after all the fishermen in the crowd had their three-beer lunches. Afterwards, anyone attending who she'd known from her youth, tried to get her to "Go out on the town" with them. That meant a total dive like the Crab Hole or some other hideous bar.

Steve showed no sign of letting her just roll on by, so Jo lowered the window. The air was cool on her face. It smelled of ocean, deep forest, and thirteen feet of rain every year.

"Hi, Steve! How are you doing?" That sounded normal, didn't it?

"Great! Heard about your dad. Sorry." He didn't look too contrite, but then he knew what her home life had been like. "Any chance of seeing you while you're in town? Marta and I eat at the Crab a couple times a week."

"Marta? Marta Benkowitz?"

"Marta Lancaster." He corrected her but his grin of pride showed she'd gotten it right. Steven and Marta? Sure, why not? Steve had always been an easy-going, cheerful guy that everyone liked. Even if he wasn't the smartest guy around, he was one of the nicest. Marta was shy, dark, and pretty enough. She was also one of the few that gave Jo a run for her money on test scores. As close to a friend as Jo ever had in Ketchikan, which wasn't saying much. An odd couple, but Steve's smile showed that it was clearly working for them.

"The Crab? Ah, sure." She was going to have to shoot herself. She'd just agreed to go back to the Crab Hole. Of course, that had been her dad's favorite bar, his second home. She'd have to go there anyway, if only to make sure his bar tab was settled.

A horn blared behind her making Steve look back at the remaining ferry load.

"Mainlander," he scoffed then returned his attention to her. "Just let Gerta know when you're in and we'll come down and join you."

"Gerta."

"Yeah. Ukrainian lady. Barely speaks English. But she showed up one day looking for work and old Fred hired her. Rumor is they're an item but it's hard to tell because Fred never talked all that much anyway and no one can understand her when she does. But the food's almost edible now which is a good change."

"Okay. Good to see you doing so well." Then she waved and drove off the ferry and into hell.

CHAPTER 26

*U*nable to eat, Jo had merely curled up in her room at the Cape Fox Lodge, hidden under the covers, and prayed for sleep. Somewhere during the third movie of an Adam Sandler marathon—she hated Adam Sandler, slapstick humor, and the world in general—she'd finally fallen asleep for a few fitful hours.

Sunday morning she tried the house, but, though the black and gold letters spelling out "Thompson" still clung tenuously to the mailbox as they always had and the same old fishing gear littered the porch, she couldn't get in. The door was locked, which was unusual. They hadn't been well enough off to have anything worth stealing, so why bother. The obvious spare key under the mat was gone, too. It had probably been used to lock the door.

Jo then went down to find his fishing boat, but didn't remember what slip it was in. Well, she thought she did, but the *Eloise* wasn't there. Maybe she'd finally sunk, though the dark waters alongside the finger pier hid any evidence if it had sunk at dock. The marina was empty of people, surprising even for a Sunday morning, so she couldn't find anyone to ask.

Right. It was June in the salmon fishing capital of the world. The run was on and every fisherman who could crawl onto a trawler, or snag a tourist, would be out on the sea or up in the fjords making a living.

Well, the hook had been baited and it had dragged her back to Alaska. Now it was time to see just how fast she could get unhooked. Since not even the Crab Hole was open at this early hour, she went for a drive through the town, a major mistake.

Two cruise ships had arrived in the night and she could see a third pulling into the Tongass Narrows even now. The population of the town had just doubled for the day. The historic waterfront was already clogged past reason, the few cars stupid enough to brave the lower streets of the town crept their way between pedestrians, even at seven in the morning. By mid-morning, the lower streets would be wholly impassable except on foot, and barely then. It took her forever to escape the congestion.

As a result, rather than cruising by some pretty little shops, she was up driving through the back roads. The middle school and high school looked exactly the same, except for another decade of age and moss on the roof. They were okay, her only refuge other than the library. She didn't go there just in case Mrs. Freson was still head librarian. The woman had given her a vision of the outer world. She'd grown up in Seattle, gone to Vassar, and for reasons beyond Jo's imagining, ended up in Ketchikan with four kids in the four grades ahead of Jo.

Mrs. Freson had fed Jo's need to know, her need to escape. Having four kids ahead of Jo, she knew which courses Jo would be taking and what books, both fiction and non, would enhance the relatively mundane teachings aimed at fisherman's and shop owner's kids. They were mostly headed to work at the fish plant or servicing the cruise ships hitting Water Street like gunshot, leaving a wide damage path and never quite enough money in their wakes.

It might be nice to see her. Sit down and visit about how Vassar had changed, about how she was doing in Seattle. Somehow it was too sensible, too rational, too normal.

The last thing Jo wanted was for anything in Ketchikan to start feeling normal.

The second to last thing Jo wanted to do was see Mrs. Freson and burst into wracking sobs that Jo suspected were lurking just below the calm outer surface she was struggling to present. She continued past the library without stopping.

At the far end of town, the fish packing plant where she'd worked part time in the gift shop during the summers was at full roar. She definitely didn't stop there, way too many former classmates and coworkers. Though she couldn't resist slowing down to see if it looked even a little different. "Severely weathered" was the standard paint job of Ketchikan, Alaska, and the packing plant was no different. Some of the cars were newer models, but not enough for it to really look different.

Finally, unable to escape the town, as the road simply ended five miles past either side of Ketchikan, she'd gone back to the lodge, lay down on the bed for a few minutes, and finally gotten much of the sleep she'd missed last night.

———

IT WAS LATE that afternoon by the time she again braced herself to venture out into the Alaskan "sunshine." A bright gray sky offered a near blinding brightness in every direction, backed by just enough moisture in the air to drench your hair if you walked through it, but not enough to justify an umbrella. That was a laugh, she had become a city girl. Umbrellas were useless in Ketchikan because rain here often rode in on gale-force winds. And she hadn't come equipped with a hood or hat. Even crossing from hotel to rental car had dampened her freshly dried hair.

Driving back through town, only touching the back roads this time, the windshield wipers squeaked and stuttered across a windshield too dry to wipe properly and too speckled to ignore. Once she reached her destination, she parked, but couldn't force herself to get out of the car.

Jo looked up through the rental car's windshield at the spitting sky. She tried to ignore the new car smell that was rapidly mutating to take on the sickening overtones of lichen and moss, no matter that the windows were sealed tight. The tall fir trees were standing stock-still against a uniform bright gray sky. No big blow coming for at least the rest of the day, probably not the one after that either.

Other than the light precipitation, this was a perfect fishing day. And she was certainly about to go fishing—for any clue she could find.

Looking back down from the sky, she glared at the bar across the street. The Crab Hole was really too nice a name for the place. It bore a notorious paint job. Fred was a cheap bastard, or maybe he just didn't care, no one could decide for sure and it wasn't a topic he bothered with. Either way, he bought the mis-mixed paints at the paint store for half price. Someone orders five gallons of peach that comes out puce? The Crab Hole's south wall will be puce for the next five years. Half the trim pale-piss yellow, the rest of it pumpkin orange. The only thing that never changed was the large, carved-wood sign. Until you knew what it was, it was hard to make sense of it.

Jo could still remember the heat on her cheeks when at the age of eleven she'd finally figured it out.

A crab hole is what the crab fisherman called a place in the ocean that crabs gathered. Often a dip in the ocean floor, it caused crabs to swarm and cluster. Good crab holes are deeply protected secrets passed down generation to generation within a family. Crabber captains lie to their crews about their actual coordinates to hide the locations. So she'd always thought the Crab Hole was named for a good place to go crabbing.

At eleven years old, Jo's mind had finally matured enough to unravel the aged, weather-softened carvings of the sign. It was a male crab mounted on a female's back. That wasn't so unusual. The Arctic Bar just down the road had a logo of two grizzly bears humping. What was out of place on the Crab Hole sign was the very obvious, once you knew how to see it, human penis that the crab was ramming up the she-crab's backside.

People thought it made the place colorful. Tourists who made it this far down the waterfront always took a picture of themselves with the sign over their shoulder in the background. Only a few, however, had the nerve to venture inside. This was completely a locals' watering hole.

Jo forced herself from the car and tried to forget how many times she'd gone through that door looking for her father. She wished she'd worn gloves, but forced herself to take the door handle shaped like a giant crab claw, painted a hand-worn electric green, and go inside.

There were almost twenty hours a day of sun here in mid-June Ketchikan, and at four in the afternoon the bar was a place of shadows and smoke. Right, you could smoke in bars in Alaska, she'd forgotten that. New York State and Washington State barely let you smoke in your own home, which was fine with her.

Here, a low cloud of nicotine stained the walls a motley brown. Mixed with the ever-constant smell of deep-fry fish and chips and grilled burgers, that were not bought for their "percent lean," it had a palpable nastiness that was bitter on the tongue and nose, stung the eyes, and left her feeling the instant need for another shower.

For "ambiance" the Crab Hole had the KTKN broadcast offering inaudible but constantly murmuring talk radio that no one listened to, but it filled any overlong silences, as if there was a busy background debate going on in the room. The other entertainment was an old Wurlitzer juke box that might have been worth something, but hadn't worked since as far back as Jo could remember. She'd dreamed for hours as a little girl of all of the places it could take her. California Dreaming, Girl from Ipanema, both the Dionne Warwick and the Frank Sinatra versions, she'd even wanted to ride The Last Train to Clarksville, wherever that was. Back then, it took an active interest to make out the faded titles through the layers of grease on the curved glass front. Probably wholly invisible by now.

The whole scene created a miasma so thick that it could have been chopped up and sold for poisoning typical house pests. The atmosphere blurred the backs of the regulars at the bar until they appeared to blend together.

But Jo didn't need to see them clearly to know who they were. Adam, Bernie, Carl, and Dan. God, had nothing in the place changed? She'd been gone a dozen years and all they'd done was get a little wider and Carl's long hair showed a little grayer where it hung down in a severely dated mullet. Dan, the massive Tlingit, so big he must be part Samoan, anchored the row on the fourth stool.

The fifth stool at the bar was empty. They always sat in alphabetical order for reasons none of them claimed to remember. The bar would have to find an Eric or Evander to sit on the stool that had belonged to Earnest Jack Thompson as surely as if he'd bought and paid for it.

From the hazy shadows she inspected the rest of the bar. A thousand, maybe ten thousand crab shells had been glued to the wall. No legs, just the shells so close together they were nearly indistinguishable. Not just Dungeness and Alaskan King. Travelers who had braved the Crab Hole went home and sent in new ones from all over the world. Blues, spider crab, stone, rock, South American land crab... She'd learned them all, when bored with sitting at some sticky table doing her homework and sipping a Coke. Floor to ceiling, the shells covered the wall.

The place looked as if some mad painter had blotched the walls with a ragged sponge then covered the whole place in dust to gray out any real sign of shape, color, or semblance to anything natural. Rather than crab shells, the ceiling had been mostly covered with dark blue mussel shells, with some gray clam and white oyster mixed in. That was almost pretty, if a little oppressive as it wasn't a particularly high ceiling.

There were a dozen or so patrons. The locals were quiet and wore tough working clothes or sensible sweaters for the cool summer day. But there were a few tourists off the cruise ships, the more adventurous ones who were seeking that "authentic Alaskan experience," all marked very clearly by the urban clothes and cruise ship attitude that was practically tattooed on their foreheads.

God, she'd hated that as a kid. Because of her half-Alaskan heritage, she looked native enough for all of the tourists to want a picture of her up against some wall of the Crab Hole as if she were an attraction placed there for their own enjoyment. She'd started charging them a quarter a shot.

Her father's sole comment about the whole situation was that she should charge a buck. She tried it and it worked. Almost well enough that she stopped minding as much, though not quite. She spent most of her take at Parnassus Bookstore which left her canning factory gift shop paychecks to go into the college fund savings account.

Behind the counter sat Fred, looking as old and craggy exactly as she'd always remembered. Near him, drawing a beer, was the woman Steve had mentioned. Gerta stood about Jo's height. She had short blonde hair, a narrow face, and athletic shoulders. Jo wondered if Fred had hired her to continue the alphabetical chain.

Gerta had noted Jo's entrance right away, though her only

reaction had been a quick glance of dark eyes. Fred must have noticed Gerta's attention, as his gaze drifted in Jo's direction.

The smile he offered when he recognized her was slow, slow and sad. He was the one who'd called her to tell her that her father was dead.

———

Jo sat on her father's stool in the Crab Hole, hoping that no one with initials "H" and "I" showed up while she was here or she might never escape. It was creepy. She'd never sat here before, not even in her dad's lap that she could remember. He hadn't been a lap kind of guy.

Thankfully he also hadn't been a drunk, particularly. Not the way she always thought of them anyway, staggering out of the Seattle clubs at two a.m. as likely to walk into walls as along the sidewalk. Or the burnout alkies begging around Pioneer Square.

Yes, her father had gotten off the boat, gone to his stool at the Crab Hole, and not moved until closing or near enough. But he nursed only a couple beers each night. It was some sort of sad male bonding that caused these five guys to perch every night in front of Fred's bar and talk sports, fishing, weather, and tourists. Which was most of their repertoire, leaving a lot of time for KTKN to drone quietly in the background.

Fred no longer got up to wait the tables. "Too damn much arthritis in my old hip." He'd practically become one of his own patrons anchored to a stool, just on the other side of the bar. Gerta serviced the tables, cooked the fry or grill orders, and tended the bar with a quiet efficiency and actually appeared to be happy with what she was doing.

"Better than nuclear specialist in Ukrainian Army," Gerta had offered in barely recognizable English when she noted Jo's attention. Actually, if Jo hadn't grown up in a town where there were many Russian fishermen, she'd not have understood Gerta at all. And once Jo had unraveled Gerta's words in her head, by which time the woman had moved on, Jo hoped that she hadn't heard them correctly.

Fred had gotten Jo a beer personally, even though she hadn't wanted one. But she was too polite to say so, and knew Fred didn't serve wine, nasty or otherwise. All of them from Adam to Fred were clearly at a loss of what to do with the empty stool, it had probably been filled nearly every night for thirty or more years. Gerta didn't appear to be bothered by much of anything.

"It was fast," Fred told her. "Funny, he wasn't the drunk one. It was the one who hit him that was out of his gourd. Twenty-two-year-old tourist kid who just totally screwed up his own life. After he hit your dad, he overcorrected and drove into that new antiques place on Madison. Busted up his leg and hip and what the Californian owner claims is about a quarter million worth of the ugliest crap you've ever seen. For a while we didn't know whether or not his old man was going to kill him before the cops let him out of the hospital on bail."

"And," Bernie chimed in, he always liked adding the last line to a story. "Rumor is he was far more pissed about the antiques coming out of his insurance than some manslaughter charge his son might get slapped with."

"Didn't come out right there, Bern." About the only statement Adam ever made was correcting Bernie.

Somehow it was appropriate that drink had been the instrument of death for Earnest Thompson, even if she wasn't going to say so in this bar.

"'Course he had less than six months to live," Carl offered.

"He what?" Jo leaned forward to look around Dan's bulk.

"Liver," Bernie offered without really turning to look at her as if he were still trying to puzzle out what was wrong with his last utterance.

"Prostate, ya' fool," Adam corrected.

Dan, as usual, said nothing. He simply dug into a pocket, set a key on the bar with barely a sound and slid it over to her. The house key. Dan was big, but he was also the youngest at the bar, probably only in his late fifties or early sixties. As such, it had clearly been his task to climb the fifty-six stairs to her father's shack and oversee what needed overseeing.

Jo didn't want the key and all that it implied, but she didn't want to offend Dan either. She nodded to him and stuffed the key in her pocket.

She'd just found out her father had been dying anyway, that he hadn't told her, and she could think of nothing to say. Oh God, she was fitting right in at the bar of the Crab Hole.

"Jo, I knew you come!"

Before she could identify the voice behind her, she was tipped back on the stool and swept into a kiss.

Yuri Andreevich!

One arm around her shoulders held her tipped back and off balance, the other started at her hip but was on her breast in a moment. He drove the kiss at her even as she shoved against his massive chest, to negligible effect.

He broke the kiss for a moment. "I know you come here when your father die. And now he no longer scare you away from beautiful Alaska and you can stay here for me and we can make many babies together."

He leaned back in and she managed to shove him aside long enough to say, "No!" Her entire system was galvanized with revulsion. She didn't think there was a way to make the Crab Hole worse than it was, but Yuri had found one.

He drove at her again with his whiskey breath and she slapped him as hard as she could, putting every inch of her workout muscles into it.

Yuri's head barely turned. He just smiled. "I knew you missed me. Now we can make love like two Russian wildcats."

Abruptly she was free, so fast that she'd have fallen to the floor without Dan's steadying hand on her back.

"The lady said, 'No'!"

She turned to see which of the alphabet gang had pulled Yuri off. They were all off their stools and moving in, but the fist that connected with Yuri's jaw hard enough to snap his head back belonged to Angelo. Angelo was a head shorter, but with shoulders just as wide as Yuri's. Yuri stumbled back into a crab-shell covered wall with a loud crunch that broke dozens of shells showering tiny flakes of calcium carbonate to the floor.

Angelo didn't give him a moment to recover. Two more hits, gut and chin again. Before Yuri could collapse to the floor, Angelo grabbed him by the hair and the back of his belt. He got him into a stumbling run and ran him at the heavy wooden entry door.

Angelo released him just as he hit. Yuri crashed through the front door, opening it with his head, and tumbled out onto the sidewalk. A short scream came from some tourist he almost bowled over as he collapsed against a car parked at the curb. A little display of local color. Another tourist snapped a photo even as the door swung shut.

Angelo came back to her slowly. The others were gathered around her asking if she was okay. Even Fred had made it out from behind the bar. But that was all a mere background buzz.

"How?" Jo gestured helplessly toward the wall of shattered crab shells.

"I grew up with Russell. He was always getting us into some *rissa*. Scuffle."

"Oh. Uh. What are you doing here?" She didn't know whether to laugh or cry or shout or throw herself at him.

He stopped a foot away, massaging one hand with the other.

"I, uh... You shouldn't be alone when family dies. Cassidy said you had no one else and she couldn't leave Russell, so I came."

"But how?" She really wasn't being very lucid was she. She pointed toward the door Yuri had so recently exited as if that would complete the question she couldn't formulate. It swung open as a couple tourists came in, looking over their shoulders at the man now up on all fours and shaking his head.

Angelo shrugged in that Italian fashion of his. "I came in and saw you at the bar. I didn't want to disturb you." He pointed at a half-finished beer sitting at a small table to the side.

She stepped in until their bodies brushed together. She ran a finger down his cheek.

"Thank you," she barely mouthed it then simply wrapped her arms around his neck and lay her head on his shoulder. Yuri didn't really matter, the alphabet gang would have pulled him off in a moment more, though it wouldn't have been half as satisfying.

But no one had ever dropped everything and come two thousand miles just because she shouldn't be alone. Being in Angelo's arms was the first rational thing that had happened to her since the awful phone call.

***

"ADAM, Bernie, Carl, Dan, Fred, and Gerta. This is Angelo." Jo couldn't stop holding his hand and Angelo wasn't complaining for a second. Gerta found him another stool somewhere in the back, and Jo had them shoved together so close that they couldn't sit without touching.

Russell had mentioned over Sunday breakfast at Cassidy's condo that Jo's dad had died and she'd gone to Alaska. Without thinking, or even saying goodbye, he'd simply walked out the door and headed to the airport. No luggage, nothing. Just two phone calls. One to Manuel that the restaurant was his for the moment. The other to his mother to help Manuel. Mama had said only one word when she heard why he was already racing to the airport, "Go." Then she'd hung up and he could only hope everything would be okay.

The whole flight north he'd been torn. A summer Sunday, he really should be at the restaurant. He'd abandoned everyone at a moment's notice. On the other side, he couldn't get to Alaska fast enough.

Russell had texted him sometime during the flight and he got the message when he landed. Cassidy had recalled some college story about a bar called the Crab Hole. Who could forget a name like that? Starting there for lack of a better idea, he'd rushed in and come to a halt when he'd seen her at the bar with an untouched beer sitting in front of her. He'd almost gone forward, but he knew this scene from a dozen different bars, though never one this oddly decorated. He recognized the slow conversation of regulars. She knew these people and they knew her.

He'd raised a single finger to the bartender and tipped his hand as if opening a beer tap. She'd brought a pint of whatever she had on draft to the side table he'd chosen. From there he could watch Jo's profile. Only sitting there watching her, did he finally realize that he could have just called her cell phone when he landed. But that didn't matter now, he'd found her anyway.

It was odd to watch. She fit in and she didn't. The conversation, so slow and sporadic as to be almost nonexistent, had continued in its way. They liked her and she them. It was so obvious that she was a part of their world. Yet, though he'd never seen her so dressed down, she still stood out like a tourist. Her clothes were too new, too well coordinated. Her jeans didn't just fit, they clung. Her hair wasn't just clean, it shone.

He'd fallen so far under the spell of watching her that he hadn't seen the big Russian arrive. Yuri had swept Jo into his arms like a long-lost lover. Angelo had been frozen in place. It couldn't be. He couldn't have so misread the situation, it just couldn't be. He'd kill himself. The betrayal hit him like a leaden weight that almost brought the half beer in his empty stomach back up as bitter bile.

Then he heard the whispered, "No," and the sharp slap. That was all the motivation he'd needed. She'd begun to struggle in earnest even as he reached her side. It had been a pleasure taking the man down. His hand still stung like hell, though not a chance he'd be admitting it anytime soon.

Gerta gave him an ice pack for which he was immensely grateful. He discretely wiggled his fingers again to make sure they weren't broken. You could cook despite cuts and burns, but a broken hand would be a whole different matter. With one hand in ice and the other clamped onto by Jo, he wasn't able to drink his beer, but that was the only fault he could find with the moment.

CHAPTER 27

*T*he stories slowly unwound around Jo. The stories of her father's friends huddled at the Crab Hole bar revealed a man she knew, yet didn't know.

"He spoke even less than old Dan here. That's why they ended up at the end of the bar. Whereas I never shut up which is how I ended up in the middle." Carl spoke after a long, comfortable pause. In any other company, he'd be the silent one, but he was definitely the talker of this group.

"Adam and Bernie, well, they're the youngsters. I think you were already born by the time they came along."

Twenty-eight years they'd been sitting at this bar and they were still the youngsters. She shared a smile with Angelo.

After another silence, Fred looked at her. "Strange seeing the two of you sittin' so close like that. Earnest and Eloise used to sit that way. Had six stools here for a pretty fair time. She came off one of the cruise ships and just didn't leave. She glowed the way you do, Jo. That's why she named you for the girl in that book Little Women. Said you had that same life in you."

Jo hadn't known that. It had seemed a little obvious, but she liked knowing it for certain. She'd taken Jo March to heart. That incredible strength. When she went into the courtroom, she kept the picture clearly in her head of Jo March taking on the entire world. Though on the inside she'd always felt more like Beth, the quiet, shy one.

"You'd sit in her lap," Fred sipped his beer to drag out the story. "The two of you would just glow. You look so much like her, it's hard to credit. You partly got your daddy's coloring, but everything else you got from your mama."

"Why did she go? Why did she leave us?" Angelo's tight hold on her hand was the only thing that gave her strength to ask the question without her voice breaking. She had a thousand questions for him too, but for the moment all she could do was hold on as tightly as she could and draw stability from his being here beside her. It felt as if she was making some commitment that she wasn't sure she was ready to make, but she'd have to unravel and straighten that out later. Her past was threatening to overwhelm her and for now all she could do was hold on.

The guys at the bar all looked at one another, as if no one wanted to speak first. The bar was quiet. Tourists didn't come to dinner at a place like the Crab Hole and the locals who did wouldn't be along for a while. With so many hours of sunlight in mid-June, dinner happened later and breakfast earlier than in the winter.

For now, it was the six of them on one side of the bar, Fred on the other, and Gerta standing behind Fred leaning casually against his back with her arms over his shoulders. Jo had found out she was older than she looked, in her early fifties, and Fred was, she knew, in his seventies. Whatever was going on there, they looked comfortable together. Clearly the bar would someday be hers and she and Fred and the other locals were fine with that.

"She faded," Dan spoke for the first time since asking if Jo was okay while Angelo threw a man half-again his size through the door. His first full sentence since she'd arrived. His deep voice made it a proclamation. The others nodded.

Carl took over. "I liked her, but Dan's right. She faded here. Faded until the light in her went out and she had to leave to go find it again. Something in old Earnest broke the day she left. But he could no more leave than she could stay."

"She never done divorce him." Again the deep declaration from Dan.

"One postcard is all Earnest ever spoke of." Carl inspected his beer then the mussel-shell ceiling as if searching his memory and finding nothing else. "Sent it the day she left. Jes' to let him know she were alive. Maybe said something about goin' to feed kids in Africa or somethin'. Don't quite recall. No return address. Postmarked at the Seattle airport."

Jo looked over at Angelo. His mother was so alive, so vital, so present. She'd been and clearly still was such a force in Angelo's life. What would that be like?

Well, that was something she'd never know.

CHAPTER 28

Over Fred's protests, Jo had settled the bar tab, though it wasn't too bad. Her father used to pay it off once the fishing season income started rolling in. Knowing he was dying, he'd sold the *Eloise*, "Which came as close to killing him as your mother leaving. Then he started into paying his tab monthly, makin' the rest of us look bad." Bernie, of course.

So, that was done. One less thing for her to worry about was all she could think. They'd already cremated him. Tomorrow evening the new owner was going to take them all out on the *Eloise* and scatter the ashes. She hadn't committed to that, but she hadn't said no either.

She had promised she'd come back through before leaving town. Still holding her hand, Angelo walked with her as she headed up Young Street, then Warren Street to her father's house.

"What day is this?" Jo's brain had already become scrambled by the events of the last two days. "Sunday?"

"Sunday," Angelo confirmed.

"How could you leave the restaurant?"

Angelo laughed and shook his head, "I don't really know, I

just had to. I wondered about that on the flight up, but some part of me must have known it would be okay, even if I wasn't thinking very clearly. Manuel can run the restaurant as well as I can. Apparently Graziella has had her eye on someone for front of house help, and she's going to do a trial this afternoon. My mother loved your idea, so she's going to be filling in for Eugene. There is no way I would ever have thought that up. How did you?"

Jo shrugged. She noticed the gesture was very unlike herself, but was one she saw on Angelo all the time. What other influences was she picking up from him?

"It simply made sense. Your mother is charming, a brilliant cook, and you clearly love each other so much that you can barely stand it. So, of course, she'd want to be with you." Now why had she phrased it that way? Of course, his mother would want to help him. But that's not what she'd said. Nor what she'd thought. "Want to be with Angelo." Why did that phrase feel as if she were speaking of someone other than his mother? She pulled her flannel shirt tighter against the back of her neck.

Angelo inspected the sky which had briefly eased from misting to merely humid. With the temperature in the sixties it only dampened the air, rather than being muggy. He looked back down, apparently he hadn't found anything up there to help him find a response to that.

They turned onto the old wooden stairs leading up to Warren Street. They slowly climbed above narrow Hopkins Alley where there were steep banks of scrub and low trees, below ranged the backs of old warehouses wearing their gray paint as if to compete with the gray sky. The stairs creaked and groaned as they climbed them, but by Ketchikan standards this was a major thoroughfare, you could walk two abreast without a problem. Once they broke free of the warehouses they had a clear view over the tops of a light industrial stretch of Water

Street and out to Pennock and Gravina Islands defining the Tongass Narrows.

Jo saw a jet lifting off the runway on Gravina, slowly filling the Narrows with its dull roar before turning south for friendlier climes. She'd pay good money to be done and aboard. Now there was the constant thought of her youth. "Get me out of here!" She could feel the shout rooted deep inside. But just as when she was a girl, she kept it bottled deep inside. Kept it there because once again her life had drifted out of her control.

No escape for today at least. All of the businesses she'd need to contact would be closed on a Sunday. Maybe she could escape tomorrow.

She squeezed Angelo's hand again, just so pleased that he was there with her. That anyone was there with her.

Because now came the hard part.

ANGELO LOOKED at the strange houses lining the uphill side of whatever street they were on. His head was still spinning at the foreignness of this place. Sure, it was technically on U.S. soil, but it didn't belong there.

Everything here was surreal.

An airport separated from the town it served by a ferry that didn't stand a chance in rough weather. And this was Alaska. He'd bet that there was a lot of waiting for the waters to be calm enough for the ferry during the winter months, which up here was probably about ten months of the year.

And the Crab Hole...he had to send some of his New York friends there, it was performance art at its finest, and most authentic. No edgy display observed by urban crowds dressed in black. That crab shell art and the patrons had been for-real surreal.

This street reminded him oddly of the Amalfi Coast of Italy.

Houses perched on the edge of impossible cliffs. Long, stick-like understructures reaching multiple stories down to the street to support the front of houses who had their backsides planted firmly against the hill. He knew where they were going before Jo even turned toward it, and he really hoped he had it wrong.

Beyond a pickup truck made of equal parts red metal and brown rust, towered a house. A house that had clearly been built before the apocalypse and somehow survived. It perched upon a structure he wouldn't trust to hold up a garden shed. Twenty-foot tall four-by-fours with a couple of two-by-four cross braces looked impossibly spindly, too little to support even the stair rail nailed into the side of them, never mind the house atop.

A long flight of stairs climbed along the sloping hillside straddled by the stick-frame understructure. The steps reached the back end of the shack where the house rested its butt against the cliff face. The only entrance was on the right side at the very back end of the house against the cliff.

The one-story structure that perched twenty or thirty feet above them might have once been white. Or perhaps blue. It was hard to tell with all of the peeling paint. He could see the green encroachments of moss or lichen or something else that wasn't supposed to be growing on buildings but had on this one. This is where James Patterson should put his next psychotic murderer. There'd be no question about what had twisted up the villain.

Angelo opened his mouth to ask if she'd actually lived here, but snapped it shut when he saw that her dark skin was almost sheet white and her jaw was clenched so hard he was afraid for her next dentist appointment. He changed tacks.

"Do you really have to go up there?"

Her nod was tight, but affirmative. She was staring up the steps wide-eyed, having stumbled to a halt with her hand barely inches from the rail.

"Okay," he'd be the stable one at the moment, even if merely looking at the place made him want to rent a flamethrower and call it done. "Let me have the key."

He didn't comment on her chilled fingers as she handed it over, merely led the way up the stairs, trusting that she'd follow. It took a few moments, but he began to feel the structure shaking with steps other than his. At the top he kicked aside a spool of rotting fishing line and unlocked the door.

Showing none of the hesitation he felt, he stepped inside, leaving the door wide open, and flicked on a light. Electricity was still working. That was a good start.

They entered at the back, where house met slope. A door straight ahead was tightly closed. A narrow, dark hallway led to the front of the house. Being braver than he felt, Angelo went down the hall hoping the building didn't collapse from under him. Another closed door to the side. Then the main room.

The front half of the house, the part perched out in space on spindly legs, was a single room. Kitchen, living, and what euphemistically could be called dining, faced a window thickly hazed with dried salt. The furnishings were old but looked serviceable. The room was clean and neat, nothing much here but a sofa, a couple of chairs, and an old television.

One more door at the far end of the room stood open. The back half of the house, other than the narrow hall to the door, had been divided into three rooms. Two bedrooms, with the bath in the center.

How had the miracle of Jo Thompson come from such a past? He turned to look at her. She stood at the threshold to the main room, posed as if perfectly calm and collected. Her hands tucked easily in the front pockets of her rain jacket. And tears streaming down her face.

"Okay, I'm getting you out of here." Angelo tried to sweep her out of the room and out of her father's house, but Jo held her ground.

"No. I need to do this now before I lose all of my nerve. This isn't hard," she spoke more to herself than Angelo. It had to be easier than the murder scene she'd had to visit and catalog as an intern, an experience that had driven her hard into corporate law where most of the crimes occurred in sterile board rooms.

"What are we looking for?"

She'd think of it as collecting evidence. That's all. Objective. She could be objective.

"A box."

"Any more guidance than that? What's in it?"

"An empty one, or a bag. We're going to make one quick pass and gather any paperwork we can find, checkbooks, stuff like that. One pass, then out."

Bless Angelo. He came back moments later with an old wooden box out of which he'd dumped a pile of broken winch blocks that her father had been meaning to repair since before she left for college.

"Could you do that one?" she indicated her father's room. She simply couldn't go in there.

He was gone in moments. She'd have to remember to thank him later. Thank God her father was a creature of habit and not a pack rat. By the time Angelo came back with the box about a third full, she'd completed her pass on the living room. Checkbooks in the second drawer of the coffee table along with two unpaid, but not yet overdue bills. A quick flip revealed that he'd gotten a hundred thousand for his boat, but medical and other outstanding bills had chewed up about half of that. He'd always lived season to season, and she remembered all too well how hard the bad seasons were. At his death, his savings were probably the highest they'd ever been in his life.

She found his spare truck keys. She'd drop them at the Crab

Hole in case anyone wanted the old vehicle. The first drawer of the file cabinet revealed neatly filed bills in the separate hanging folders that she'd set up for him long ago. She pulled the most recent from each folder so that she'd know who to cancel. The other drawer included the truck title, which would go with the keys, and a small life insurance policy in her name. How hard had it been for him to maintain that? It wouldn't have paid for a year of her college or what she now made in a month or two, but she was touched nonetheless.

Finally, she found what she'd really been wanting, his will. The old envelope cracked with age as she opened it. The paper had yellowed, but was otherwise fine. Jo flipped to the back page, signed and witnessed, dated shortly after she was born.

She flipped back and scanned down the first page. Dan was named as the executor if Jo was under eighteen, otherwise Jo was executor. That simplified matters immensely.

Jo made it halfway down the next page before her knees let go and she dropped onto the couch.

Her father's will named both Jo and Eloise Thompson as beneficiaries. Fifty-fifty split if they were both surviving and Jo was over eighteen.

Now she was legally required to find her mother, the woman who had abandoned her before she was three.

CHAPTER 29

"Together." Angelo said when Jo froze at the last room. The door by the entrance must be Jo's bedroom.

He opened the door, turned on the light, and stepped inside. There was a narrow, north-facing window that had been over-grown by moss. A tree in full leaf pressed hard against the cracked glass. The overhead bulb behind a faded papier-mâché shade did little to light the room.

It was perhaps the most depressing place he'd ever been. A desk, a narrow bed, and a closet that stood empty. The walls had posters curling from the damp, of astronauts and the space shuttle. Of the Martian surface and fantastic science fiction spaceships.

"Those were from my 'How far can I really get from Alaska?' phase," Jo stared at them blankly.

"I would say that culturally, you succeeded."

"I don't know," she kept staring at the curling posters. "Ketchikan doesn't look quite so bad as an adult. You couldn't pay me to live here," she threw up her hands, normally so quiet, in a very Italian gesture as if to block the possibility of such a thought. "But there is community. There are good people here.

They're just not my people. When I was a kid, I swore that I would never again set foot on Alaskan soil for as long as I lived."

Angelo eyed her carefully. "Yet your legal practice is mainly Alaskan."

"Don't remind me." She shuddered. And to Angelo's eye, what she'd intended to be mock horror had turned to very real distress.

This was not the time or place to ask about that particular problem. So, instead, Angelo looked about the room, narrow enough to touch both walls with out-stretched arms and barely twice as long.

"Anything in here you want? If not, I'm getting you out of here."

"Let me go through the desk drawers just in case."

Nothing surfaced, and Angelo was going to shoo her out when he spotted a picture on the wall that didn't seem to fit the others.

"What's that one?" He pointed at the one image. It was small. A postcard of a penguin Photoshopped to be flying above the clouds with a little thought bubble. "Look Ma, I'm an eagle!" You could see the penguin's trajectory was failing and headed for a splashdown in the ocean far below. The "Ma" had been crossed out and replaced with "Jo" in faded pen.

Jo reached out slowly and pulled out the thumbtack holding it to the wall.

She turned it over and held it so that they could read it together.

Dearest Jo, I could find no way to fly in K-kan. By the time I could remember even how to crawl, it was too late for us. Say hi to Dan for me. All the best! Eloise (not the boat)

And a somewhat pathetic smiley face.

It was dated five years ago.

SHE AND ANGELO had a quiet night at the Cape Fox Lodge. They ate a meal at the restaurant, with no seafood involved, as if they'd both been overwhelmed by the Salmon Fishing Capital of the World. Jo had the Russian Chicken and Angelo the Pepper Steak. They split a piece of Chocolate Cheesecake, but had been unable, or unmotivated to finish it.

She slept like the dead, curled against his chest, wrung out to her very core. Somewhere in the middle of the night she'd needed more. He'd woken easily, in that quiet way of his, and been gloriously good to her, kissing away her tears of exhaustion that found their way out even as her body released the spring wound so tightly inside.

In the light of morning, with room service pancakes cooling on the small table, she'd finally faced the task of sorting through the box. Angelo stayed out of the way, pretending to watch a baseball game with the sound turned way down, which she appreciated. When she had it sorted and started on the phone calls, he'd gone for a run. A dozen phone calls later she'd arranged for someone to clean out the house, someone else to sell it in the name of the estate, the land had to be worth something. She cancelled utilities, medical, and car insurance. By the time the first round was done, she had a couple of pages of a hotel pad covered with notes.

She could draft her first motion for probate, except for the conditions of the will that mandated she find a woman twenty-six years gone. She could argue for probate in absentia and probably get it. Even throw her mother's half into a trust in case she ever surfaced. But was it worth the pain and aggravation? She didn't know, couldn't think. So she set it aside for the moment.

Angelo drifted back in just as she started digging into what he'd recovered from her father's room. No letters. No strange postcards from the past. Mostly junk she could just throw out once she'd looked at it. Near the bottom, there was a photo. Her father and a woman she didn't recognize, or at least not completely.

She'd snooped often enough as a child trying to find some evidence of her mother, and found none. Yet here in a cheap wood frame stood a much younger version of her father, his face and hair dark with Tlingit blood. Behind him, the newly painted prow of the *Eloise*, her name in bold blue lettering on the white hull. Beside him, a pretty woman with her own dark hair almost down to her waist, but fair features, perhaps of the East Coast, perhaps California. She wore bright yellow fisherman boots, jeans, and a plaid flannel shirt. Though her eyes seemed hidden, hazed in some way that Jo couldn't quite discern, her smile appeared bright.

And she cradled a tiny child in her arms. A child, Jo now knew, who had skin the color of her father's and the features of a mother she'd never met but would recognize in the mirror.

"ONE LAST STOP, then we're gone." It was early in the afternoon and she and Angelo had managed two seats on the evening flight back to Seattle.

Jo pulled up in front of the Crab Hole and cursed when she saw the "Closed for Funeral" sign. She checked her watch and cursed again. Regrettably, there was still plenty of time.

They drove down to the docks; the *Eloise* still floating in the slip. A small group had clustered on the dock. Jo parked and took the truck title and keys with her, and the postcard.

"Engine's conked," Carl informed her. "Doesn't matter a damn, crematorium screwed up the preserve-the-ashes order, so there's not a damn thing to scatter anyway. Didn't know you could get a cremation with no ashes, but seems you can order it that way. We figured we'd go down to the end of the pier, drink a pint, and piss inta the Narrows."

Jo managed a laugh. It was so fitting that it was sad and funny and touching all at the same time. Her body didn't know what to do with the collision of the conflicting feelings and so she just nodded her head in approval.

She pulled out the title and keys, "Do you need a truck?"

"Aw, shit. Yeah, one of us will take the damn thing. Best thing to do for that beast is drop her off the end of the pier to make a fish reef for divers, like them old battleships."

Jo hugged him. She knew that was as close as any of them would get to saying they'd liked her father and would miss him. He held her lightly when he returned the gesture, patting her back like a child's.

"He was damned proud o' you. Even when we didn't understand what you were doin', he was so proud of you. Missed you as much as Eloise, but know he was damn fucking proud."

She wondered if he meant Eloise her mother or *Eloise* the boat after he'd sold her. She decided the politic action was not to inquire.

Then Carl was gone and turned into the wind so that he'd have an excuse to wipe at his eyes.

Each came to hug her goodbye and pat her back. Fred groused about his arthritis and that if anyone else was gonna die before him they'd better be doin' it soon or he wasn't comin' to any of these shitheads' funerals. Gerta offered Jo a nod. Bernie said something about it being a good thing they didn't have any ashes or old Earnest might get pissed when they pissed on him." Adam just rolled his eyes at Bernie's back and shook her hand.

Angelo, bless him, was hanging with them by the *Eloise* easing any awkwardness. He gave them someone to speak to besides Earnest's daughter after they'd already said goodbye to her.

When Dan came up to her last of all, the others had moved off a bit to check on the status of the engine repairs and to get a beer. Dan gave her a big, hard hug as if she were his own daughter somehow. Being hugged by Dan was like being enfolded in the arms of a gentle papa bear, someplace warm, soft, and very safe.

He started to turn away, and Jo almost let him go. It was an option. Burn the will and postcard, turn her back, and let the state take it all. She was technically in violation of the laws of probate for doing what executor tasks she'd done so far, by canceling utilities and removing items from the house. She should first have filed the death certificate and will with the state who would then certify her in the role of executor.

However, she was licensed to practice law in Alaska and while this wasn't her area of specialty, she knew the Alaskan laws well enough to know the penalty wouldn't amount to much more than a scowl from the judge, if that. At this point, she could take the wooden crate back and dump it on the living room floor, throw the key in behind it, and walk away clean.

Except it wouldn't feel clean.

Instead, she stopped Dan with a hand on his arm, and pulled the postcard from her coat pocket. His broad, dark face went bright when he saw the writing, then sad before he could possibly have read even the few lines there.

"You were closest to her, weren't you?"

Dan nodded slowly, "In coupla ways." He rubbed a meat cleaver-sized hand across his face. "Earnest sat ta' end. Eloise sat twixt us'n. He wanted her included."

"She stayed in touch."

"Birthdays an' such. Yours and mine. I kep' in touch on hers."

"You know where she is." Jo had figured that must be the message, "Say hi to Dan." Her mother had stayed in touch with Dan, knowing he'd be in touch with Earnest and so could hear how her daughter was faring.

Her father had been smart enough to understand that when he'd seen the postcard, but he'd still been hurting enough to not forward it. There'd been nothing on the card for him. But he hadn't been angry enough to throw it out either.

She'd give good money to know if he'd tacked it to the wall when it arrived, almost a spit in Jo's eye of "you'll never see this because you never come home" or had he tacked it up when he found out he was dying, specifically so that Jo would find it.

Dan didn't look away.

In that look, she saw the pain of knowledge. Earnest had sat next to him for the last five years knowing for a fact that Dan was in touch with Earnest's departed wife, the wife he'd remained married to until death did he part. Her father must have mentioned the postcard. She could almost hear the conversation at some moment when only the two of them were there at the bar.

"Got a postcard."

Dan waiting in silence.

"For Jo."

A slow turn and meeting of their gazes.

"From her mother."

A long silence, followed by a slow nod on Dan's part.

A mutual turning away.

Then five more years of sitting side by side with that conversation now hanging between them.

Jo scrubbed at her arms to remove the chill of that on a warm day, knowing full well that's exactly how it had been.

"March," Dan said after such a long pause that Jo almost didn't catch it. "Eloise March." Then he turned, joined the others, and they headed down to the end of the pier to drink together and piss into the Narrows. Angelo hung back, waiting for Jo.

"March" for Jo March, for Little Women and the strong mother, Marmee March, who Eloise must have wished she could be. Everything done in the literary tradition, as Eloise had been part of that tradition before her daughter.

That Dan had said nothing more meant that her mother either couldn't be found, or could be found very easily.

That in turn meant…

In Seattle, by looking in the phone book. All Jo had needed to find her mother all this time was her chosen last name.

CHAPTER 30

"*I* love you."

Jo was shocked to stillness at the whisper. The jet had just slammed on the power to roar down the Ketchikan airport runway and get her out of this place. She turned to Angelo praying she hadn't really heard it. But he wasn't facing out the window with a first-time visitor's curiosity, he was looking right at her.

She shook her head slowly once as the jet's roar peaked and then the plane abruptly rotated its nose off the runway and pointed for the sky.

Angelo nodded.

"You can't."

His face pained. Obviously not the answer he wanted. Well she didn't have that answer. He simply couldn't.

He didn't ease his grip on her hand.

"I can. And I do. And, before you go there, I'm not one of 'those' guys. You're only the third woman I ever told that. The first two were my mother and Cassidy on the day she married Russell."

Jo swallowed hard. It actually hurt to do so, but she couldn't work up any moisture. The dry air brushing across her face from the little overhead vents didn't help at all. The jet continued to roar almost as loudly as her pulse thundered in her ears.

She tried to remove her hand, but Angelo held onto it.

"I love you, Jo Thompson."

"But," this was crazy. "But why?" He'd just seen her at her very worst. Ketchikan had almost killed her. It probably would have if not for his presence.

Angelo's laugh was soft and, thankfully, not bitter.

"Okay, let's ignore the fact that you are easily the most beautiful woman I've ever been with."

She doubted that, looking all gorgeous and Italian the way he did.

"The most fun in bed."

Jo had to admit she'd never had such a incredible time with a man, not ever.

"And you're far and away the smartest. We can also ignore the fact of how you smell." At that he leaned in, using the fact of her incarceration in the narrow plane seat by the bright "Fasten Seatbelts" sign as they continued the climb out, and inhaled such a long sniff by her ear that she almost giggled.

"I take that back. I can't ignore how you smell. It is a flavor I can never fully understand but could gladly spend a lifetime trying to reproduce. God, you smell so good, Jo."

"I did take a shower. It's called soap."

He didn't deign to answer that with more than an Italian wave of the hand to dismiss her attempted misdirection. It was hard to argue, he smelled amazing to her as well. That's why she kept curling up with her face pressed against the center of his chest. It was like someplace she'd never known, like…she didn't have the word for it.

"What I also can't ignore was watching you with the alphabet gang."

"What about them?" Defensive. She could feel her spine stiffen and her chin rise as she prepared herself for their defense. She was feeling protective of her father's drinking buddies, which was utterly ridiculous, but an undeniable fact as well.

"You were so kind to them."

That knocked her back in her seat.

"They were in so much pain. They aren't sure who they are without your father there. You sat at that bar on his stool and you stood on that dock and told them it would be okay. That came straight from the heart, Jo. Straight from a really amazing heart."

Jo tried to imagine who Angelo was talking about, it wasn't anyone she recognized. All she'd done in Ketchikan was find out that her past hadn't been neatly left behind. Instead it had risen like a specter of evil until her past now blocked every path forward. Like the case she'd managed not to think of for forty-eight hours, the one burying her desk. The case that would bring her back to Alaska.

That was it. There was her defense.

"Angelo, you're really sweet. But you can't love me. Besides, I'll be in Alaska for a lot of the next three to five years." No matter how awful that fact itself sounded.

The plane leveled out and Jo could see the steward starting down the aisle with the drink cart.

"You can't do that," Angelo declared as if it was any kind of an option.

"My case is in Alaska. North Slope. There is an immense amount of relevant information there, both documentation and individuals who will need interviewing. I'm going to have to be there, and at the capital in Juneau, as well as New York. So you can't love me, because I won't be here."

COULDN'T Jo see the pain it caused her each time she mentioned going back to Alaska, even as the plane was, at this moment, setting her free of the place? Angelo could see it written on her face. If he ignored, no, if he set aside his own pain at the moment, he could see hers as plain as a crack in an eggshell.

It was so hard to think straight around her. He could kick himself for saying he loved her when she was so emotionally strung out. He hadn't meant to. Hadn't known it was there to say until he did. It had been such a surprise he wasn't even sure he'd said it aloud until she turned to face him.

Now, not only had she thrown it back in his face unanswered, Counselor Thompson had turned it into a full-court defense and was now performing courtroom dissection on it.

Gods, who knew that loving someone could hurt this much? *Sì*, it was too soon, too fast. If it felt too fast for him, no matter how true, how must it feel for her? He'd even screwed up falling in love.

Jo had just been through emotional hell. He'd never been someone's lifeline like that before, at least not a woman's. He'd smacked Russell a couple of times during his courtship of Cassidy, or rather his non-courtship of her, but the guy had needed it.

Jo was a wholly different matter. For Russell, it had literally been a smack on the head. He'd wager that Jo wouldn't appreciate that at the moment, even if she needed it.

Having Jo hang onto him as she had these last two days had left him feeling pretty damned powerful. In some ways, punching Yuri had been the least of it no matter how good it felt. Standing beside her in that hauntingly sad house, sitting with her father's friends at the bar, waiting at their crazy but somehow appropriate funeral so that she could touch each person's heart. They were so good together as a couple, they hadn't even had to talk about it.

Okay.

Angelo took a deep breath.

Okay.

Another breath.

Jo's emotions were stirred up and he'd just have to accept that.

And his timing sucked.

He could admit that too.

He'd have to shut up at the moment about how much she filled his heart. It was like heat and ice flashing through his body in alternating waves with each beat of his heart. But he could keep quiet about that for her sake. For now.

What he couldn't ignore...

"Jo! How can a woman so smart as you even think of going back to Alaska? It tears you up."

"No, Angelo." Jo was gone. Counselor Thompson now sat in the airplane seat beside him. Somehow she'd recovered her hand from his without his even noticing. "I know you want me to stay in Seattle. I like you. We have fun together."

"Fun!" he cut her off. "Fun? I tell you I love you and you tell me we 'have fun' together?" Okay, maybe he couldn't keep his mouth shut.

He tried again.

"I'm not talking about me, Jo." He waved away the drink cart lady. When she tried to distract Jo, he waved her off again. "For the moment, I'm not talking about how much I love you and how much you fill my heart."

The drink cart lady now wasn't going anywhere. She made a show of serving the threesome on the other side of the aisle, but had to ask them to repeat what they wanted several times. Well, he was the one who'd decided to confess his love on an airplane, now he'd have to live with that for the rest of his life.

Angelo closed his eyes to concentrate. Jo was so big on words. He had to be careful and choose just the right ones. He opened his eyes and looked at her, really looked. But those dark eyes only showed clear and cool rather than the soft warmth they usually radiated.

"I'm not talking about my heart, Counselor Thompson. I'm talking about yours."

"I think I know my own heart."

"Then how can you go back to Alaska?" It burst out of him. It was so damned obvious that she couldn't go. Not for three to five years. It sounded like a prison sentence. She'd die just as some part of her mother had, though he was smart enough to not use that argument.

Even if she didn't end up at the Crab Hole bar, she might as well. Her heart would shrivel and die, like those old men who didn't even know how to say goodbye to a companion who had sat with them every night for decades.

"I can go back to Alaska because that's my job," her voice was rigid. "I'm very good at my job."

"But is your job good at you?"

———

Jo FLAGGED the steward who was only just moving away and asked her for a ginger ale on ice. It gave her an excuse to not look at Angelo. She wished she had a book that she could read, or at least pretend to.

She reached for the in-flight magazine, but there wasn't one in the seat-back pocket before her. There were two of them in front of Angelo, but she wasn't going to reach across or ask for one.

Instead, she took her soft drink and peanuts and stared straight ahead.

Her job was just fine.

She'd won her first class debate in high school. She'd led the Vassar debate team to a statewide victory, even if a little school in Maine had won the regionals. Editor of the Law Review at the University of Washington. Partner at an elite law firm at an unprecedented twenty-seven years old.

Her job was just fine. Though it did feel as if she were protesting perhaps a little bit too much.

But really.

Her job was just fine.

And anyway, Angelo didn't love her. He was a guy. He was a really decent guy for coming to Alaska to be with her, but he was still a guy. He'd just tangled up loyalty and lust with deeper emotions. He didn't love her, he only thought he did.

Jo closed her eyes, leaned her head back against the seat, and let the humming of the engines fill her head, ignoring the pleading look on Angelo's face.

He didn't love her, she assured herself. Especially when her career started taking her places he couldn't follow.

CHAPTER 31

"*I* got the call."

Russell's voice was loud in the empty restaurant kitchen followed by the clomping of his crutches as he pushed in through the back entry door. Front-of-house service had ended two hours ago, cleanup had finished the hour before, and the restaurant had been Angelo's alone since. He'd shooed his mother out and started working on the menu for the new restaurant.

It needed a different feel, a different flavor. Perhaps northern. The Piedmont region of Italy was in the north, but so was Venice, though he was less of a fan of east Italian flavors. Lombardy was a possibility; everyone had heard of Lake Como now that George Clooney had his villa there.

"What call?" Angelo added a pinch of rosemary to the cream sauce, stirred and tasted it again. It tasted flat. No matter what he did, it—

Russell whacked Angelo's leg with one of his crutches.

"Hey! Ow!"

"What call? Think, man. I'm married to your girlfriend's best friend. You did something to freak out Jo. She cuts off all communication with any of her friends and for some reason I don't pretend to understand, it's now up to me to fix the whole screwed up mess. So, I'm figuring we'll deal with it tomorrow instead of half an hour to midnight tonight. Then the stupid phone rings. Guess who's on the line?"

"The Pope."

Russell hobbled to the cooler and pulled out a couple of beers.

"No, worse than that."

"I don't know. Who?"

Russell slowly eased down onto one of the stools by the prep table with a groan. "Never break your goddamn leg, Angelo, it's a real pain in the ass."

"And the leg."

"And the leg," Russell agreed with him.

"I'll remember that." For lack of any better idea, Angelo opened the beer Russell had set out on the counter and poured some into the sauce. A stir, a taste.

"Well, that takes care of that."

"Awful?"

"Godawful." Angelo turned off the burner, dumped the pot in the big steel sink, and splashed some water into it before sitting on the stool facing Russell. "So who was on the phone worse than the Pope?"

"Maria Amelia Avico Frickin' Parrano."

Angelo swore and knocked back some of his beer. Definitely worse than the Pope.

"So, I'm half undressed for bed and more than halfway to coaxing Cassidy to join me when the call comes in. Then what the hell happens? Next thing I know, I'm dressed, and my loving wife is closing the door on my ass telling me not to bother coming back until I fix it. Hell of a honeymoon."

Okay, he'd felt like shit before, but this was perhaps a new low.

"So," Russell leaned back and folded his hands in his lap. "What the hell did you do to her?"

"I told her I loved her." Damn, he really had to work on not saying that out loud. It took too much out of him.

"No shit?"

"No shit."

"And you do?"

Angelo could only nod. He couldn't even speak. Like his soul had been taken out, run through a blender, then turned into a really crappy cream sauce.

"What did she say?"

Angelo didn't even bother to shrug. To hell with her. Let her go back to goddamn Alaska. He closed his eyes. That thought hurt even worse.

"Oh man," Russell groaned.

Angelo couldn't agree more.

"WHAT THE HELL, JO?"

Jo yelped and dropped her briefcase which thudded onto the deep pile carpet, clipping her foot hard enough that she fell into a leather armchair.

As she'd entered the lobby of Stanley, Tu, Rolfmann, and Thompson from her office, the lights had sensed her motion and turned on. They'd revealed a very tired looking Cassidy Knowles slouched low on a dusky blue leather sofa.

Jo rubbed her foot a moment longer, but nothing appeared broken.

"What are you doing sitting in the dark? Why didn't you come back to my office?" Jo's heartrate was still up. Interestingly, seeing Cassidy, she should be feeling joy at seeing her friend or chagrin at how she'd been avoiding her. Instead she felt a little depressed. Some conspiratorial part of her mind had been waiting for Angelo to come by and visit her. He hadn't even called. Not that she could really blame him.

"I did come back." Cassidy pulled in her feet enough for Jo to sit at the other end of the couch.

Jo recovered her briefcase from the middle of the floor, set it on the coffee table then sat.

"But you were on the phone to some crazy place..."

"The Chairman of the Danish Maritime Authority's Shipping Tribunal."

"Too much stratosphere for me."

"Says the woman trained in wine by Robert Parker."

Cassidy shrugged, "Wine tasting. Creators of international maritime law. We each have our comfort zone and that one sure isn't mine. So, I backed off. You took so long to finish your call that the lights decided I wasn't here and turned off. Didn't see any reason to argue with them."

"It is," Jo checked her watch, "past one a.m."

"What are you doing working this late?"

"Well, it's a big and important case and I—"

"Blah. Blah. Blah." Cassidy made her quacking duck hand sign from college whenever she caught Jo over-defending her position. It had actually been exceptional training for trials, as she now automatically heard Cassidy's quacking noises whenever she was about to say too much. Her main challenge had been to not smile at the image during a serious courtroom moment.

Jo bit the inside of her cheek, then tried again. "It'll be the most important—"

"Wah. Wah. Wah." More quacking duck.

Jo knew from experience of many years that Cassidy could go all night and never repeat a sound. Even when they were drunk, Cassidy somehow kept track.

She knew why Cassidy was here. Jo wanted to confide in her, but it wouldn't work that way. Cassidy was newly married and through those eyes, thought that in order to be happy, everyone else should be as well. Perrin was a total romantic, which meant she was of the same mind, only more so. If she mentioned Angelo's declaration of love, which was still freaking her out, she'd never hear the end of it.

"I was offered a new job." Jo had already decided to not take it, but she didn't need to tell Cassidy that. At least not right away.

"Whacka. Whacka. Whac—Uh, what?" Cassidy blinked.

"Renée Linden is retiring and wants me to take over her job."

Cassidy jerked upright to stare at her. She gestured toward the Market. "That Renée Linden? The one behind like, I dunno, everything?"

Jo nodded. "That Renée Linden. She's retiring and thinks I should replace her as the Executive Director of the Pike Place Market. She's been courting me for a couple of weeks."

"Weeks?!" Cassidy's voice whooshed out and she dropped back on the couch. "I once managed to hold out for forty-three minutes when she wanted me to serve on a board for the Friends of Emerald City Opera. The other board members actually made me a plaque in honor of my holding out for so long. It ended up being fantastic and fun, but it sure didn't look like it from the outside. Weeks? Really?"

Jo nodded. She'd forgotten about that connection. When Renée retired, that position would probably be opening as well. Except Renée wasn't just a member of Friends of the Opera, she headed that board which placed her on the board of the Opera itself. Jo's head throbbed.

"You're turning her down?"

Jo did her best to remain impassive.

Cassidy squinted her eyes. "You are. Okay, Thompson. That one you're going to have to explain."

"Cass, it's one a.m. and—"

"And you're going to explain this one to me in short, simple, unlawyerly words because it is, as you say, one a.m."

"I'm sure Russell—"

"Is presently with Angelo. He's having some kind of meltdown. His mother got so worried that she called Russell a couple of hours ago."

Jo closed her eyes and counted to ten. It didn't help, so she counted to twenty with no better results.

"Oh shit, Cass. It's all so screwed up." At thirty she rose to her feet.

"I can't do this." Jo picked up her briefcase. She straightened her jacket. Straightened it and tried not to think about how much fun Angelo had made of taking it off her. He'd made her feel so desirable, so important, so...

"I can't do this. I have a phone conference with the under-secretary of the United Nations Division of Oceans and Law of the Sea tomorrow at seven a.m. I..." They were real reasons she couldn't talk about everything that was screwed up with her personal life, aside from the fact that it would take all night and she needed the sleep, but even those felt as if she were making excuses.

"I..." She made it one step toward the door and got stuck again. "I can't do this."

Cassidy came up to hug her, and some preservation instinct had Jo stepping back. She ignored the pain on Cassidy's face.

"I'm sorry. I just can't. You— Renée— Angelo— The will— My mother—" She was stuttering worse than her father's old truck engine which had refused to turn over when she and Angelo had tried it. She finally slapped a hand over her mouth to stop herself.

"I can't, Cass. I just can't," she mumbled through the hand over her mouth.

"You'll call me when you can?"

Jo nodded, blinking hard against the tears.

"I'll be the first?"

Jo nodded again.

"I mean it Thompson. Repeat after me, 'I'll call Cass first.' Right? Say it."

"You first," she mumbled.

"Okay," Cassidy nodded to herself, pulled her sweater straight like Captain Picard readying himself for battle. "Okay. Now, you're coming home with me."

"But—"

"But nothing Thompson. I'm not having you drive. I'm not leaving you alone tonight. I live two blocks away. You're coming with me and that's final."

Jo could only nod and keep her hand in place. There'd never been a friend in the world like Cassidy Knowles.

And God, did she need a friend right now.

Even if she couldn't speak to her.

CHAPTER 32

"*H*i, honey." Jo heard Russell call out from the living room as Cassidy opened the front door to their condo. "Can you believe that goofball told her that he loved her?"

Cassidy spun to face her as all the blood drained from Jo's brain. Only the power suit kept her from simply fainting to the floor.

"Even worse, Jo clearly lost her mind and told him she didn't care for him."

She braced a hand on the still-open front door as her stomach heaved. She was about to barf the energy bar she'd eaten ten hours earlier all over Cassidy's perfect white carpet.

"He was somewhere between murdered and so mad I'm glad he doesn't own a gun. Once I got him really drunk, he started mumbling that she was killing her soul, but he wouldn't explain that one. I dumped him in the guest bedr—" Led by his long-hair black cat, Russell came around the corner of the hallway on his crutches and stopped dead.

He and Jo stared at each other for an eternity that may have lasted less than five seconds but they were seconds stretched beyond all reckoning.

"Shit! Jo. Hi. I'm... Oh, shit!"

Jo turned and ran.

Cassidy called after her, but Jo bolted into the emergency stairwell and almost tumbled down the concrete steps.

When she heard Cassidy's call getting closer, she turned and sprinted up the nearest steps. It was a mistake. She'd meant to go down. She thought she'd be trapped, but it was all that saved her.

Cassidy roared into the stairwell the same moment Jo turned the corner onto the next landing up.

Cassidy went down.

Jo collapsed on the stairs a half flight above where Russell held the door open. Separate but together, they listened to the pounding echoes of Cassidy's downward footsteps and frantic calls.

"Shit!" She heard Russell in such pain she almost went to reassure him. "I'm such an idiot!"

He wasn't the only one.

Jo DIDN'T dare go home, for Cassidy would surely follow her there. And she didn't want to find a hotel room, and be one of those red-eyed weeping women trying to hide some deep unhappiness for everyone at the front desk to see and whisper about.

She did the only thing she could think of after she heard Cassidy return and tell Russell she was indeed going to check Jo's apartment.

Jo walked down the twenty flights and out into the night. Four blocks into Bell Town, she arrived at Perrin's Glorious Garb. The shop's lights were out, as was the studio light in the back. She went around to the side door and pressed the buzzer that served the six upstairs apartments.

She leaned on the buzzer.

A sleepy and distorted, "Who?" crackled out of the speaker.

"Jo." Her throat was so tight that it ached to create the single word. All she could taste was the salt of her tears that must have started again without her noticing. All she could see was the tiny squawk box.

The door buzzed sharply enough that Jo almost fell backwards off the low stoop, but managed to stop herself by grabbing the door handle.

Perrin met her at the head of the stairs.

One look at Jo's face was apparently all she needed. She led Jo down the narrow hall painted an improbable lime green and through a chartreuse door.

Perrin didn't cross-examine her. Didn't prod or poke. She only asked one question, "Should I call Cassidy?"

Jo could only shake her head before she pitched face first onto Perrin's couch and cried herself to sleep.

CHAPTER 33

*J*o made it to the morning phone call. Kept Muriel in the room for it because she knew she wouldn't remember a word of what was said. Afterward, over her protests, Muriel sent her home.

Per her assistant's instructions, which she'd written down and handed to Jo, the first thing she did was take a long, hot bath. Despite doing so, she remained numb to the core. Then she made coffee and ate the large apple muffin with the crunchy crumb topping that she always avoided, which Muriel had made her promise to pick up on her way home.

Now she sat out on the balcony with her unopened John Grisham book in her lap. She glanced down at Muriel's list.

Buy decadent muffin

Go home

Take hot bath, a long one, with bubbles (recommended: get undressed first)

Muriel's voice came through loud and clear.

Make coffee

Get that book you keep talking about not having time to read

Go to balcony (clothing optional)

Jo had pulled on shorts and her Vassar t-shirt which felt impossibly decadent for ten in the morning. Hearing Perrin in the back of her head, she had not put on a bra, which left her feeling unclothed despite being covered.

Eat muffin and drink coffee (you got dressed, didn't you? Knew you would.)

Open book (you're almost there)

Read book

Do not come back to the office today (Would tell you not to think about the office, but that would only make you think about the office, so I shouldn't have written this sentence to begin with, but it's too damn late and I'm not rewriting the list.)

She'd signed it with her cell phone number, a clear invitation if she needed to talk. But Jo didn't. She needed to think. But every time she tried, it all got snarled up in her head.

Her phone rang. That would be Cassidy. By now Perrin would have woken up and called Cassidy to let her know that Jo was alive.

She let it ring.

She couldn't seem to achieve Step 8: Open book. It was simply too much effort.

Instead she sat and watched Seattle from on high. Truly little street noise reached her twentieth-floor condo. Big diesel trucks climbing the steep hills of downtown Seattle, the occasional siren, nothing else reached her from the ground. Instead, there was the distant roar of the jets climbing north out of SeaTac airport. Some headed to Ketchikan, and some just headed the hell away.

Jo knew the latter was a false sanctuary, but it attracted her nonetheless. Wing off to Europe or New Zealand. Change her name and become a beach babe in Costa Rica like they'd always joked about in college to escape finals week. The three of them breaking hundreds of hearts in some tropical paradise. Probably be a lot less fun than it sounded.

The main sound on her balcony was the gentle breeze brushing past her, kicked into merry swirls by the shape of the building. Below and before her, the city and the Sound glittered under the bright morning sunlight. It had been some time since she'd simply sat and enjoyed.

She tried to think of the last time she'd totally stopped. And couldn't. No run, no swim, no bike ride. No case law, no social outing, no Angelo.

It tore away her breath to even think his name.

God. She sounded pitiful. In that moment, some part of her rose up and decided she was sick of whiny Jo Thompson.

She was not some whiny female.

She just wasn't.

Jo opened her book.

The bookmark was caught by the breeze and threatened to flutter out to sea. By the time she trapped it in the corner of the balcony, she'd lost her place in the book. A sudden urge to throw the whole thing off the balcony ran through her until she had to clamp her hands hard and set the book down carefully on the small steel table beside her half-finished muffin.

Action. She was an action person, and here she was taking none. That's why she was feeling so overwhelmed. She'd take this day off and deal with everything: past, present, and future. And she'd been avoiding the easiest one.

Do that one, then she'd get herself back on track without any problem.

She went inside and picked up her cell phone. A voicemail and a text from Cassidy. She didn't bother to listen to the voice-mail. To Cassidy's texted, "You okay?" she replied, "I'm fine now. Will call tonight. Tell Russell he's still fine with me."

She dropped the phone before Cassidy could respond and pulled out the phone book from where it gathered dust in the bottom desk drawer. Doing a simple Internet search was too personal, too close to actual contact. It felt as if it risked letting the person know you were looking them up, even if it didn't really.

Good old White Pages. "March, Eloise." Just one. Redmond, Washington. She was here. Ten miles across the lake. Jo noted down the address and phone number. Now she just needed to decide whether to have some probate attorney contact her or do it herself. She could file initial probate with the Alaskan court and simply include the contact information, it wasn't as if it was a complex estate with any decisions to be made. The court would send notice and, barring protest by either party, cut everything in half and issue a pair of checks.

Jo pulled the Alaska documents out of her In Basket, they'd left the wooden crate at the Cape Fox Lodge along with most of the trash. Such a pitifully thin stack to define an entire life. She pulled out a couple of empty file folders and organized the information quickly. Closed accounts, open items, estate documents. No death certificate. She drafted a quick note requesting a copy of the death certificate and put it in an envelope to the Ketchikan Coroner's office.

For lack of anything better to do with the postcard, she dropped it in with the will and ignored the slight pinch of filing away the only contact she'd received from her mother.

The only thing that didn't fit in any file was the photo. She propped it in the middle of her desk. She wasn't afraid of the past. Bring it on, she told the photo. Nor the future. Bring it on.

Next she started drafting a nice, "Thank you but no thank you," note for Renée. She rapidly filled a whole sheet on a yellow legal pad with phrases and cross outs, reasons and desires. She slashed a big "X" across the whole page, flipped that page over to the back, and glared at the blank sheet now in front of her.

It was a relief as visceral as a cold shower when her phone rang with the tone she'd programmed for the main lobby.

That wouldn't be Cassidy, Perrin, or Angelo. She'd given the elevator code to each of them. She picked up her phone trying to remember if she'd made any recent online orders.

JO HAD BARELY PULLED on decent clothes by the time the elevator whisked Maria Parrano into her apartment.

"What a beautiful picture."

Of course, it was the first thing Angelo's mother had gravitated to in the entire condo.

"You look wonderful, Mrs. Parrano."

"Maria."

"You look wonderful, Maria." And she did. The flowered summer dress and flat, strapped leather sandals made her look both comfortable and elegant. The yellow leather purse was bright and cheerful. She did nothing to hide her age, but it was hard to credit her with a thirty-year old son.

"Is that you?" Maria had picked up the cheap frame as if it were something precious.

"No, it's my mother."

"I meant in her arms."

"Oh, yes. That's me. Only child."

"She looks so sweet."

"Me?"

"Your mother."

Jo finally caught up with the conversation. "I wouldn't know. She left when I was two."

Mrs. Parrano, Maria, lay her fingertips over her lips for a long moment in apology. "I'm sorry. Do you know much about her?"

As she told Maria what little she knew, Jo poured them both a fresh cup of coffee and led them out onto the balcony where her novel remained unopened, her place still lost.

"Redmond is close, isn't it? Really? Have you called her?"

"I don't know if I'm going to."

Maria nodded. "It's hard. When Angelo was in high school I received a note from a friend. My Angelo, his father, had contacted her to find out how I was and how the baby was doing. He didn't even know baby's sex or that I was gone to America. I decide that someone who care so little about me and about my beautiful boy that he waits fifteen years to ask the question, he does not matter. So I tell my friend to tell him nothing. If she ever hear from him again, she does not tell me. There are times I doubt myself, but it was good. It was right."

Jo wished she had that kind of strength, but she'd never had a parent to teach her. She'd learned to put up the façade, to pretend she had strength, so that no one could see through her. Well, none but Cassidy and Perrin.

Yet somehow...

Angelo didn't see through the façade, but neither did he see the façade. He saw her as strong to begin with. As if it actually were a part of who she was.

"I just found out that my mother, Eloise, stayed in constant touch with a mutual friend through all the years. I don't know if Dan asked my father's permission or not, but he liked her and answered her back." Her mother had at least cared more than Angelo's father. That wasn't much in her favor, but it was something.

"She sent me a card, which my father left on my old bedroom wall for me to find." She'd decided that was how it must have been. Her father didn't have any meanness in him. Useless, lazy, disconnected? Yes. Mean, no. She went and fetched the postcard from the file.

Mrs. Parrano read it several times then brushed at the corners of her eyes.

"I wish my Angelo had done so much. She made the choice yours. You could have asked this Dan or tear the card to tiny pieces and throw it away. She leave it all up to you. That is a very hard and brave thing to do." She handed back the card carefully. "I hope I have a chance to meet this woman someday."

Jo looked at the card for a long moment and then tucked it into the Grisham novel. She still didn't know if she wanted to meet her mother or not.

———

JO HAD CERTAINLY SAT with enough witnesses over the years to know that Maria Parrano was sitting on some topic that was extremely uncomfortable and struggling to find some way to say it. Jo sighed inwardly.

Well, she had decided this was her day scheduled to deal with things. If she remembered correctly, and she'd have to call Muriel later to be sure, she'd be on a flight to New York tomorrow afternoon. So, now was the time.

"Sometimes, Maria, it is easier if you just say it."

Maria sipped her coffee again, but didn't look away. Jo was learning that Angelo had inherited his directness fair and square from his mother. Or was it something ingrained in the Italian genetic code?

"I don't know you, Jo Thompson. I would like to, but I do not."

"Yes, I'm sorry about missing dinner, but my father—"

Maria's hand wave of dismissal was so like Angelo's that Jo had to bite her cheek not to smile.

"What you did was more important and we will eat together soon, you and me. I like to think that we would be friends."

"I would like that too." And Jo was a bit surprised that she wasn't just being polite. Maria Parrano was a very pleasant person to sit with.

"You're sweet," she patted Jo's knee without making it belittling. "But I have come to ask you a favor."

A chill crept up Jo's spine. A deep breath. A nod. She didn't dare speak.

"I know there is something between you and my boy. I know that it is deep and important to both of you, and I don't want to pry. But my Angelo is hurting so much. Can you at least tell me why so that I can help him somehow?"

This wasn't what she'd expected. She'd thought Angelo had sent his mother to plead on his behalf. Instead, the mother had come herself out of love for her son.

"You love him very much, don't you?" At Maria's knowing nod Jo had to look away. It wasn't enough, so she stood up and walked the ten feet to the far end of the narrow balcony and back.

How would her life have been if she'd had a mother like that? Who could guess? If her mother were still in Ketchikan, would Jo have ever left? Would she have been driven to become who she was? Oddly, she could trace nearly every success in her life back to that moment of abandonment. Her motivation to learn, to excel, to be better...

To be better than her own mother? To show her...what?

She sat abruptly.

"What is it, my girl?" Maria's words shifted strangely in her head, combining oddly with her thoughts.

"I suddenly don't know why I do the things I do."

Maria took her hand, and massaged it as if to warm it. Her hands were like her son's, slim, but strong. Calluses where a knife was held, dozens of tiny scars from a lifetime of cooking.

"I cook for thirty years. I raise two boys, as much mother to Russell as Julia was mother to Angelo. Suddenly one day their boy is married and they decide to retire. John and Julia, they suddenly don't know what to do. I worry, but I listen to my heart and I know what to do. I know to go be with my Angelo."

Maria pulled her over and kissed Jo's cheek.

"And you help him see that I can help him. Tell him to let me make pastry. Oh, I think he would have found out the idea himself, but sometimes that boy moves so slow."

"Sometimes he isn't so slow." Her voice felt dreamy and distant. As if it belonged to someone else. Maybe Counselor Thompson had deserted her for the day, leaving only a lost Jo behind.

"Oh?"

"He told me that he loved me." It didn't kill her to say. It didn't even leave a bitter taste. It was simply a fact, a fact too unreal to, well, be real.

"When do he say so?"

Jo cast her mind back until once again she was sitting on that impossible flight.

"Right after my father's funeral, while the plane was taking off." She could feel the shuddering of the jet and taste the dry air pumped into the cabin as she worked her jaws to pop her ears.

"No," Maria breathed it out as little more than an astonished whisper.

Jo could only nod. Here it came, the defense of her boy and why wasn't Jo sensible enough to—

Maria Parrano slapped her hand sharply against her thigh with a loud smack.

"That *idiota*. I can no believe he do that to you. Is my son so *stupido?* He must be. Well, serves him right his heart is all hurt."

Jo could only watch her wide-eyed as her rant continued.

"Men, they are so..." Maria tapped her own temple sharply. "What is the word I want?"

"Dense?"

"Yes," Maria squeezed Jo's hand. "Dense that is good word for my Angelo. You not have enough on your mind, so he must add love just then? Dense. Dense. Dense."

Jo couldn't stop watching the woman in amazement. Jo couldn't have said it better herself. And it felt amazing to have

Maria on her side. It helped confirm that she hadn't lost her mind simply because she didn't love Angelo back.

"Of course," Maria put her other hand over Jo's. "You are so crazy about him. That is so easy to see, except I think he can no see that or he not be so miserable. You make him wait Jo. You make him wait until you are good and ready to say you love him. Oh, I do like you. It will be so fun to have you as a daughter. So fun!"

Easy to see? Sure she liked Angelo but—

Now Maria looked directly at her with those dark warm eyes that sparkled with inner light.

"You take your time, Jo Thompson. You are too busy, too many things, they push at you. When you have time. After you decide about your mother and settle all of your father things, then is time to decide you love him. Not before then. Not now."

Then she smiled again so strongly that Jo could feel herself smiling back despite the cry of protest that lurked inside, but couldn't seem to find traction to leap off the tip of her tongue.

"After you do, oh, then you and me, we will have so much fun!"

CHAPTER 34

*J*o never did get the note to Renée finished. She had an acceptable first draft, but it wasn't near to sufficient. It wasn't a matter of polishing the language, she simply had to throw it out and start over yet again. And she definitely wasn't going to see Angelo, but she called Cassidy and Perrin for a get-together. The first of them she'd promised, and both she owed.

"Somewhere new. Somewhere different. Not near the Market."

Cassidy picked Vito's and by seven they were tucked side-by-side into a deep, burgundy faux-leather booth on the opposite side of Seattle. They had two glasses of a local red that Cassidy recommended. On the other side, Perrin had a rum drink of the unlikely name Janky Panky that had turned out to be a nice mix of sweet and mule kick. They had a Beef Carpaccio and steamed clams with sausage that might give Cutter's a bit of a challenge.

"It's like Angelo's place gone bad." Perrin squinted up at the black wall and acrylic-painted Italian landscapes barely revealed by the dim candlelight. "Like I keep expecting a mob boss to show up in a '40s zoot suit carrying a violin case." She leaned out of the booth and looked around the restaurant. "But here it would have a violin in it."

The jazz pianist at the grand was far enough away to make it easy to talk, but close enough to reveal that she was good.

Perrin leaned out and looked toward the pianist this time. "Hey, she's cute, too. I like long blondes."

"What is it with you and women?" Cassidy's tease was an old one. Anyone who might look good in one of Perrin's designs elicited the cute comment.

"Oh, I've tumbled a girl or two in my time."

Cassidy almost snorted her wine.

"Didn't stick. I'll take the guys." Perrin winked at Jo when Cassidy glanced down to see if she was wearing any of her wine.

Cass had always had a slightly narrow view of the world, and every now and then Perrin found a way to give it a good sharp poke.

"So," Perrin settled in her seat. "Are you better now?"

Jo nodded, "Much."

"Good. Then let me just say, What the fuck was that?"

Jo could do this. She'd told Mrs. Parrano, Maria, a nearly complete stranger. She could tell her best friends. And, as she'd advised Maria, she'd just say it before she could second guess herself.

"When I was up in Alaska, getting on the plane, Angelo told me that he loved me."

"And that shorted out your brain for what reason?"

Not quite the reaction she'd been expecting. Neither showed shock and amazement.

"Because my father had died seventy-two hours before. And at his funeral, which was five geriatric guys and an ex-Ukrainian Army woman pissing off the end of pier in his honor, I found out my mother lives in Redmond."

"Which Redmond?"

"The one like ten miles that way." Jo pointed over her shoulder. Or was it the other way? Vito's was partly below street level, dark and dive-like. There was no obvious view of Puget Sound to provide direction. She took a breath and just said it again to see if she could.

"Then he tells me that he loves me." It came out, but it still wasn't easy.

Cassidy studied her wine.

Perrin just shrugged, "Okay, minus ten points for timing but about plus five gajillion for having the good sense to fall in love with our Jo. So what's the problem?"

"What did you say?" Cass spoke softly. Right at the heart of the matter. If she hadn't been so involved in food and wine, Jo might have tried to convince her to go for law. She had the right kind of mind, but her palate was world class.

"I'm not ready. I didn't say anything."

"What?" Perrin took up a clam on her small fork and waved it at Jo, dribbling garlic butter–white wine sauce up and down the middle of the table. "Tell me one thing wrong with him other than lousy timing. Wait, does he have good timing in bed?"

"In the bed, in the shower, on the floor. Exceptional timing." She knew how to make Perrin crazy. "He's talking about Russell's sailboat, especially since Russell can't really use it with a broken leg."

Cassidy's grin was easy. "Yes, his sailboat offers many, many possibilities."

Perrin groaned in voyeuristic delight, placed a hand over her heart and panted a few times.

"That was good for me. Was that good for you? So," she waved her clam again and dribbled some more. "Tell me one thing wrong with him." She finally ate the clam.

"I'm not ready."

"Evading the question, Counselor. Naughty, naughty lawyer. Are you in love with him or not?"

Jo tried to answer the question. She really did. She opened her mouth and nothing came out. She closed it then tried again.

"Maria Parrano thinks I am."

Cassidy twisted to look right at her. "You talked to Angelo's mother about Angelo being in love with you?"

"He's not in love with me, he only thinks that he is."

Perrin pointed another clam at Jo, but faced Cassidy. "Is it just me, or is she avoiding every question we put to her?"

"It's not you." Cassidy's voice was grim. Grim enough that maybe she was thinking of changing over to law.

"She trapped me."

"How?"

"She was nice. Okay? Are you happy? She was nice to me. She told me how excited she was that I was going to be her daughter and how much fun we'd have together."

Now that she'd started Jo couldn't stop. Her voice kept rising and she couldn't reel it back in.

"What am I supposed to do with that? Tell me one thing I want more in my life than that? I want my mother to be there for me and for us to have fun together. Then my mother's lover offers…" She waved a hand helplessly.

"Your…mother's…lover?" Perrin was grinning. "I thought we were talking about your lover's mother. Or is there something going on between Eloise Thompson and Angelo that we need to know about? Because we all know how Perrin loves salacious tidbits." In the middle of the last sentence Perrin started tipping over into giggles despite her best efforts at a straight face.

Cassidy's cough didn't sound one bit like a cough.

Jo gave up. What could she do? In moments all three of them were howling with laughter.

Jo WAS SITTING on the plane, the country rolling along beneath her. Now she had two missions in New York.

Her primary purpose was a meeting with the Undersecretary of Maritime Law at the United Nations tomorrow morning. It was just a preliminary meeting. Information gathering. It would be six long months of research and planning before she'd be ready for even the first meeting with the lower-level representatives of the nations with Arctic claims. Most of that six months would be split equally between Juneau and Barrow. She needed to switch that. Hitting Barrow in mid-winter was not part of her plan. Barrow first, then Juneau. Even if Barrow would make Ketchikan look like paradise.

Jo ignored the sudden knot in her stomach, putting it down to airplane food.

Her secondary task was a last minute "favor" for Renée Linden. Jo really had to hand it to the woman, she was a spectacular strategist. After days without any contact whatsoever, she managed to drop by Jo's office as she was double-checking her briefcase and gathering her coat before leaving for the airport. Again, not enough time for a proper conversation.

But somehow, as a favor to Renée, Jo was now hand-carrying a folder of ad proofs to New York for the supermodel's approval. Not FedEx, not Internet. It was to be a hand carry and a personal meeting.

Melanie, the supermodel, was going to meet her at the airport so that they could go over the proofs together. Something about Russell refusing to release them without her final approval. It made sense if they'd been friends. It sort of made sense.

Actually, it made no sense at all. Apparently Melanie was flying out of JFK shortly after Jo was flying in, so that part worked. But none of the rest of it did. Renée had clearly slipped another fast one by her, but Renée's hidden strategy eluded Jo the rest of the way across the country.

"Russell, he does such beautiful work." Which sounded even better in Melanie's exquisite voice.

The Palm Bar and Grille at JFK was pleasant with dark wood decor and prompt service. They'd opted to split a Crab Louie Salad, and even though Jo had only had the one glass of wine last night, she opted for a diet Coke as did Melanie.

They had a spread of six different ads that could be based on The Glass Shoppe photo shoot in the Market on the table between them.

"I like this one the best."

Jo had to agree. "You do look incredibly sexy in that one. Good for a Playboy or a GQ placement. But what do you think of this one for Condé Nast?" It was more playful. Rather than the flirty punch that Melanie delivered so consistently, it had captured her with a smile just being surprised from her lips as she turned to a vase of the deepest red that arced like a tulip petal.

"You are good at this." Melanie tipped her head one way and another. "I have to think about this one some more. I usually go for the sexy, but this is interesting. You are right of course, use this for them. I need to think about other demographics of my market. I won't be the most beautiful one forever."

Not on display, Melanie actually had little accent or affectation. Her hair was hanked back in a long ponytail. Her skin with minimal makeup was more human. And her accent, rather than suggesting France, hinted ever so slightly at New York. Upper East Side perhaps.

They went through the rest of the ads relatively quickly in between slow bites of crab salad. Then they reached the ads built on the images that had been shot at Angelo's. The difference was immediately obvious.

"Those are all Claude's, aren't they?" Melanie indicated the reject pile.

Jo checked the photo index list and compared the photo numbers. "Every one."

"Russell is so good. I'm glad he picked up the camera again. It is a part of who he is. He had such a talent. I never look so good as when Russell takes the picture."

There was some note in her voice that Jo couldn't help noticing. "You love him very much, don't you?"

Melanie glanced at her then looked away. But she didn't need to say any more.

Jo rested a hand on her arm. "I'm sorry. That was rude of me. I didn't know."

Melanie stared for another long moment at the far end of the bar before turning back to Jo. Then she shrugged those perfect shoulders helplessly.

"At first, I fell for Russell because he is sooo handsome and we look so good together. Then I find that he is worth many, many millions. I liked the sound of that also very much."

Even without the French accent, Melanie had clearly hidden inside its mask so long that it shifted her speech patterns.

"I grew up poor. I terribly liked the sound of that money. And then I liked Russell. And then..." Again the elegant shrug. "I was not strong enough or challenging enough or something I no understand. He is good with Cassidy, better than he would be with me. We would have had one of those two-year marriages on the front page of the Enquirer with all of the ugly at the end. It is better that we did not."

Jo squeezed Melanie's arm.

They sorted the ads based on Angelo's in an easy accord that required few words.

There was one more folder at the bottom of the box. Melanie opened it while Jo made notes for Renée.

"Oh," Melanie's soft exclamation drew Jo's attention.

It took her several moments to make sense of the images Melanie was spreading out across the table.

She vaguely remembered Russell snapping photos during the meal, just some quick candids. No flash umbrellas, no makeup artists, no clothier.

There were two shots of Melanie and Perrin both looking stunning in Perrin's designer clothes. Russell had done one mockup of each, the first one for Pike Place Market, and the other for Perrin's Glorious Garb. The second one was the killer. They were huddled together as if conspiring to break every heart they came upon. Bare shoulders, a deep, deep V-neck on Perrin, an amazing length of leg from Melanie.

"Oh. Perrin, she must use this one."

"She'd can't afford your rates, Melanie. And she never takes charity, not even from her friends."

"Nonsense. You tell her I have already taken payment for this; I never gave her back the green dress. I like it too much."

Jo's attempts to thank her were lightly brushed aside.

"It is done." To prove her point, she tossed the ad using the two of them for the Market into the reject pile.

"Now, what are these?"

Jo looked down at them and blushed. It was her and Angelo. Jo in her power suit and Angelo in his immaculate charcoal dress shirt sat shoulder to shoulder, sharing Panna Cotta. They had lifted their spoons at the same moment as if they were about to feed each other, though Jo knew they hadn't.

"This one, it sizzles. It makes me feel hot all over." Melanie fanned herself with her hand.

Russell had faded the table under the text. The walls were a soft haze. All that remained in focus were the identical desserts, the identical espresso cups, and the identical expressions.

"No," her mouth was dry and a sip of Coke did nothing to ease the sensation. "We can't use this one."

"Why the hell not?" For just a moment, Melanie's voice took on a Lower West Side grind.

"It's… I don't know. It's just…"

"It is lovely," Melanie insisted, her soft French firmly back in place and a slight blush on her features that Jo tactfully ignored.

She tried to look at it and see the two people on a date, not herself and Angelo, but couldn't manage it.

Melanie picked up a cherry tomato and bit down on it.

"There is a photograph that Russell took of me. He is such an *imbécile* that he does not understand what he took a picture of, until much later. Then he sent me a copy with a lovely apology that cut like a knife in my heart." She reached over to her purse and slipped it out of an inside pocket, then slid it across the table.

Jo had seen Melanie look many ways in many ads. Tantalizing, distant, teasing, voracious, but this was different.

It was a close-up of Melanie's face, her features lit from below by the bright blue of a bubbling hot tub. No bathing suit straps where her perfect shoulders rose just above the water. A vase of red roses the color of Melanie's lips floated nearby. Her eyes were wide and her smile soft.

"It looks like…you're in love." Jo regretted it the moment she said it, but that's how it looked.

"*Oui.*" Melanie agreed sadly. "And so I was, with the *imbécile* behind the camera. He is such a good man."

Then she put one finger on her much-handled photo and slid it across the table next to the ad Russell had made of Jo and Angelo eating dessert together.

Jo's gaze drifted from Melanie's photo to the ad.

She looked at both of her and Angelo's expressions. Now it was easy to see what showed there.

CHAPTER 35

$\mathcal{A}$ ngelo kept his attention divided between his sauce and the woman auditioning to be the new aboyeur.

As the expeditor, she would direct all communications between the tables and the cook line. A single mistake could snarl the entire line and cause a cascading wreckage of service that could take hours to recover from. However, a good expeditor could improve the line's efficiency and front-of-house service dramatically.

He'd given Graziella a free hand to at least test an assistant. She'd been working as hostess, head waitress, and expeditor. Far too much for one person in a busy restaurant. She was very social and enjoyed the front of house, so she'd brought in Luisa to try out for aboyeur.

Luisa could almost be Graziella's twin. They were both tall, sleek, and dark haired with classic, straight Italian noses gracing their pretty faces.

The main difference rapidly became apparent. Graziella always asked and cajoled, even pleaded in a pleasant tone. Luisa got flirtatious, funny, caustic, whatever it took to get what she needed to make everything run smoothly.

Angelo liked her already. If Manuel approved her after today's test, he'd hire her on a two-week trial. She'd just moved back to the States from two years studying in Italy. Rather than spending time in cooking school, she'd worked restaurants in different regions for three months at a time. She knew food well enough, but it appeared that she understood restaurants intimately.

Her Italian, she admitted, had remained fairly miserable. But when Angelo had pretended to totally botch an order to gauge her response, she'd proven her command of at least the invective portion of the language. She could swear better than Russell, and she made it sound much more pleasant. For one thing, Russell's accent sucked.

His mother came over for a taste of the new sauce he was fooling with on the side. She let it roll on her tongue for several long moments.

"That is for the seafood linguini at the new restaurant?"

He nodded.

"So, you decided to go Piedmonte without asking your mother?"

Her tone no longer struck fear into his heart. "Piedmonte and Lombardia. They're close. I still need to work on the name. Angelo's Nord Italiano Hearth or maybe Angelo's North Italian Hearth."

"The second one, your *patroni* are in America. The sauce, it's good."

She turned back to her pastry station where she was making chocolate biscotti for dipping in a thickened vanilla-coffee cream she'd created.

Angelo waited for the other shoe. For the "a little soy sauce would make that nice" or "maybe if you added a bit of elk meat." But she didn't.

"Love you, Mama," he called to her.

"You only love me because I no insult your beautiful sauce," she shot back and they shared a smile.

A smile that froze on his lips when he looked up and saw who stood at the kitchen door. The kitchen volume dropped by half as his staff spotted his reaction and then its cause. They might not know the whole story, but Angelo supposed his own rocketing and crashing emotions had been hard to miss.

"Jo." It wasn't even a whisper, but it was all he could manage. He hadn't seen her since they'd parted in stiff silence at the airport to find their separate cars. It hadn't even been a whole week and yet it felt like a year.

She wore the power suit, but the jacket was open, the floopy bow tie missing, and the blouse open just one button. She looked exhausted from travel and nervous to be in his kitchen. He'd never brought her back here and felt suddenly very self-conscious. She looked so incredible, standing there shifting from one foot to the other. A small, practical, wheeled suitcase rested beside her, her briefcase in her hand.

"I thought you were in New York."

"I was."

"I thought you were supposed to be in meetings all day."

"I cancelled them."

He opened his mouth but closed it with a snap that nipped the end of his tongue painfully when his mother poked his ribs with the handle of a wooden spoon. Before he managed to turn on her, she gave him a shove that almost sent him stumbling into Marlys. His grillardin stepped out of the way and let him pass down the line and around the end of the cook stations until he stood close in front of Jo.

"Here. You'll get run over if you remain there." He took the suitcase and rolled it under the side prep table, its little plastic wheels making loud thumps on the seams between the tiles, so loud they seemed to echo about the kitchen. The table was presently covered with piles of vegetables and iced filets of sole to prep for the dinner service. She slipped her briefcase under the table as well.

"This is out of the way for the moment." A waiter came through the swinging door they'd just cleared, bearing an armload of dirty dishes. Graziella didn't believe in trays and tubs on the floor and Angelo agreed. The waiter delivered them to Marko with an ear-ringing clatter.

Angelo glanced over and saw that Manuel had shifted to cover his position on the line and had turned down the heat under his sauce as well. Good man. Now he had to face Jo.

"I'm sorry to interrupt. You're busy and—"

"Look, I'm the one who's sorry. I shouldn't have blurted it out like that. I wasn't thinking. It just came out."

"Did your mother or Cassidy chew you out about that?"

"No." He glanced toward his mother. "Were they supposed to?" He waved the question away.

It meant she'd told his mother and...he turned back to Jo with a shrug.

"They didn't have to. I sort of figured it out slowly on my own." It had taken him most of the last four days, but he wouldn't mention that. He tried to read her expression, but he couldn't make sense of it. Counselor Thompson, he could read her pretty well. And when she was Jo, everything was so obvious on her face that they could have whole conversations without a word. This woman standing before him, he was less sure of.

He wanted to shout out how much he'd missed her, but he couldn't. It would simply kill him.

He'd drifted through the week, shopping, cooking, sleeping, and then doing the same thing again. It was as if someone had dropped him in a vat of gelatin that was slowly setting to solid around him. He kept struggling against it because he didn't know how to stop. Now that she stood in his kitchen, it was as if the gel had never been and he'd come back to life.

"I shouldn't have said it and I wanted to formally apologize." He folded his arms over his chest to keep his hands still. He knew it sounded stiff, but it was the best he could manage.

She waited, shifted again.

What more was he supposed to say? Cast the remaining shards of his broken heart at her feet and watch them be stomped again like tiny grapes?

Jo looked around her, but not as if she was seeing anything. Her hands, those beautiful, elegant, calm hands that could drive his body to such distraction...weren't calm. They were practically fluttering about her lap.

She was nervous. He'd never seen her nervous. Frustrated at work, out of place and confused in Alaska, but never nervous.

"I've been in the air for almost sixteen hours with only three hours on the ground in New York before turning back around. I had really lousy connections coming back, but it was the fastest I could get here."

"Fastest?" He didn't dare to hope, squashed the glimmer of it as well as he could, wrapped his arms tighter across this chest.

She pulled out one of the stools from under the prep table and sat down on it.

Angelo kicked one loose and sat facing her. A glance showed that most of the line was watching them surreptitiously, except for his mother who was making no bones about what she was paying attention to. He was glad the patissier station was at the far end of the cookline. The kitchen had never in two years been so quiet while a meal was in progress.

"I've had sixteen hours to think about something you said. And you were right, Alaska would kill me. Another multi-year lawsuit would do me in, too, even if it made my career. By the end I would be bitter and angry. I don't want to be that."

"That, uh, that sounds good. Does that mean that you'll—" He couldn't finish the sentence, but Jo nodded anyway.

"I called Renée Linden last night just before I got on the

return flight. You are now talking to your new managing land-lord, the Executive Director of the Pike Place Market. Still sounds crazy when I say it. Well, I'll have some time to get used to it as that will take most of a month to switch over. She's informing the board of her retirement right now. Muriel and I have to go meet them in fifteen minutes but Renée assures me that's just a technicality."

"Oh my God, Jo. That's incredible!" Angelo wanted to shout. He couldn't think straight. He'd now have time to court her. She wouldn't be running out of his life to a place filled with bad memories for her. He wanted to reach for her, but it was too much. He rested his hands firmly on his thighs and clamped them there.

"And you're closed Mondays and Tuesdays still, right?"

"Uh, right." That was a real problem he hadn't been able to solve. Maybe he could shift some of his hours somehow so that he could see more of her. But he hadn't come up with a solution yet.

"New restaurant, too? Same hours?" She was switching over to that Counselor Thompson role that had so captivated him.

"Hadn't thought that far ahead, but, uh, sure. Probably. Why?"

"Good. I only have," she checked her watch, "twelve more minutes and I have a bit of ground to cover."

"Okay. You're in Seattle. You're quitting your job as an attorney. Are you okay with that?"

She reached out and touched his hand for a moment. A simple contact that rippled up his arm so powerfully it made his breath catch in his chest.

"Bless you, Angelo, for thinking of me and my feelings. It's not something I'm particularly good at. Actually, the Market's business is so complex now, that being an attorney is a distinct advantage. Apparently it is one of the reasons Renée first considered me. I'll still be practicing law, I will simply be doing it on a more reasonable schedule. Speaking of schedule…"

"I can—"

"Shush! Ten minutes to go."

God, but she simply slayed him when she was in this mode. There'd never been another woman like her.

"The Market has a number of vendors who only work on the weekends. I'll be telling the board that my hours are Wednesday through Sunday. I'll have Monday and Tuesday off as well. I'm not sure what I will do with a career that fits into only five days a week, but that's a different issue."

Angelo couldn't help himself. He leaned forward and wrapped his arms about her in a quick hug. He'd be able to see Jo. They'd share weekends.

Wait! That was if she wanted to keep seeing him. Well, she was here, wasn't she? Talking to him. Had cancelled her meetings back East. He held her a moment longer, reveling in the magical scent that was Jo Thompson, praying he was even partly right about what was happening.

All his anger, all his hurt was sliding toward the floor drain like old dirt in soap suds. And if he was wrong, he'd go right down the drain after them. That cooled down his heart a bit.

He managed to sit back, but felt like an overeager little boy. He kept reaching out a hand to touch her knee, or her hand where it rested on her thigh, just to prove to himself that she was here, real, and so warm.

"Seven minutes. Well, I've spent most of the last seven hours practicing this." He saw her take a deep breath then she whispered to herself, "I can do this."

Clearly, whatever was next came hard. He took one of her hands in both of his.

"You are the strongest woman I've ever met, Executive Director Jo Thompson. You can do anything."

She nodded several times as if slowly building layers of reassurance like a layered torta.

"Melanie told me I could."

"Melanie?"

She waved his question away for another time with a perfect flick of her fingers.

"Would you come with me tomorrow morning after you finish your shopping for the restaurant?"

"Of course—"

Jo held up a hand to cut him off. He couldn't help himself, he kissed her fingertips. She actually caressed his lips and he almost wept with how good it felt.

"I'd like you to come with me to go see my mother."

He couldn't be prouder of her if she were a new restaurant. It was a shock, not what he'd been expecting her to say, but it was still fantastic.

"Yes, of course I will go with you."

Then she took another deep breath, glanced at her watch, then glanced down the now silent cookline toward his mother.

Maria Amelia Avico Parrano nodded some silent answer to whatever Jo's silent question was.

Then Jo turned back and took both of his hands in hers and held them tightly.

"I was thinking… If we like my mother… I was thinking we could invite her…" Another deep breath. "We could invite her to the wedding."

"The wedding?" Angelo's ears were ringing. "Whose wedding?"

"Well, Perrin made me this absolutely killer wedding dress. It would be a waste not to wear it, especially as you claim that you love me."

"I do," Angelo couldn't believe his ears. "Oh Jo, I love you so much I don't know what to do with all the feelings inside me. I'm like a potato in a microwave without enough vent hol—"

She leaned in and kissed him as a roar of applause rang through the kitchen. Pots and pans were banged with ladles, the butts of knives were pounded against cutting boards.

She shifted back just a little, just enough for him to see her lips as there was no chance of hearing her over the cheering.

"I love you, Angelo."

It was all he ever needed to know.

KEEP READING

Keep reading for an excerpt from book #3:
Where Dreams Are of Christmas
And reviews are a HUGE help.
Thanks for joining my journey, Matt.

IF YOU ENJOYED THIS, YOU MIGHT
ALSO ENJOY:

WHERE DREAMS ARE OF CHRISTMAS
(EXCERPT)

A WHERE DREAMS SEATTLE ROMANCE

*M*aria *Amelia Avico Parrano* sat at the take-out window of her son's restaurant in the heart of Seattle's Pike Place Market. Outside her window, the morning bustle of Post Alley would just be starting. Inside, the kitchen sounds of the busy prep crews of Angelo's Tuscan Hearth were already echoing behind her. Manuel, Angelo's *sous chef,* was pushing his new assistant Nora to see if he could make her panic. Maria smiled to herself, no luck yet.

Luisa and Graziella were rehearsing the new menu items for the daily fresh sheet. "Black sea bass poached in a Piedmonte Roero Arneis, that's a slightly sweet white wine of northern Italy, with a rub of basil..."

Maria let the words drift into the background. Served with a surprise pairing of a young Barbaresco red, it would be an innovative pleasure on the palate. The other noises were starting to sound so familiar, it was if she'd never been anywhere else. Six months she'd been in Seattle since her retirement. Retired at forty-seven, it still made no sense.

But the couple she'd cooked for the last three decades in New York had retired and didn't need a resident chef any more.

They had rewarded her most comfortably and now she had a place here at her son's restaurant. And it was time.

She flicked on the heater switch, in moments a warm wash of air blew onto her legs. When she slid up the kitchen window to face the chill first day of December, the cold wasn't bad. Russell, her son's best man at the beautiful fall wedding, had installed another heater over the outside of the window to radiate a wall of warmth down onto the customers and an awning to keep Seattle's December rains at bay.

Russell was such a sweet man, she really didn't need that much protection. She had helped raise both Angelo and Russell, her son and her former employer's boy, so of course they saw her as old and frail. That was their role in life. Youth was supposed to think that way. But she didn't feel that way. Not even a little.

Besides, she had far too much fun selling coffee and pastries at her take-out window to stop merely because of the weather. Already some of her regulars were loitering on the wet brick-work of Post Alley and quickly clustered around the window as soon as she opened it.

"Good morning, Maria." The near chorus was music to her ears.

"Hello Clara, Joseph, and William. I don't see you as much as I do when the weather is nice. Don't you love your Maria any more?" She handed William his cappuccino first to soften the tease. He dropped a five dollar bill in the jar she'd set out. She'd made a decorative tile with "Breakfast $5" worked in lavender against a yellow glaze at one of those paint-it-yourself pottery places. "The price," she would tell people, "she is fixed in stone." Then she gave William a fresh *cornetto*.

"What's in it this morning?" he took a big bite without waiting for an answer. "Oh my blessed heaven!" He managed to mumble with his mouth full, a smile on his face, and crumbs clustering on the lapels of his sharp lawyer's suit.

"It's a sweet *Prosciutto di San Daniele* with a fresh, tangy *Robiola Bosina* cheese."

By that time Clara had bitten into hers and had her eyes closed, as usual, to relish the tastes. Joseph went for the cappuccino first, still looking more asleep than awake. Other regulars had queued up as they paid and chatted, only moving to the edge of the awning and the radiant heat as others pressed inward.

The milling, happy crowd attracted other Pike Place Market tourists. Inside of five minutes there were more people that she didn't recognize than ones that she did.

Henry came over from the fish market and she refused his money, as she had a hundred times before, but he always offered. Henry always held back the best of the day's catch for Angelo or Manuel each morning, today it was the black sea bass.

"Maria, when are you going to marry me?"

"I could never marry you, Henry. You always smell of fish. I could no marry such a man." He of course knew that was a little joke. His fish were always so fresh and he kept everything so clean. He was a vendor, and a very smart one, not a fisherman.

"I'll give it all up for you." He flashed her one of his smiles.

She was half tempted to at least date him. He was such a nice man, and good looking, even if a bit round in the belly. His graying hair would go silver and make him a very handsome older man. But, though she liked him, there was no spark.

Maria wanted spark. She wanted electricity, lightning bolts. She only hoped that she hadn't waited too long and missed her chance.

She served and chatted with a dozen more tourists after Henry left. Her son had found lightning. And Russell too. The two boys were so cute in married life it was hard to credit that they were men grown, always doting on their wives while trying desperately to appear the strong men they couldn't help being if they tried. Their wives, Jo and Cassidy, were both such exceedingly competent women, they made her feel out of her depth. All she had ever done was cook and raise the two boys.

But she'd felt that spark once in her life. She'd felt it right to the very core of her being. A love for a no-good, useless man who had walked away after taking her virginity and leaving her pregnant with a son. Maria had been forced to come to America to hide the shameful pregnancy of an unmarried Italian Roman Catholic girl. She'd never gone back to Manarola for more than to visit.

She wanted fire. She wanted someone who made her blood burn and her heart race. For an hour, perhaps two, she smiled and teased and enjoyed herself immensely. It had become her contribution to her son's success. He was the great chef, but she knew how to charm the people.

The morning always went too quickly; another dozen *cornetti* and she'd be sold out for the day. She made her usual bet with herself. Today she guessed that nine, perhaps ten of the people she'd served would be back for an Italian lunch when the restaurant opened. Even one additional customer would pay for the minor loss she took on each breakfast she sold.

She served a young Chinese couple who didn't speak a word of English, or Italian either. It didn't matter. She helped them figure out which bill to put in the jar and they left ready to explore the waterfront with their breakfast in hand.

A man drifted to the take-out counter window during a momentary lull.

Maria Amelia recognized him. Lately, he'd often wandered by in the mornings, slowing down but never stopping. He always appeared to want to, but never quite managed.

Her greeting elicited little more than a friendly nod. A shy one. He wore old sneakers with white socks, dark-brown khakis that had started to fray where the hems scuffed along the ground, a red flannel shirt under a faded jeans jacket, and a baseball cap with some computer-looking logo. The whole outfit had clearly been worn several years too long, probably from a Goodwill store. He didn't have a beard, but needed a shave badly. It was long enough she could see it would have a little salt in the pepper if he let it grow.

For all that he was quite the handsomest man she had served that morning. Not the prettiest, so many of the young men were pretty. Those fresh clean faces that thought they knew the world while having seen none of it.

This man had seen much of it. Perhaps too much, perhaps not, but it showed on his solid features and in the soft brown eyes that didn't skitter aside despite his unease, or downward despite her low-cut dress. She wouldn't mind much if they did, after all, why was a woman built the way she was if not to share it a little bit. But she liked that he didn't go there.

He stopped uncertainly several steps from her window, just at the point where she could see the rain dripping off the awning, splashing onto the brim of his hat, and trickling off the brim and into his open jacket.

The man pulled out a wallet, made a back-and-forth motion with his fingers as if searching for money, then shoved it back in his pocket.

As he turned away, Maria called to him.

"Don't go."

He stopped, this time with the drip falling down the back of his neck. When he looked back at her, his nice eyes looked just a little wild. Fear that he couldn't afford to pay even so little for a breakfast.

"Here, it's my last. You should have it." She held out a *cornetto* and cappuccino.

He hesitated, so shy it was almost painful to watch.

"I always save the best for last. So these must be for you."

The man came and took them, careful not to touch her as he did so. His nails needed trimming, but the hands were good ones. He didn't use them for manual labor, but they showed a man who had used them for more than office work his whole life. A few small burns and nicks she recognized as someone who cooked, and wasn't very good at it, which only made her like him all the more.

He almost managed a smile before turning away and hurrying into the rain.

HIS CHEEKS BURNING WITH SHAME, Hogan Stanford hurried down Pike Place Market's Post Alley until he was out of sight of Maria's window. Then he circled around to the antiques place at the corner of Post and Stewart and peeked back toward Angelo's Tuscan Hearth.

It was a gray, drizzling December morning, freezing water was trickling down his back, and he was a complete and total idiot.

He hadn't been able to say a word.

He'd first noticed her from his condo's window which faced Puget Sound. Watching the tourists mob up and down the four short, bricked blocks of Pike Place Market had become one of his favorite pastimes. Even if he didn't like to join the fray, it always seemed so full of life.

And in the midst of it all there had been a flash of color, of sky blue and gold that had glittered in the crowd. That was what had finally drawn him outdoors to wander the streets of the Pike Place Market. On his third outing, he'd spotted her again. It had been a warm day for December and she'd worn her tan camel hair coat open. That day she'd been wearing a red skirt, a vivid orange blouse, and a sunny yellow kerchief over her dark, curling hair, like a flower in bloom. But he had no doubt that it was the same woman. It simply had to be, there couldn't be two women in the world who glowed so brightly.

He'd been so stunned by her beauty that he'd lost track of her when she must've ducked into a store. It took him another week to spot her again, though at least now he had a face to go by. This time she sat in the window at Angelo's Tuscan Hearth Ristorante, framed by the wood-and-brick window frame, like a Botticelli.

Today she'd been dressed in brilliant blues as she served up breakfast and charm in equal portions. She shone like a ray of sunshine in an otherwise dark world on this dreary December day. At least he was pretty sure it was December now.

He peeked again around the brickwork corner and back up Post Alley. She was bantering happily with another customer. Leaning her elbow on the counter and resting her chin on her hand, she looked as if she could happily visit away the whole morning. It was an ability he had never understood. He didn't know whether to be impressed by how natural she was, or be nervous that she would talk everyone to death and be a bore. Yet she never appeared to bore anyone, though he had watched her many times. He decided that she had an uncanny awareness of the mood of each individual she met.

Hogan noted with some chagrin that she served the woman a *cornetto* and a paper cup. The one still warm in his hands hadn't been her last after all. Thinking him homeless, she said it to make him feel less embarrassed. People were never that nice. It had to be an act...but again, it didn't feel like one.

Being stupid, Hogan. It was one of his trademarks, but he just couldn't approach her. Half a dozen times over the few weeks since he'd spotted her, he'd walked by while she was serving, trying to work up the nerve. Finally this morning he'd managed it.

Now she slid her window down. In moments, the soft red glow of the overhead heater faded to black. Finally sold out. He shifted back around the corner and out of sight of the restaurant, then rested his back against the wet brick. The moisture slowly seeped through at his shoulders and rear end.

She was so different from the dark and brooding Vera who had totally wrecked his life.

He knew he had to get out and speak to someone. All he'd wanted was one moment in the glow of a woman as bright and cheerful as the one in the restaurant window.

And then he'd looked in his wallet and realized that the smallest bill he was carrying was a hundred.

Then she'd decided he was homeless.

How sad was that?

And he'd let her think it.

Really sad, he answered his own question, knowing it was absolutely true.

Keep reading.
Available at fine retailers everywhere:
Where Dreams Are of Christmas

ABOUT THE AUTHOR

USA Today and Amazon #1 Bestseller M. L. "Matt" Buchman has 70+ contemporary and military romance novels, and action-adventure thrillers. Also 100 short stories and lotsa audiobooks.

Booklist says: 3x "Top 10 Romance of the Year" and among "The 20 Best Romantic Suspense Novels: Modern Masterpieces." NPR and B&N say: "Best 5 Romance of the Year." PW declares: "Tom Clancy fans open to a strong female lead will clamor for more."

A project manager with a geophysics degree, he's designed and built houses, flown and jumped out of planes, solo-sailed a 50' sailboat, and bicycled solo around the world...and he quilts. More at: www.mlbuchman.com.

Other works by M. L. Buchman: *(* - also in audio)*

Other works by M. L. Buchman:

Contemporary Romance (cont)

Love Abroad
Heart of the Cotswolds: England
Path of Love: Cinque Terre, Italy

Where Dreams
Where Dreams are Born
Where Dreams Reside
Where Dreams Are of Christmas*
Where Dreams Unfold
Where Dreams Are Written
Where Dreams Continue

Science Fiction / Fantasy

Deities Anonymous
Cookbook from Hell: Reheated
Saviors 101

Single Titles
The Nara Reaction
Monk's Maze
the Me and Elsie Chronicles

Non-Fiction

Strategies for Success
Managing Your Inner Artist/Writer
Estate Planning for Authors*
Character Voice
Narrate and Record Your Own
Audiobook*

Short Story Series by M. L. Buchman:

Romantic Suspense

Antarctic Ice Fliers

Delta Force
Th Delta Force Shooters
The Delta Force Warriors

Firehawks
The Firehawks Lookouts
The Firehawks Hotshots
The Firebirds

The Night Stalkers
The Night Stalkers 5D Stories
The Night Stalkers 5E Stories
The Night Stalkers CSAR
The Night Stalkers Wedding Stories

US Coast Guard

White House Protection Force

Contemporary Romance

Eagle Cove

Henderson's Ranch*

Where Dreams

Action-Adventure Thrillers

Dead Chef

Miranda Chase Origin Stories

Science Fiction / Fantasy

Deities Anonymous

Other
The Future Night Stalkers
Single Titles

SIGN UP FOR M. L. BUCHMAN'S NEWSLETTER TODAY

and receive:
Release News
Free Short Stories
a Free Starter Collection

Do it today. Do it now.
www.mlbuchman.com/newsletter

www.ingramcontent.com/pod-product-compliance
Lightning Source LLC
Chambersburg PA
CBHW020604110726
47899CB00002B/362